T0032599

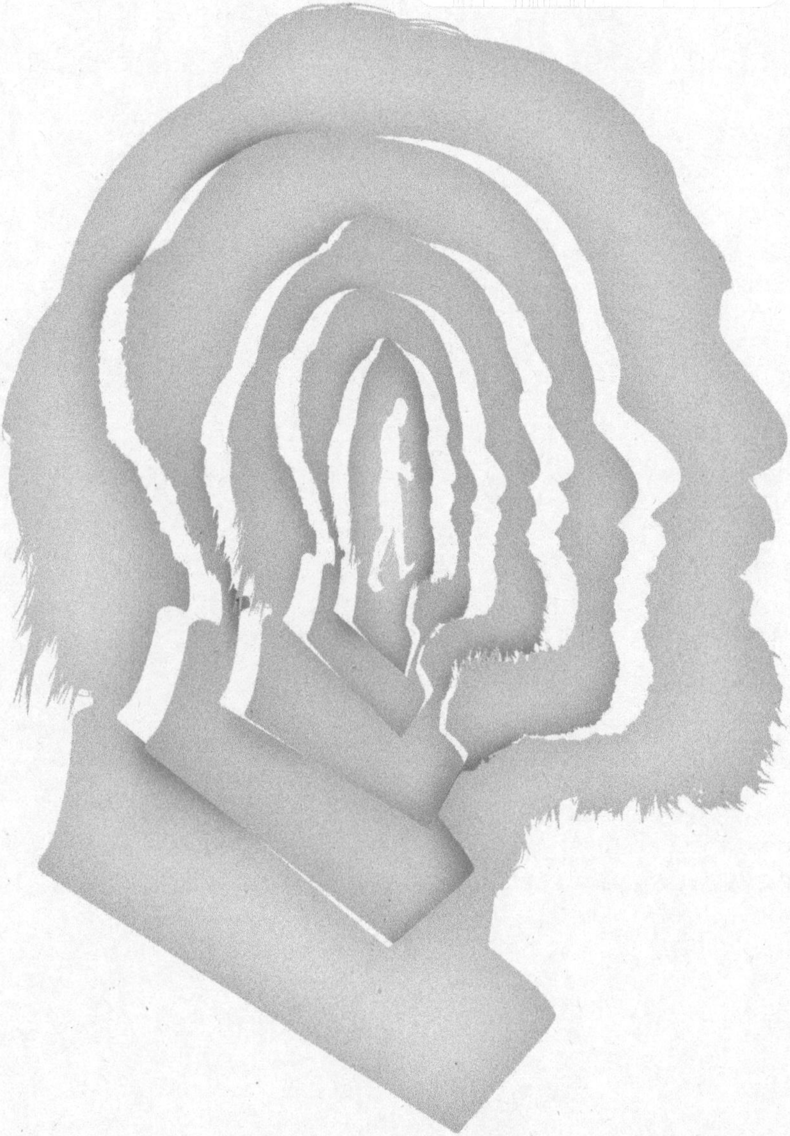

Praise for

PROFESSOR SCHIFF'S GUILT

"Liberal hypocrisy is furiously implicated in Israeli writer Agur Schiff's *Professor Schiff's Guilt*... He also portrays a more concrete inheritance of racism, mostly in the presence of undocumented African workers in Israel... This shrewd masquerade has real bite."

—*THE WALL STREET JOURNAL*

"A daring post-colonial satire about a professor who inadvertently gets wrapped up in human trafficking in modern-day Tel Aviv... The author takes a clear-eyed view of the horrors of slavery and its present-day consequences... It's a blistering skewering, and as sharp as it is funny."

—*PUBLISHERS WEEKLY* (Starred Review)

"A writer contends with slavery's legacy, and his own link to it... Daring in both scope and imagination."

—*THE NEW YORK TIMES*

"In this very funny, wise, and rueful novel, the cranky hero thrashes around in the coils of guilt, atonement, desire, and shame once he learns that a distant relative was a slave trader. (There's other bad stuff, not nearly so distant.) But really, he's no more culpable than we all are—and no less."

—JAMES TRAUB,
author of *Judah Benjamin: Counselor to the Confederacy* and *Foreign Policy* magazine columnist

"Deftly raises important contemporary issues—including how accountable should we be for the sins of our ancestors—without losing sight of the comedy that lies at the heart of tragedy."

—WAYNE GRADY,
author of *Emancipation Day* and *Up From Freedom*

"Not only a hilarious satirical novel full of self-deprecation, but also a topical and very relevant book, which cleverly ridicules the self-righteous and should finally place its author alongside the most prominent writers."

—*HAARETZ*

"One of the most thrilling and thought-provoking novels I've read in the past year . . . Schiff writes with simplicity, full of charm and humor."

—*ISRAEL HAYOM*

"A wonderful and brilliant book . . . a very entertaining book, rich with imagination and literary innovations."

—*WALLA*

PROFESSOR SCHIFF'S GUILT

A NOVEL

BY **AGUR SCHIFF**

TRANSLATED FROM THE HEBREW BY JESSICA COHEN

NEW VESSEL PRESS
NEW YORK

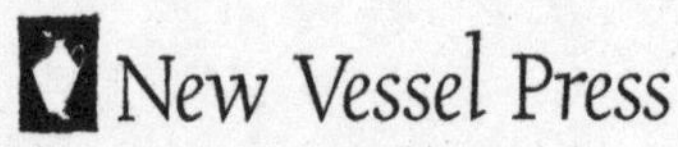

www.newvesselpress.com

Published by arrangement with The Institute for the Translation of Hebrew Literature

Library of Congress Cataloging-in-Publication Data
Schiff, Agur
[Ashmato shel Professor Schiff, English]
Professor Schiff's Guilt/Agur Schiff; translation by Jessica Cohen.
p. cm.
ISBN 978-1-954404-16-8

Library of Congress Control Number 2022943250
I. Israel—Fiction

"When a white European author writes about Africa, he is unwittingly reenacting an exploitative act. Literary colonialism, I would call it. I have no better description."

—George Aboagye

1

Yes, it's true: my grandfather's grandfather's grandfather was a slave trader.

I cannot deny it. Nor do I see any point in obscuring this embarrassing fact. After all, I feel no affinity with the man, who departed this world almost a century and a half before I entered it. And I trust you will believe me when I say that our genetic linkage arouses more than a shred of discomfort in me.

Ladies and gentlemen, there are those who claim that the past always makes surprise appearances. Indeed, that is sometimes true. Except that what we have here is not a long-forgotten parking ticket that crops up out of nowhere and, if not paid—with interest, of course—might result in your bank account being seized. Nor are we dealing with an old woman who stops you on the street to remind you that she was the girl you were once madly in love with. No. The past I am being asked to submit to you, distinguished members of the Special Tribunal, is my family heritage, for good and for bad, and when it rears its head, I cannot pretend to be surprised.

Because I have known for years about my great-great-great-great-grandfather, Klonimus Zelig Schiff. About his business affairs, the fortune he amassed, and his mysterious disappearance. I have read about him. I have written about him. I have dreamed about him. I even know what he looked like.

In a portrait that hangs in the Surinaams Museum in Paramaribo, he stands upright and rigid, wearing a tricorn and a stern expression. He is flanked by his wife Esperanza, her head covered with a snood, and although she is not beautiful, she certainly is—how can I put this?—charismatic. In the background, a ship with billowing sails glides across a flat, gray sea that glistens like a sheet of zinc.

Naturally, almost instinctively, one seeks out the resemblance. It's a bit like searching a baby's face for the parents' features. And when one persists, one always finds something. A certain glint in the eye. An angle. A contour. Generally speaking, though, ladies and gentlemen, perhaps you will agree that a face is an asset we tend to overvalue. Particularly if we take into account how quickly it withers and loses its capacity to do justice to its owner.

Then again, why should anyone care what the slave trader who was my great-great-great-great-grandfather looked like? As far as I'm concerned, you are entitled to think that Professor Schiff—namely, I—am him, as long as you can maintain your judicial objectivity. Not that I doubt your integrity, distinguished members of the tribunal. Not at all. I trust you unequivocally.

Members of the Special Tribunal, Madam Attorney General, Head of the Investigation Team:

I stand here before you.

It is hard to believe that up until a few weeks ago, I knew nothing of your existence or of the existence of your lovely country. Truth be told, I could barely have placed it on a map. And so you see, there was not even the slightest chance of me ever landing here.

Besides, I am a truly wretched traveler. I have not the foggiest sense of adventure. Zero aspiration to self-transport. I prefer to stay at home, in my own private disarray, surrounded by the illusion of safety among familiar landscapes. The disruption, the waiting, the carrying, the pushing, the ups, the downs—all these, for me, are torture. I detest airports. Sitting on airplanes. Flight attendants' saccharine smiles. Small talk with potential partners to an aviation disaster. Explanations about life jackets in two languages I do not speak. Immigration officials. Standing in line. Staying at hotels—oh yes, sleeping on mattresses that are too soft and smell like too many honeymoons. Special effects from an American action movie blaring from the television in the next room. The impossible modulation of hot and cold water in the drizzle of a shower . . .

Not to mention the sojourn itself: city maps that rip down the middle, streets with impossible names, incomprehensible information flashing on a cellphone screen, the fear of pickpockets and overzealous vendors and relentless self-appointed tour guides. And the endless yearning—for shade, for shelter from the rain, for a bench to rest on, for a cup of espresso, for a toilet! The mere thought of battling a full bladder while traipsing around a foreign city causes me unimaginable suffering. And what about sustenance? Yes, that is also a challenge for the likes of me, an aging man set in his ways.

Be that as it may, precisely when I had made the decision to never again travel more than a two-hour drive from home (that's gross hours, including traffic jams), I came across a small story in the newspaper. And this inconspicuous item, on the back page of an old daily, is what led me to be standing here before you.

It happened during my summer break, in the public library. I sat there one morning, leafing through newspapers from June 2006, as part of my research for a book. A different book, of course. Not this book that I am writing now, the one in which you yourselves are playing a central role. I was flipping through the papers idly. Languidly. My eyelids were drooping, as I recall. My head lolled. You can imagine the scene: a summer afternoon in the reading room, a large but musty space lit with fluorescent bulbs, where the air-conditioning's frequent death rattles disturb the readers as they try to doze at the long tables. In fact, my municipal library somewhat resembles this chamber, at least in climate and soundtrack.

And then, in front of my half-closed eyes, there appeared a small, marginal item, at the bottom of the page, a sort of trivial curiosity that the night editor must have fished out from the slush pile to fill in a gap between two other articles.

I woke up at once.

The piece was about the remnants of a nineteenth-century merchant ship that had been unearthed off the coast of a West African city—none other than this very city, the capital of your charming republic. But at the time, as I said, I knew very little—almost nothing, to be honest—about your country, your capital, or even this vast continent. In short, ladies and gentlemen, we have here a coincidence: the ship was found in your territorial waters, and the items dredged up from its crumbling body by a British archeological delegation are housed here, in the Museum of African Culture. The ship was identified as a cargo vessel with a 200-ton capacity that is thought to have been built in the Rotterdam shipyard in 1780 and christened the *Esperanza*.

Ladies and gentlemen, there is poetic justice, even a certain logic, in the new law recently enacted by your parliament, the lengthy title of which is the Law for Adjudicating Slave Traders and their Accomplices, Heirs, and Beneficiaries. I might even have welcomed it, if not for the fact that I myself have been chosen to serve as the law's first test case.

When it comes to identification, you are not mistaken. There is no shortage of Jews bearing the last name Schiff. Most of them acquired the name (which means "ship" in Yiddish) because they traded in pickled herring or repaired sails for a living, or because their wanderings led them to some damp port city where one could not escape the whipping winds, the noise of the waves, or the dreams of ships at sea. But this was not the case with my ancestor, Klonimus

Zelig, who gave the name "Schiff" to the shipping company he founded in faraway Suriname, at the southwest reaches of the Caribbean. He owned a fleet of four multipurpose trade ships, which crossed the Atlantic back and forth between the Americas and the Bight of Benin in West Africa. Three of his vessels were named after his daughters: the *Rachel*, the *Rebecca*, and the *Sarah*. The fourth and largest, which was also the most elegant of the small fleet, was named for his beloved wife: the *Esperanza*.

Esperanza Schiff, my grandmother's grandmother's grandmother, died in the prime of her life, before her young son, Solomon, had even celebrated his bar mitzvah. I, Professor Schiff, am Solomon Schiff's great-grandson's great-grandson's son. Or is it his great-grandson's son's grandson? Please forgive me, as the counting back of generations can be confusing, even when the genealogical sequence is simple to track.

Incidentally, you might be interested to learn that my father kept a family tree. It was a yellowing parchment on which, rather than the customary tree diagram, a wave at the base rippled out in smaller waves, like some sort of watery cactus. At the frothy end of each wave-branch was a tiny illustration of a sailboat, inscribed with a name, date of birth, and date of death. I found this scroll a loathsome artifact, with its grotesque design and musty smell. I hated it. And so when I took it to school one day, in the second or third grade, I made sure to lose it. How? I simply gave it to the most popular girl in my class, in return for a quick peek at her forbidden zone. After some time, stricken with remorse (but mostly driven by my father's terrifying fury), I asked for the document back. But the girl, who turned out to be a shrewd businesswoman, demanded that, in return, I give back what I had seen. Namely, that I return to her the sight revealed to my eyes and imprinted on my memory. Are you following the logic, ladies and gentlemen? Do you understand how a peep show engraved in one's memory can be of equal value to a family heirloom passed down from generation to generation?

In any case, it was clear to me then that I had inherited none of my late forefather's business acumen. Not even a smidgen. What he did, perhaps, bequeath me was hubris, and a burning desire for glory and honor—although in me the syndrome has manifested in a humbler form, expressed only in the publishing of books. It is a troubling but tolerable obsession. But with my forefather, Klonimus, it was bona fide megalomania: when he finally comprehended the magnitude of suffering and injustice he had caused, he made up his mind to atone by repairing the entire world.

But, of course, none of this alters the fact that the man was a criminal, at least by today's standards. Moreover, were he standing here today before this distinguished tribunal, the way he chose to absolve himself might have merely served to amplify his guilt.

I assume all this will be clarified at a later point.

2

Today, in hindsight, it is clear that Professor Schiff's road to Africa began even before that newspaper story. Before he discovered, thanks to a peculiar coincidence, that some of the sunken *Esperanza*'s remnants were housed in the Museum of African Culture located in a certain African capital. Before he decided to travel to that metropolis to demand what was rightly his, in his capacity as heir to the slave trader, and to take the opportunity to delve into his genealogical roots and perhaps write a book in the process.

His road to Africa began with the tumultuous yet jubilant emergence of Mrs. Lucile Tetteh-Ofosu in his life. And Professor Schiff—who tends to wax nostalgic about the past, both distant and near; who incessantly looks back; who busies himself by scanning images on a celluloid film stretched between his hands before a bright light—has been trying for months to pinpoint the precise moment he was captivated by her.

He remembers a long Nefertiti neck and a face so round it seemed to have been drawn with a compass, heavy eyelids over slightly slanted eyes, and smiling lips. She looked petite on that day when they first met, shorter than she really was, because, as he later learned, she was precisely as tall as he and perhaps even slightly taller. She wore a yellow T-shirt that hung over her breasts like a robe, and very baggy gym shorts. It was as though she had indiscriminately grabbed a few clothes from an adolescent boy's closet and quickly put them on. Her frizzy hair was tied back with a white ribbon. And since the "enchantment" (this was the word he chose to explain what he'd experienced) made him ignore the pervasive signs—including, for example, a broom, bucket, and mop—Mrs. Tetteh-Ofosu struck him as an indecipherable and slightly clownish illusion.

In retrospect, it was *he* who was the illusion. Because he walked into Attorney Melchior's home without being asked—simply opened the door and marched in—and the lady in the boyish clothes was well within her rights to be startled when he appeared out of nowhere right before her. His silver beard glistened in the dim hallway as if it were on fire. In the large mirror on the wall, he saw her reflection standing next to his.

"Can I help you?" she asked in English, in a quiet voice. But Professor Schiff was too busy looking to hear. He was assembling her, one might say, segment by segment, from the flip-flops up, past the shiny gym shorts and onward to the shirt, up the wonderful neck, until he beheld the canny spark dancing in the whites of her eyes.

Pulling himself together and remembering that English was the appropriate language for the occasion, he asked in the slickest accent he could muster, "Is Attorney Melchior at home?"

But then something strange happened. At any rate, Professor Schiff found it strange at the time. The lady walked over to the doorframe and kissed the mezuzah affixed to it. Or rather, she did not exactly kiss it so much as touch the mezuzah and then put her fingertips to her lips, as is the custom. After performing this ritual, she said to Professor Schiff, "For you."

"For me?" wondered Professor Schiff. He himself was not in the habit of kissing mezuzahs or any other object, nor was he familiar with the custom of kissing a mezuzah by proxy. The notion amused him.

"Yes, for you," said the dark-skinned woman in the boyish clothes, and gave him a forgiving smile. Or so he imagined.

And then another figure appeared in the semi-dark room. But this was a familiar person. Not immediately recognizable, but certainly familiar: the master of the house, Attorney Yoel Melchior himself.

"What are you doing here, Schiff?" Melchior grumbled, and his disgruntlement immediately broke the spell. Yet it was Professor Schiff who should have been disgruntled. And he was. In truth, Professor Schiff had arrived at Melchior's home in a state of fury. In even greater truth, Professor Schiff felt an ardent desire to murder Attorney Melchior, chop up his body, and throw the pieces in the gutter.

"I was forced to come because you won't answer my calls," said Professor Schiff. His trembling voice divulged the violence mounting in his throat.

"It would have been better if you'd left me a message at

the office," replied Melchior. He was clad in the profession's finest attire, namely, a well-tailored gray suit and socks whose pale-pink shade matched his expensive tie.

"I left you eighty-five messages. I've been phoning your office twice a day. Sometimes three."

"Cold water?" offered Melchior. "Or perhaps a beer?"

"Let's start with my check. We can get to the party later."

"Lucile, do me a favor. Could you bring our guest some water? He needs to calm down," said Melchior in clumsily accented English to the lady who gazed at Professor Schiff from beneath her heavy eyelids. And that was how Professor Schiff learned that her name was Lucile. Melchior then turned back to Professor Schiff: "I have two pieces of news for you, Schiff. The bad news is that, as of now, under the current circumstances, and considering the sum total of the data, I am unfortunately prevented from being able to fulfill my financial obligation to you." He plunged into an armchair and made himself comfortable. Professor Schiff stubbornly remained standing, even when Melchior waved at the couch. "The good news is that I've decided to meet you halfway, and I should therefore like to offer you, as an act of goodwill and beyond the letter of the law, something else instead of money." He gestured magnanimously at the woman, who had since reentered the room carrying a tray with a bottle of water and three glasses. "Something of equal value, as they say."

"What?" Professor Schiff asked feebly. "What are you offering me? I don't understand."

"Her," said Attorney Melchior. His hand was still suspended in midair, like the wing of an angel. "I'm offering you her."

Lucile sat down at an angle on the armrest of one of the chairs, crossed one leg over the other, and dangled a flip-flop from her toe. She slowly sipped her water, eyes closed, with the same intensity with which she had kissed the mezuzah.

"Wait . . . What?" Professor Schiff stammered. "I'm not sure I understand." He realized there must be some trick being played here, the nature of which he had yet to grasp. "Her?"

"Exactly," confirmed the lawyer with a nod.

Professor Schiff had all but given up on ever getting the four thousand dollars he was owed by Yoel Melchior and his partners. He was well aware of what everyone knows: battles against lawyers always end in defeat. Even when they end in victory. And yet, if he saw no chance of the debt being paid, why had he insisted on coming here and entering this house uninvited? To be humiliated, in all likelihood.

No, this was no trick. Melchior was simply making a mockery of him.

"Bravo," said Professor Schiff and slowly applauded, "excellent work. An outstanding joke."

Melchior looked at Lucile. "Professor Schiff thinks you're funny," he said, in English.

"No, that's not what I think," said Professor Schiff and attempted to smile at her. He shook his head heavily and felt his brain rattling from side to side in his skull.

"Very well, then, let's proceed, Schiff. This is not a negotiation. Take it or leave it." Melchior pulled a phone out of his pocket, glanced at it, and clucked his tongue. "And I don't have much time. I have to be in court in forty minutes."

"Unbelievable. Are you seriously offering me a human being instead of the money you and your friends owe me?"

"I admit that when you put it that way it doesn't sound very good. But yes, the idea is that you will take this woman, as . . . as a personal assistant, in return for erasing our debt."

"But I need the money, I have bills to pay."

"Then let her work for you."

"Work for me?" Professor Schiff shouted. "How exactly? Should I have her develop screenplays for people like you, who don't pay? Or perhaps she could write my next novel for me? Besides, the whole idea is crazy, utterly scandalous, and completely against the law."

The volume of his voice made no impression on Melchior. "What do you know about the law, Schiff?" he asked dryly, and promptly answered, "Nothing whatsoever."

But the woman's eyes sent a reassuring signal to Professor Schiff. He wasn't sure how much Hebrew she could follow, but she looked as though she'd understood everything, and now appeared to be informing him that the result of this ridiculous negotiation would be beneficial to all concerned, including her.

"Listen, Schiff," said Melchior with a theatrical clap of his hands, "I really can't understand the discrepancy between your talent, which I truly admire, and your complete lack of creativity when it comes to conducting your life."

Professor Schiff's headache was of the type that grips one's skull in a slow squeeze of the vise. For some reason it occurred to him that if only Lucile were to place the pink palm of her hand on his forehead, the pain would instantly vanish. It was not just her long fingers, at the tips of which, he believed, was a comforting coolness. Professor Schiff began to notice that the very presence of this woman filled the entire space of the room. The house. The yard. The street.

He heard himself ask, "And will she agree?"

"I see no reason why she wouldn't," said Melchior.

Professor Schiff found the proposal despicable and the situation repugnant. The conversation he was having with Melchior was absurd and embarrassing. Nevertheless, he nodded feebly.

"Very well, then," said Melchior, "the matter is settled." He stood up, walked over to Professor Schiff, caught hold of his limp right hand, and shook it. "My secretary will send you a copy of the agreement, you sign it and send it back."

"Agreement . . . ? " Professor Schiff murmured. He held the glass of water up to his forehead. The cold tempered his headache slightly.

"Something along the lines of, you know, the standard wording. It's not very complicated." Melchior focused his eyes on a point in space and recited as if he were reading off a teleprompter: "The agreement . . . entered into between the grantee, hereinafter 'Schiff,' and the grantor, hereinafter 'Melchior,' also known as Attorney Melchior, Franco and Co., on such and such date . . . Whereas Melchior is interested in repaying his fiduciary debt to Schiff, and whereas Schiff has expressed his consent to accept an item of equal value in lieu of the funds to which he is entitled, it is hereby agreed and declared between the parties as follows. One: The preamble to this agreement is an integral part hereof. Two: Schiff shall receive from Melchior one Mrs . . . um . . . Lucile . . . so and so, passport number such and such, hereinafter 'Lucile,' who shall be placed in Schiff's service for an unlimited period of time. Three: It is hereby agreed between the parties that Lucile is a renumeration of equal value to the fiduciary debt in the amount of four thousand United States dollars, which Melchior owes Schiff. Four: At such time as Lucile shall be transferred to Schiff's proprietorship, all of Melchior's debts to Schiff shall be considered terminated, and Schiff shall have no further financial claims whatsoever on Melchior. Five: Schiff is entitled to make any use of Lucile as he shall deem desirable in his sole discretion. In witness whereof, the parties have signed and so forth . . ."

Professor Schiff looked up at Lucile Tetteh-Ofosu. A serene smile covered her face. She nodded calmly and slowly, essentially confirming that the transaction, ludicrous and reprehensible as it may be, was agreeable to her.

She kissed the mezuzah twice as they walked out of Attorney Melchior's home.

One might hold, justifiably, that the aforementioned events portray Professor Schiff as a weak man. Or, alternatively, as an ineffectual opportunist, the kind who, despite the humanist principles he holds dear and makes a point of preaching, was, at the moment of truth, capable of collaborating with inconceivably heinous acts. One might also conclude that the avocation of his great-great-great-great-grandfather had somehow, against all reason and biological determinism, managed to flow through the genealogical chain as a hereditary trait. And yet one must allow Professor Schiff the benefit of doubt. Under the extraordinary circumstances in which he had been placed, it was precisely his overcautiousness that scrambled his common sense.

Attorney Melchior did not forget to hand Professor Schiff Mrs. Lucile Tetteh-Ofosu's passport, since according to the terms of their agreement she was now supposedly subject to his authority.

The green plastic cover of the document was imprinted with gilded, ceremonial letters spelling the name of a country whose existence Professor Schiff recalled only vaguely, and at this point was not quite able to place on a map. But at his age, of course, memory plays tricks. A name that sounds completely new, like a sudden flash as unexpected as a shooting star, might actually have been hovering forever in the dim recesses of one's consciousness.

Professor Schiff gave the passport to Lucile immediately. He asked her, in fact begged her, to forget—and to do so as quickly as possible—the disgraceful episode in which he had—wholly against his will, he repeatedly emphasized—been caught up. And if there was even the briefest impression that he was in fact responsible in any way at all for the embarrassing affair, he most wholeheartedly apologized and was willing to back his sincere apology with any necessary compensation. And, of course, he offered to call her a taxi and pay for her to be taken to wherever she wished.

But Mrs. Lucile Tetteh-Ofosu was in no hurry to go anywhere. "How is your headache, Professor?" she asked in a nurse's matter-of-fact tone.

How did she know his head hurt? He did not dare to ask. Instead of answering, he simply gave a grateful smile.

They walked down the sun-drenched street, a black woman in a teenaged boy's clothes beside a bespectacled man with curly gray hair and a beard. She moving in an elegant dance of supple bounds, he with his feet splayed as he swayed with distracted clumsiness. Passersby gave them curious stares, and Professor Schiff, aware of the intriguing, disturbing contrast between him and the woman beside him, felt a painful shame at the ownership attributed to him by observers. And yet, at the same time, he was proud of the covert, embarrassing, inconceivable connection that now existed between them. In this respect, again, he was torn between two sensations: the desire for her to vanish along with the memory of the embarrassing incident, and the desire for her to remain in his company. At least for a few moments longer.

Without turning to look at her, he said, "Either way, you're welcome to come to my home. I mean, to our home . . .

Mine and my wife's, Tami . . ." From the corner of his eye he noticed that her shadow was no longer accompanying his. He stopped. Had she heard him? "And by the way," he added, "purely by chance, we happen to be looking for someone to work for us, unrelated to what happened today . . ."

He reached into his wallet and took out a business card, to which he had only recently added the prefix *Prof*, which seemed to squeeze his name toward the edge of the card. Then he turned around and saw her hurrying away to the crosswalk, where she was swallowed up in a crowd that seemed to spitefully close in on her. He ran, actually chased her, and when he finally caught up and stood blocking her path, he said breathlessly, "Here's my business card. I enjoyed meeting you, really, don't hesitate to call, for any reason, at any time . . ."

Lucile listened patiently, and only when he'd stopped stammering did she take the card from his hand and shove it into the back pocket of her gym shorts. "Okay," she said.

"Okay," said Professor Schiff. And what now? What now? Was he going to simply let her leave? Vanish into the crowded, urban infinity? Or into his memories? The list of time's insignificant moments?

"So where are you headed now, Mrs. Lucile?" he heard himself ask.

"To the sea," said Lucile Tetteh-Ofosu.

"Oh," said the surprised professor. Then he said it again: "Oh." He tried to picture her among the joggers, Qigong practitioners, and sanitary workers of Gordon Beach.

"For physical maintenance, I presume," he said in a haughty, professorial tone that was completely out of step with the desperation pulsing through his aching head.

She seemed confused. "Physical maintenance?"

"I mean, it's your exercise, isn't it?"

"No, it's not exercise," said Lucile with a forgiving smile, "I collect seashells."

Very simple, yes, very simple and entirely understandable.

"May I join you?" asked Professor Schiff.

3

After months of deliberations, Professor Schiff finally decided to travel to the African city where the remains of the sunken *Esperanza* were housed. He looked up the Museum of African Culture and sent Dr. Samuel Baidoo, the director and chief curator, a letter in which he outlined what he knew about his great-great-great-great-grandfather. He signed off with these words:

As far as I know, I am the legal heir of Klonimus Zelig Schiff, and it is therefore worth looking into the implications of my status as regards the Esperanza *and its contents.*

Less than three weeks later—the blink of an eye by the standards of the country to which he was headed—Dr. Baidoo's brief reply arrived:

Dear Professor,

I would be happy to offer you whatever help I may. And of course, if at any time you are intending to travel here, simply relay a message to me and we shall arrange to meet. I would be honored to host you at the museum and introduce you to a selection of our magnificent collection.

Yours truly,
Samuel

In early February, Professor Schiff set off on a journey brimming with layovers. After fourteen hours, he emerged from a cool airplane into the sweltering, viscous, heavy air of Africa.

On his first day, he took his map and ventured out alone to wander through the exhaust fumes and florid dust that covered the city. He ambled among street stalls, carts, shiny motorcycles, pedestrians who all seemed to be carrying things on their heads, goats, dogs, and chickens. More than once, he miraculously avoided slipping into the gutters that ran along the sidewalk-less streets.

Surrounded by this wonderful hubbub, Professor Schiff narrated the experience to himself, impressed himself with accounts of his visit to Africa, boasted to himself about the remarkable touristic accomplishment, and never stopped snapping pictures. He photographed the coconut vendors who lopped off the tops of the green fruits with large machetes; he photographed the dumpling vendors who announced their wares by honking horns; he photographed women in colorful outfits who grilled plantains on charcoal; he photographed women selling pineapples and mangos stacked on aluminum platters perched atop their heads; he photographed the gangs of children who ran after him and left him in peace only when he handed out yellow bills of money; he photographed a funeral procession that inched alongside the vehicles crawling through traffic, making sure to capture the mourners as they sang and danced, as well as a picture of the smiling deceased man held aloft at the head of the procession.

As expected, after a few hours he was ready to give up on the adventure in return for a strip of shade, a bench to rest on, and above all, a place where he could relieve himself. Finally, when he could tolerate his torments no longer, Professor Schiff took refuge in a cafe that also served as a sort of grocery store and souvenir shop. He was forced to give the cheerful proprietor a brief autobiography, to tell him where he had come from and where he was going, and only then, after having purchased a beaded necklace, was he permitted to use the toilet. This was a doorless structure in the backyard, where he urinated into a hole in the ground.

The next day, Professor Schiff hired a car and a driver.

The driver, a potbellied man named Duke, with almond eyes whose whites were yellow, took it upon himself to show Professor Schiff all the essential tourist sites: The ancient neighborhood that tumbled into the sea. The lighthouse. The fish market. The mausoleum where the nation's founder was buried. The independence monument: an arm reaching up to the sky with a tightly clenched concrete fist. The new presidential palace with its architectural boldness. And, of course, the famous fort.

They reached it at midday. The white building perched sleepily on a cliff at the edge of the bay, its modest glory hidden behind walls that glistened in the sunlight. The Republic's flag hung heavily on poles along a boulevard of tall palm trees, casting their shadows on the bare asphalt road. Above the gate was an extinct European royal family's coat of arms and curly numbers indicating a distant year. A man in an undershirt sat on the steps smoking. A dog sprawled lifelessly next to him. Without a word, the man tore off a ticket from a book and handed it to Professor Schiff.

Through the silence, he could hear fishermen calling, cellphones ringing, a cicada grating.

Professor Schiff joined a small group of tourists. The guide, wearing rubber flip-flops and a floral shirt, led them among staircases and balconies overlooking the gray ocean.

"Why is everything so dilapidated here?" Professor Schiff plucked up the courage to ask the guide, in the grumbling tone of a disappointed customer. He pointed to the ancient iron cannons rusting in the yard, the peeling paint on the walls, and the sagging ceiling beams.

"Yeah, how much could a gallon of anti-rust paint cost?" groused one of the tourists, a man with a flushed face whose silky hair clung to his forehead. The arrogance of this red-faced man irritated Professor Schiff. But in fact, it was his own conceit that irked him.

"Not every memory requires a renovation," replied the guide with a snort.

And this, of course, was a hint at the next stop on the tour, the really important spot, the thing everyone had come to see. Including Professor Schiff. Because now, after each of the sweaty tourists had amassed a huge quantity of photos, they were finally taken to the fort's dungeons: the heart of the matter, the holy of holies.

In these horrifying, airless spaces, where only a single beam of light penetrated through a barred porthole, slaves had been housed before being led through a narrow passageway to the shore. To the ships. To their journey across the ocean.

The guide turned on a flashlight. In the corner of the room, on the floor, were flower wreaths, velvet hearts, candles flickering on and off, and framed family photos. These were offerings left by American tourists. The dampness gave the objects a gray-brown veneer and united them with the slippery layer of mud covering the stone tiles.

"This mud," said the guide, "is residue from the biological product left here by the slaves two hundred years ago."

Biological product, yes, that was exactly what he said. Professor Schiff felt dizzy and lost his balance. He leaned against the damp wall.

"Are you all right, sir?" asked the guide.

"Yes, I'm fine."

When they reached the "point of no return" at the end of the passageway, the tourists were welcomed by an ocean breeze that carried an odor of fish and decay.

Back in the main area of the fort, a group of schoolchildren in green and yellow uniforms crowded into the room. They were clearly fascinated by the rusty chains and cuffs hanging from the wall (in between a model slave ship and a painting of slaves chained together with iron collars) and couldn't help reaching their little hands out to pull, rattle, and touch the ancient relics. The children filled the gloomy display area with raucous giggles, and their eagerness infected Professor Schiff, lifting his spirits slightly.

On his way out, the guide stopped Professor Schiff and handed him a bottle of ice-cold water. "Don't forget to drink, sir, it's important in this heat."

Professor Schiff pressed a crumpled bill into the man's hand. In thanks. And apology.

"And as for the renovations," the guide remarked, "I wanted to let you know that we have received a grant from the European Union. It's in next year's budget."

In the parking lot, under the shade of a massive mahogany tree, Professor Schiff and Duke stood watching the schoolchildren leave the fort and clamber onto their bus.

Professor Schiff asked Duke if he'd been brought here on a school trip when he was a boy.

No, Duke replied, he hadn't. There were two reasons, he explained in his slow cadence: A, because he hadn't grown up in the capital but in a small town up north. And B, because he hadn't gone to school regularly, even though schoolchildren were given a hot meal and therefore never went to bed hungry.

Professor Schiff asked why Duke hadn't gone to school, but the driver simply shrugged his shoulders.

Afterward, though, in the Toyota, Duke opened the glove compartment, dug through the tools and rags, and pulled out a fat and dog-eared Bible. Holding it up, he declared, "Here—this is my school." This was the book, he said, that had taught him everything he needed to know about the world: about love, about hate, about reward and punishment.

Professor Schiff could see dozens of paper bookmarks sticking out from the Bible's pages.

"Jesus was the only teacher I ever had," Duke added, "and maybe that's all you need."

"Maybe."

"Every day, I try to do one good deed. That way, I don't go to bed hungry."

On their way back to the hotel, Duke stopped to buy three birdcages from a peddler who stood right up against the car window. Then he drove to Independence Park, where he set the birds free. One of them, a tiny creature with a red chest, took flight and perched atop the memorial statue, on the thumb of the concrete fist.

Professor Schiff took a picture.

4

Ladies and gentlemen, members of the Special Tribunal, Madam Attorney General, Head of the Investigation Team:

In 1830, my great-grandfather's great-grandfather, the Jewish millionaire who resided in the city of Paramaribo in Suriname, Klonimus Zelig Schiff, ceased all his business activities. He sold three of his four ships (the *Rachel*, the *Rebecca*, and the *Sarah*); transferred his shares in the plantations, the refinery, and the rum distillery to his partners; gave up his upholstered, silver-leaf-adorned pew at the synagogue; handed over the keys to his palace (actually a capacious wooden house painted white, which had survived Paramaribo's two big fires and still stands today) to his three unmarried daughters; made them promise—collectively and separately—to tend to the welfare and education of their thirteen-year-old brother, Solomon; and then boarded the *Esperanza*, his only remaining vessel, and set sail to an unknown destination along with five families of freed slaves.

He did not say when he might return, nor did he make any formal farewells. Not even to his daughters and his beloved young son. He left no clues, either in writing or in any utterance.

And so, even before the *Esperanza* had dwindled into a dot and disappeared across the horizon, conjectures and rumors tantalized the residents of the remote Dutch colony at the edge of the Caribbean. Most believed, quite reasonably, that Schiff had grown tired of provincial life and decided to return to his native city of Frankfurt, and that his daughters and son would soon join him. But there were those who insisted that Schiff had sailed to the other side of the world only to kiss the soil of the Holy Land.

The *Esperanza* was spotted in various places around the Atlantic Ocean, and at least two reports of encounters with the vessel made their way to the port of Paramaribo. If someone had bothered to track the ship's course, they would have located with relative ease where it had sailed, where exactly it anchored roughly two months later, and what became of it afterward. But public interest in the enigmatic disappearance of the millionaire Schiff faded quickly. And as happens so often, the mystery made way for new scandals and more burning issues, and the story was eventually forgotten.

And now, ladies and gentlemen, I must relate the tribulations of my great-great-great-great-grandfather's daughters after his disappearance, and most especially those of his son, Solomon. These details are necessary to clarify more precisely my position in the family dynasty.

Klonimus's daughters, three fashionable young ladies with fine taste and a fondness for leisure, managed within a decade to fritter away the entire sizeable estate with which they had been charged, down to the very last gulden.

Yes, I know what you're thinking, distinguished members of the tribunal, and needless to say, I couldn't agree more. According to the doctrine on which I was raised—and I hazard a guess that you were as well—wasting money is not only permissible but desirable. That, after all, is the engine that drives our finest economies. But wasting money produced through exploitation and the inflicting of unimaginable suffering—that is a crime! On this matter we are in complete agreement. In fact, I do not believe there could be anyone, either in this air-conditioned room at the Attorney General's offices or anywhere else in the world, who would not concur on this matter. It is such a blessing that we, citizens of the twenty-first century, can so easily distinguish between good money and bad money.

Either way, as they swirled with ever-increasing speed around the typhoon of profligacy, the young ladies Sarah, Rebecca, and Rachel did not forget the pledge they had made to their father, and they made sure that their young brother, Solomon, received the finest education available in those days in a far-flung colony at the edge of the Caribbean. As well as the finest medical care, when it turned out that the young boy's lungs were afflicted by the tropical humidity. But in those days, even in places frequented by ship doctors on leave (whose main areas of expertise were sawing off limbs and disinfecting wounds caused by lashings), medical science could do little for Solomon Schiff except offer a diagnosis: tuberculosis.

The young man was doomed to live a short life. It ended on a ship (as befitting the family's leitmotif) on his way to Europe with his wife and infant son. He had planned to start a new, healthy life in Danzig, with the help of distant relatives.

That, incidentally, was a rare occasion on which common sense coincided with medical advice. But fate, as they say, had other ideas.

Solomon Schiff was almost thirty when he was buried at sea, lowered into the waters of the Atlantic with no pomp and circumstance except a salute from the captain in his blue uniform. The Kaddish prayer was recited for him only two months later, when his widow and son reached Danzig. All I know of the widow, whose name was Theresa Schiff, was that she moved from Danzig to Riga, where she opened a haberdashery. Under the management of her son, Baruch, the shop grew into a commercial business with branches throughout Prussia.

And Baruch begat Abel. And Abel begat Hezkel. And Hezkel begat Yedidia.

And Yedidia begat me.

As for the three Schiff maidens who remained in Suriname, I do not know what became of them. I would like to believe that they managed to preserve their good names, as well as that of their father the slave trader, even when they lost all their other assets.

5

No, Professor Schiff did not walk along the beach with Lucile Tetteh-Ofosu that morning. He was called to take care of his wife, who'd thrown her back out while driving home. Professor Schiff tried to explain the emergency to Lucile, but he couldn't come up with the right words in English, so he simply told her in a doleful voice that, regrettably, he had to leave, but she had his card and of course he would be happy to hear from her, etc.

It later occurred to him that he might have asked Lucile to use the special powers he attributed to her—though he wasn't sure why—to relieve Tami's back pain, but he didn't think of it in time. That missed opportunity, of course, spared him from having to explain to Tami how and under what circumstances he had met Mrs. Lucile Tetteh-Ofosu, and thereby also exempted him from an embarrassing—and futile—attempt to hide the excitement that still pulsed in him. Yes, he managed to avoid that, too.

Professor Schiff went home, extricated Tami from the driver's seat of the Honda, and helped her hobble inside, doubled over and groaning in pain. Then he called the doctor, who arrived quickly and exhibited no clinical hesitation before emptying a syringe into the folds of Tami's back and promptly departing. Tami fell asleep, and Professor Schiff took the dogs for a walk, made himself a cup of coffee, and kept thinking about Mrs. Lucile Tetteh-Ofosu.

Was there any way to find her?

That very evening, he phoned Attorney Melchior's office. He had no intention, of course, of signing the imbecilic deed conceived and written by the lawyer, but he was hoping to get a phone number, address, or any other clue that might lead him to the magnificent lady.

Much to his astonishment, Melchior called him back. "Schiff," he said, "I'm glad you called. I wanted to let you know that I've added a few clauses to the agreement. Minor stuff. There's a certain issue related to ownership rights, you see, since according to the law you can't transfer property whose ownership can't be proved. But it's just a legalistic hindrance. Not the kind one can't overcome with the right language."

Professor Schiff held the phone away from his ear, walked over to the wall, pounded it with his fist, then sat down out of breath in his armchair. He could hear Melchior's faint voice coming from the receiver: "Schiff? Schiff! Are you there?"

The next morning, while drinking his first espresso, instead of stitching together the shreds of a dissipating dream, as he usually did, Professor Schiff saw an image of the woman from yesterday and felt a distraught sense of longing. If he were to have any chance of meeting her again, he would need to come up with a practical and rational way for it to happen.

He asked Tami for help. This, he knew, would involve a certain awkwardness. Because, after all, candor between a husband and wife is marked by fairly clear boundaries, especially when it comes to other women.

This is what he said to her: "I was at Attorney Melchior's yesterday . . ."

"Really?" said Tami, raising an eyebrow curiously.

"At his home . . . not at his office . . . to make sure he couldn't avoid me."

"And . . . ?"

"No, he didn't pay me."

"So . . . ?" Tami tried to spur him on, knowing full well that there must be another story beneath the story. A bigger one. The story due to which he had sat down on the edge of the bed and was irritably raking his curly hair.

"Anyway, there was this woman there . . . his cleaner . . . who said she was looking for more work."

"But you don't trust anyone. You're the only reason no one has come to clean this house for two months now. Are you willing to let go of your paranoia?"

"I think it'll work out with her."

He could tell immediately that Tami understood. Perhaps not everything, but she saw the gist of things.

She laughed, and her laughter shook her aching back. "Then call her and ask her to come," she said, groaning with pain.

"That's the thing, I've lost her number and I don't know how to find her."

"Ask Melchior."

"I tried, but he said she just disappeared."

"Disappeared?" Her face took on that expression. The one with irony but no smile.

"Gone."

"Maybe she decided to go back."

"Back?"

"As in home," Tami said, "we're talking about a migrant worker, right?" She furrowed her brow and the two deep creases above her nose made a V shape. "Where's she from—Africa?"

"Maybe," said Professor Schiff, "does it matter?"

"Then go hang around south Tel Aviv for a few days and you'll run into her eventually."

"A few days?"

"It's not like you have anything to do anyway. Tell yourself you're doing research for a book," Tami said with a snort.

"Maybe it really is the beginning of a book," Professor Schiff mused.

"It's definitely the beginning of something. But when you find her, think twice before you bring her here to clean our house."

Tami was a good advisor. Her ability to play the part of his oracle validated the merits of their long marriage. Or at least so he liked to think.

6

Ladies and gentlemen, members of the Special Tribunal, Madam Attorney General, Head of the Investigation Team:

I would like to remind you, or myself, that until not long ago, not long at all, I knew nothing of your vibrant country. A quick glance at the atlas, some pictures online, and a handful of accounts on travelers' forums added very little to the general knowledge I had acquired about the entire continent in the sixty-three years of my life.

What I knew was zebras, giraffes, and lions. When I was a child—and that really was a long time ago—the zoo, a neighborhood attraction that emitted a stench and the screeches of captive wild beasts, was located near my home. The zoo was my favorite pastime—and that was Africa. There were chimpanzees, lions, a pair of elephants, and a lone hippopotamus lounging in a pool of filthy water. In a popular children's book that I read, white people searched for a treasure hidden by a cruel, black king who hanged his subjects from baobab trees. Later on, I discovered Tarzan. After that, it was children starving to death in Biafra, passengers on a plane that was hijacked and released at the Entebbe airport, and people from a nation called Hutu murdering people from a nation called Tutsi in a country named Rwanda.

And so, you see, I did manage, with absolute disinterest and no true curiosity, to gather a few more images and words over the years: the snows of Kilimanjaro; Victoria Falls; "Doctor Livingstone, I presume"; Kurtz in the heart of darkness; a herd of gnu crossing a crocodile-infested river; tsetse flies; apartheid; voodoo; Boko Haram; a python swallowing a deer; an elephant cemetery; gorillas in the mist; Ebola; gold mines; blood diamonds; locust swarms; dead rhinos; kidnapped girls; a despot in a leopard-skin hat; children bearing arms; men dancing in raffia skirts. And once, on a visit to Amsterdam, I bought an African mask at the Waterlooplein Market that still hangs on the wall in my office.

That's more or less it.

I can sum up my relationship with Africa in one sentence: this continent, with all its evergreen forests, its wild animals, lakes, rivers, beaches, its 11.73 million square miles, and above all, ladies and gentlemen, you, the 1.2 billion human beings with your hundreds of cultures, languages, customs, and faiths—you have not aroused any particular interest in me. And so it is strange, very strange, that after spending a mere three days here, I was overcome by the sense that I have always been connected to this continent, to this land. To you. And I must emphasize, ladies and gentlemen, that it is not merely an affection for a people and a place I never knew, but a genuine metaphysical affinity. A primordial emotional bond. Would you believe it?

Yes, it is strange. When you issued an arrest warrant for me under the Law for Adjudicating Slave Traders and their

Accomplices, Heirs, and Beneficiaries, and forced me to stay here, I began to amuse myself with the notion of settling in this place, even if our unusual affair ends with my unconditional release. I admit, though, that I haven't looked into the practicalities of the idea.

7

Finally, after a week spent getting to know the bustling tropical city, Professor Schiff managed to reach Dr. Samuel Baidoo, the director of the Museum of African Culture, on the phone. Dr. Baidoo was extremely friendly and asked how Professor Schiff liked his country.

"It's a sad country, where people are always smiling," said Professor Schiff.

Dr. Baidoo sighed. "How true. How true." Then he apologized for having been absent and making the professor wait, remarked on the dust and humidity, asked if the professor's hotel was satisfactory, and recommended an Italian restaurant on Nasser Street, just around the corner, five minutes' walk from the hotel. Then, after a hesitant pause and a nervous clearing of the throat, he asked if Professor Schiff might be interested in purchasing a few items.

Professor Schiff was confused. "Items? Which items?"

"Items salvaged from the ship," said Dr. Baidoo.

Professor Schiff was having trouble following. "But if I understand correctly," he said, "all the items salvaged from the ship are part of the museum collection, aren't they?"

"Our collections are dynamic," Dr. Baidoo replied, "that is to say, they change, they are not fixed, if you get what I mean."

It was no misunderstanding, then. The vague hint was in fact an unambiguous offer. Dr. Baidoo made a point of adding, politely yet pointedly, that Professor Schiff would be advised to come to their meeting at the museum with cash in hand. Without, of course, any obligation.

To Dr. Samuel Baidoo's credit, it should be noted that he did not bother engaging in the standard game that usually starts with a phrase along the lines of, "please consider my situation" and an eye roll. In the next stage of the game, one holds a bill of money up against an item or document and passes it—swiftly, smoothly—to the recipient. Once the money has changed hands, there usually comes a demand for more. But only through hints. A slight movement of the chin. Or of the eyebrows, if such exist. And then, to bring the procedure to its culmination—because, after all, it has patterns and rules, perhaps even a certain beauty, as does any ritual—comes the expression of gratitude. A few polite words, a handshake, a courteous salute.

But Dr. Samuel Baidoo was completely frank. His job, he explained to Professor Schiff, was getting harder and harder, because the museum was subject to chronic fiscal problems. The Ministry of Culture had promised to transfer the annual budget, which had been cut by thirty percent, but would not cover the deficit from prior years. Now the museum's coffers were simply empty. And it is impossible to run an institution—he whined bitterly—when even the janitors can't be paid. "Did you notice that the museum is only open on Saturdays?" he asked rhetorically, and promptly answered,

"It's because we have no capacity to clean the toilets more than once a week." And so he had no choice but to put up items from the collections for sale once in a while. Not too often. And only ones that were not in the permanent collections, of course, so as not to negatively impact the museum's "conceptual quality" or "design integrity." Professor Schiff must understand, Dr. Baidoo explained, that he was forced into this course of action out of genuine concern for the fate of the institution he directed.

Dr. Samuel Baidoo was a large man with a polka-dotted bowtie. He sat opposite Professor Schiff with his legs splayed wide and stroked his sparse beard while a ceiling fan with four large blades whirred and creaked above them, subjecting him to a roulette of light and shade. The second-floor windows of the gray building, designed in the neoclassical pastiche so beloved by the architects of the British Empire, looked out on a sandy lot where tin shacks clung to each other. A woman bathed a baby in a tub. Dwarf goats darted among laundry lines. A pot steamed over a fire in which coconut husks burned.

"You may buy any item you choose," said Dr. Baidoo, "but let us agree that in light of the delicacy and extreme complexity of the matter, the transaction must occur discreetly."

Sitting on the desk were the objects extricated from the wreckage of the ship in the summer of 2006: a compass, the helm, a decorative chest, bowls and cups inscribed with the name *Esperanza*, china plates illustrated with what appeared to be scenes from Creation, china teacups also adorned with the ship's name in blue letters, a silver kiddush cup, a sextant, three English muskets, a copper board shaped like tablets with the ten commandments engraved in Dutch, and also, miraculously, three leather-bound volumes: the ship's logbook, all of whose pages were waterlogged, wrinkled, and covered with light-blue stains; an enormous Bible (twenty by fifteen inches and at least six inches thick); and a *siddur* (which Dr. Baidoo called "a Jewish prayer book") that was also extremely worn, so much so that the pages had hardened into an inseparable clump. Dr. Baidoo also showed Professor Schiff a few pages written in Dutch and Hebrew, which seemed to be remnants of a personal diary, as well as three small drawings: two of a young girl, and one depicting an elderly man with a disheveled beard. The diary pages were amazingly well preserved, their contents easily readable.

Professor Schiff was drawn, of course, to the texts and the drawings. It was these he wanted—he had no doubt of this—very much. He examined the ancient documents with supreme care. Could his great-grandfather's great-grandfather have held these papers in his hands?

Then again, how could they have survived deep underwater for decades? The doubt that gnawed at Professor Schiff was an integral part of the meeting's clandestine air of criminality.

Dr. Baidoo had an answer, of course. These pages, he explained, had been protected in a special copper chest, a safe of sorts, that was coated with lead and sealed with wax. A work of art that was a wonderful specimen of the way early nineteenth-century ships were outfitted. Unfortunately,

Professor Schiff would not be able to see this miraculous chest, since it was on permanent loan to the naval museum in Newport, Virginia, and so on and so forth . . .

Dr. Samuel's fluid monologue only increased Professor Schiff's suspicion. Nevertheless, his desire to own these objects was overpowering. First, he decided to purchase the diary pages and the drawings, for two hundred dollars—a tolerable, one might even say reasonable, price—and after a brief negotiation he also managed to obtain the logbook for a bargain price of one hundred dollars. Over time, Professor Schiff promised himself, he would buy the remaining items, too, all of them, drib by drab, and become their legal owner.

The transaction was sealed with a ceremonial handshake.

"I'm a very bad businessman," said Dr. Baidoo bitterly, counting the bills, "but of course, I took into consideration that you are no mere collector. These items are of personal interest to you."

Professor Schiff gingerly picked up the pages and drawings and placed them in a manila envelope, which he inserted between his backpack's rigid back and his laptop computer.

It is unclear why it never occurred to Professor Schiff that in the country he was visiting—as in any lawful country haunted by its heritage—there was sure to be some interest in the fate of archeological findings. Including those fished out of sunken ships.

It was the arrogance, most likely. The arrogance was what made him belittle the Republic's supervision and enforcement apparatus. At least during his first few days. Because if he had only given it a little thought, he would have immediately seen that the artifacts of which he was now in possession were national treasures of historic value. On the other hand, was it not *he* who was the sole legal heir to Klonimus Zelig Schiff, the owner of the *Esperanza* and everything in it? And did these items, therefore, not belong to him according to law and logic?

As soon as he returned to his hotel room, Professor Schiff photographed the diary pages covered with crowded, neat, beautiful, error-free handwriting, and sent the pictures to his friend Margo in Amsterdam. He asked her to translate them for him.

Late that night, Professor Schiff fell asleep with a deep sense of satisfaction: the satisfaction of a man who had fulfilled his mission and earned a peaceful slumber. He wasn't even bothered by his usual heartburn.

But he was awakened at dawn when the door to his room was slammed shut. He turned on the lamp and leaped out of bed. Three men in colorful shirts and fashionable sneakers moved about the room with exuberant cheer, their faces smeared with the grins of latecomers to a party. They circled around the suite, stepped onto the balcony, moved furniture, turned on the television, and emptied Professor Schiff's suitcase onto the floor. Their glee as they danced this way and that was accompanied by a sour swell of sweat and alcohol.

Professor Schiff was terrified. His brain was busy trying to pull the brakes on his rapidly swirling thoughts, its rhythm seemingly synchronized with the pace of the three men's movements. Only when one of them stepped, accidentally it seemed, on his bare foot, did the fear change to anger.

"What do you want?" Professor Schiff yelled. "Who are you anyway?"

The mad dance stopped at once, and the guests froze. One of them, the man standing in the balcony doorway, pulled a badge with a small photo out of his pocket. He flashed the badge at Professor Schiff and said, "We're from the national security unit, and you, sir, are suspected of stealing national treasures with the intent to smuggle them out of the country."

There was no point in denying this, of course, and it did not even occur to Professor Schiff to resist or protest. It was, after all, simply a matter of paying the requisite price (fifty dollars apiece), which Professor Schiff handed over with trembling hands and a sigh of relief.

For some reason, they decided to confiscate the *Esperanza*'s logbook, apparently believing they could get a good price for it on some black market or other. And it really was a most attractive item, even though its pages were splattered with indecipherable ink stains.

Fortunately for Professor Schiff, they let him keep the diary pages.

8

Honorable members of the Special Tribunal, Honorable Madam Attorney General, distinguished Head of the Investigation Team:

Yes, my grandfather's grandfather's grandfather, Klonimus Zelig Schiff, was a slave trader. I have briefly described to you his life up until his sudden and mysterious departure. Please be patient. We will get to that. It's a long story. What's important for me to mention now is that apart from being a slave trader, Klonimus Zelig Schiff was also a missionary. But not just any missionary—not another uncompromising, honest, naive, cruel representative of Christ (on the matter of which I need not say another word to you Africans), but a Jewish missionary.

Schiff's guilt, then, is twofold. Not only did he abduct hundreds of people from Africa, enslave them, and deny them their rights, he also persuaded them to convert. It is true that, considering all his misdeeds, this one does not equal the other villainies attributed to him. Yet still, his insistence on converting his slaves to Judaism added insult to injury. Even if his intentions were pure (and the intentions of missionaries always are, of course), it was a despicable act. At least to my mind. Atheists like myself sometimes have trouble comprehending that for people of faith, religion is the soul itself. (Incidentally, distinguished friends, there are those who claim that religious conversion can instigate clinical depression, along with its typical symptoms of insomnia, loss of appetite, decreased libido, apathy, and even suicidal ideation.)

It is important to note that the conversion of Schiff's slaves was not coerced but brought about solely through peaceable persuasion. However, even if Klonimus Schiff's business acumen—namely, superlative salesmanship and charisma—was instrumental to his missionary project, the way he presented these miserable people with his preferred religion was not particularly sophisticated. I assume his winning line was: "Come and join us—a nation of liberated slaves." A deceptively simplistic sales pitch, aimed at a target audience that would in any case have bought whatever product it felt a rapport with.

At any rate, the minute Schiff's slaves gave up their voodoo traditions and disavowed the pantheon of ghosts who managed their arduous lives, or, alternately, dismissed the Holy Trinity from their jobs (some of the slaves had joined the Dutch Reformed Church by then) and decided to convert to Judaism, they took upon themselves the whole folklore package offered by the ancient tribe they were joining, from dress and accessories through national myths and messianic hallucinations.

Including, of course, a yearning for the Holy Land—namely, Zion. With your permission, I should like to expand on this topic shortly.

To Schiff's credit, he did not force the converts to undergo circumcision (even though it would seem, after having been put through countless physical punishments, that they might have easily been able to tolerate this torture, too), nor did he demand that they learn the holy tongue, the language through which one communicates with God. Only those who wanted to win the big prize, the prize of freedom, had to prove their ability to read three chapters of Psalms in Hebrew, as well as answer a few questions posed by the examiner, Klonimus Schiff himself. And indeed, the senior workers at Schiff's estate, practically all of whom were freed slaves hired as secretaries, managers, and personal butlers, observed the Jewish commandments and could chatter a little in the holy tongue. As could their families. And if Schiff caught them covertly sacrificing a chicken to some voodoo patron or revered spirit, he would promptly order that they be whipped. Not too hard, I hope.

There were some twenty such senior workers at Schiff's estate. A few had served him for over two decades and so it is no wonder he felt very close to them, and also a great sense of responsibility toward them, just as a patriarch feels toward his family. He housed them in comfortable apartments, fed them with the estate's best produce, spoiled them with rum, pipes, and spiced cakes, dressed their wives in fine dresses, made sure their children learned reading, writing, music, and arithmetic, and provided medical care. Since he was a thorough man and imbued with a sense of purpose, he also built a seminary on his estate, where on the first of every month he gathered the small tribe, read a chapter from the Torah, and delivered a sermon.

Oh, what a peculiar bunch they were.

And now, ladies and gentlemen, as promised, I return to the topic of Zion.

You are surely familiar with the famous lines, "By the rivers of Babylon, there we sat down, yea, we wept when we remembered Zion"? Of course. I knew you would be. Who isn't? I'm sure you also know that this well-known verse from Psalms voices a central theme in the Jewish ethos: the yearning for Zion.

Klonimus Schiff made a point of ensuring that each of his converts adopted this ethos, instilling a yearning for that mysterious swath of land, that magical, sweet, mythological destination where—and not in any other place on Earth—all hopes would come true. In other words, ladies and gentlemen, not only did Klonimus turn his slaves into Jews, he also made them Zionists.

Do you understand what happened here? Astonishingly, my ancestor was almost fifty years ahead of the Zionist movement! Admittedly, he was at the wrong time, in the wrong place, and with the wrong people, but in my opinion he certainly deserves the title "Herald of Zionism." Even if there is no street named after him in Tel Aviv.

Ladies and gentlemen, members of the Special Tribunal, Madam Attorney General, Head of the Investigation Team:

You might be thinking, You're being evasive, blurring

and bleaching out the background pictures. After all, what we have here is a slave trader, not merely a shrewd tradesman engaged in the business of buying and selling a desirable commodity. Even if your ancestor was only interested in acquiring capital, you say, and even if he was no bloodthirsty sadist by nature, it is nevertheless unlikely, in fact truly implausible, that he did not witness horrifying acts of cruelty with his own eyes. And these acts, you say, even if he did not commit them himself, even if he neither implicitly nor explicitly instructed that they be committed, were still his absolute responsibility.

He was a slave trader, you say. A slave trader!

He saw, you say, how the captives were dragged out of his ships after their hellish journey, sick, starved, humiliated, their will to live beaten out of them.

He saw them, you say, in forced labor.

He saw them in pain, sick, dying of exhaustion. He saw them beaten and whipped to the point of unconsciousness. Horrifically executed. Losing limbs. Bleeding to death.

He saw them heartbroken when they were torn away from their children and loved ones.

He saw them worn down, bedraggled, prematurely aging, dying in destitution, and buried anonymously. He saw them, you say, erased into oblivion. Disappeared. And the faint echo of anguish that was all they left behind—he saw that, too, you say. He saw it and allowed it to evaporate into the wind like an offensive odor.

You ask, and rightly so, why I do not recount these things here, before this distinguished tribunal.

Well, ladies and gentlemen, I did not intend to blur these horrors. Nor would I be able to. Simply because they have been spread out behind me as a powerful background since the moment I took this stand. And of course, the entire life story of Klonimus Zelig Schiff is entangled and intertwined with these horrors, and they are what led him—yes, perhaps too late—to atone for his deeds in such an unusual way.

Please allow me to continue.

9

Professor Schiff searched the streets for a woman he didn't know, a woman he'd only met once, a woman who had left little more than a hasty impression in his memory. He searched, knowing that even in this overcrowded city, where acquaintances were always cropping up around the corner, his chances of running into Lucile Tetteh-Ofosu again were slim. After traipsing around for hours, he collapsed on a bench in a dusty park, where tired tamarisk and bowed palm trees grew out of the remnants of a filthy lawn. Squinting at the whiteness of the buildings surrounding the park, he tried as hard as he could to envision the ghost he was looking for. It had only been seventy-two hours and already he was willing to admit defeat. Or rather, to admit what he in fact knew: only a compulsive gambler would believe that coincidence could repair a plan gone wrong. And Professor Schiff did not have even a sliver of the gambling temperament. In fact, he was the opposite of a gambler. The complete opposite.

His eyes drooped shut, and he might have dozed off, but a few seconds later he opened them because he sensed someone standing next to him. He blinked at the colorful figure leaning over him and blocking the shabby view. It took a few seconds, perhaps even minutes, for Professor Schiff to grasp that the person talking to him was Lucile Tetteh-Ofosu. But this was certainly not the cleaning lady in boyish clothes. Standing before him was a splendid woman in a brightly colored dress that reached down to her ankles. A necklace of white glass beads dangled on her dark chest. A red silk scarf was tied around her tower of hair. Her feet were clad in golden flats.

"You're early, Professor," said Lucile Tetteh-Ofosu.

Had she really known he would come here, precisely to this spot, to wait for her, precisely now, on the bench in this dusty park in south Tel Aviv? Could that be possible?

Professor Schiff pulled himself together. Despite his racing pulse (he could almost feel the blood pushing its way into his calcifying arteries), he managed to adopt a professorial tone. "Oh yes, I'm always early for meetings," he said. Which was true. He was one of those people who always arrive early and then kill time in a park, on a bench just like this one.

"So I understand your proposal is still valid?"

"Which proposal?" Professor Schiff asked with some alarm. He couldn't remember proposing anything. He only remembered very much wanting to see her again, and that his wish had now come true.

She sat down next to him. Professor Schiff looked at her sideways and saw her fingers playing with the beads around her neck.

"Which day would you and your wife like me to come?"

The next day, while Tami Kushner conducted a businesslike interview, a few important details about Mrs. Lucile

Tetteh-Ofosu emerged. For example, that she was forty-seven years old; that she had five adult children who were scattered around the world; that she was a certified bookkeeper; that she was the scion to a modest but ancient royal family in which she was seventy-fourth in line for the crown—or would be, if the crown were ever given to a woman.

"And crowns are not given to women," Lucile explained with a giggle, "not with us, at any rate. Because you can't carry a pail of water on your head if you're wearing a crown."

"But still, you are a princess," said Professor Schiff, his deep voice seeming to resound on a different frequency.

Tami scowled. Her irritable finger picked stale crumbs off the table. "The problem is," she said, "that even if Mrs. Tetteh-Ofosu is a princess, or has some sort of royal title, she still has to produce a work permit, or a document stamped by the Ministry of the Interior. Otherwise, with all due respect and goodwill, we can't employ her."

"Of course," Lucile agreed, "my family pedigree is a completely private matter."

The forced meeting took on a truly hostile tone, Professor Schiff felt. He tried to decipher his wife's expression. What was the significance of the small, sweet-and-sour smile suspended on her face? Based on the clock's ticking, he knew her finger had been fiddling with the breadcrumbs for three minutes now.

Finally, Tami said, "But don't misunderstand me, Mrs. . . . um . . ."

"Lucile," said Professor Schiff.

"Please don't think, Lucile," Tami continued, "that I have any special regard for official permits or passports or identity papers, or any other document meant to enable or prevent border crossings. I really don't."

"Either way, I have no official document, if that's what you mean," Lucile said and shook her mane of curls in their red scarf.

"It's fine, Lucile, it's really fine," said Tami, "the truth is that I really hate the idea of certificates and identity papers." She narrowed her eyes at Professor Schiff. "As my husband once wrote—he's an important writer, you know—a passport is nothing but a comic strip with one picture." She sniggered. "And a border, he wrote, is just a line of ink, which if you bend and twist into loops gives way to the word *freedom*. That's nice, isn't it?"

"Yes, nice," said Lucile with a blank expression. After a short pause, she rolled up her sleeve, exposing a white scar all the way down her arm. "This is a line, too," she said, running her finger along the scar, "a fence I once crossed. My sleeve was completely ripped off. I turned it into a hair ribbon."

Something in Tami's expression suddenly changed. "Don't worry," she said, "you're among friends here, Lucile. Everything will work out in the end." She placed her white, bony fingers on Lucile's tightly clenched fist. "And I'm very happy that my husband offered to help you. Sometimes I forget how generous he is."

Professor Schiff was confused by this reversal and suddenly felt neutralized at the dining table gathering.

"Coffee?" he asked desperately. "Or tea, anyone?" When there was no reply, he declared, "I'm making some for myself. Anyone want some?"

It was as if he were merely the matchmaker, and now that the two women had been introduced—his wife of thirty years and a strange woman for whose charms he had fallen three days ago—he had completed his mission and, as far as they were concerned, could step aside. And keep quiet. At least for the time being. At least until the introduction phase was over and all the necessary questions had been asked, such as, "How many years have you been here?" and "Where do you live?" Questions it hadn't even occurred to him to ask and which had therefore been reassigned to Tami. And also, "Are you here alone?," a question he had deliberately avoided.

Either way, the metaphysical forces continued to rattle Professor Schiff as he decamped to the kitchen, made himself a cup of coffee in the moka pot, and slipped out onto the small balcony.

Tami followed him there unexpectedly. "The woman says she has nowhere to sleep because she just had to leave her apartment . . ." Before continuing, she examined Professor Schiff's face, and he moved his eyes from the coffee cup in his hands to the urban dusk growing darker among the balconies. His hands were trembling. Little waves slapped the sides of the cup.

"We could ask her to stay here for now," said Tami, "but I know how much you dislike houseguests . . ."

Phrased as it was in the general plural, the word *househ-uests* seemed to encompass the whole world, including, of course, Lucile Tetteh-Ofosu.

Tami's gaze bothered him. "Your hands are shaking, Aguri," she said. "Be careful not to spill coffee on your pants."

10

He'd arrived at the height of the dry season, the harmattan, and the northern winds from the Sahara covered the city with haze. In daytime the sunlight barely broke through the pale-yellow shield, and at night the air was heavy with smoke.

Professor Schiff by now viewed himself not as a tourist but as a guest. He straggled through the teeming, frenetic, noisy streets that never stood still for a second; he was swallowed up by the crowds along with peddlers, porters, children, and women in colorful dresses, in each of whose faces he looked for Lucile; he sampled delicacies at street stalls and then flushed his scorched throat with bottled water; he tried to befriend people and strike up conversations by asking stupid questions (his favorite opener was, "If you could live in a different country, which one would you choose?" and he was not surprised when every single person replied, "Our country is the best in the world"; everyone, that is, except a woman with a box full of glasses frames perched on her head, who said, "Canada. I hear they have snow there. I've never seen real snow"); he drank white palm wine that was just starting to ferment, ate fufu with peanut soup, and spent a whole day and night in his hotel suite, stricken with diarrhea and abdominal pain. When he recovered, he decided he needed to venture beyond the capital.

When Professor Schiff saw Duke, his driver, he was as delighted as he might be upon meeting a beloved childhood friend. But the familiar, sweaty face waiting in the Regent Boutique Hotel's lobby showed no expression. Duke simply asked, without any apparent interest or enthusiasm, "So what's the plan, Professor?" Then he crushed his cigarette out on the marble stair, kicked the butt onto the gravel path, and wiped the sweat from his brow with a plaid handkerchief.

Professor Schiff was slightly disappointed by the cool reception: in this huge city, where three and a half million humans blended noisily together, Duke was thus far his only friend. "An excursion," he said, "south, to the shore."

They settled on an itinerary for the day trip, agreed to a price (not without a circuitous negotiation that ended in Professor Schiff's utter defeat), picked up a few bottles of water, and set off.

Their first stop was Coconut Beach Resort, opposite which, out at sea, lay the *Esperanza*'s ruins underwater. The resort was a compound of two-story residential structures and coconut palms, surrounded by a concrete wall. Hidden speakers played rhythmic music that echoed all along the bay, overpowering the sound of the ocean waves.

After passing a thorough and pedantic security check at the gate, Professor Schiff and Duke found themselves walking along a path made of wooden boards. The familiar flags of various European countries flapped in the wind atop poles running along the path. A sheltered concrete square buzzing with people looked out onto the beach. There were golden-haired girls with their shoulders tattooed, well-groomed women in stylish beach attire and sparkling platinum jewelry adorning their suntanned bodies, potbellied men in clouds of cigar smoke, and waiters darting among low tables, serving cocktails and bowls of shrimp. On the beach, cleaners were picking up beverage cans and muscular volleyballers shouted, leapt, hit balls, and rolled around on the sand.

At the resort's diving club, the main attraction—or perhaps the only one—was an underwater tour of the wrecks of the sunken ship. The office wall displayed sun-faded photographs of the site, in which divers in masks and oxygen tanks swam among debris covered with sand and seaweed. There was also an expressive oil painting of a schooner, with cannon barrels visible through its slits. This was not, clearly, the *Esperanza*.

The diving club's manager, a man with poached skin, a long yellowing beard, and blue eyes encircled by white lashes, welcomed them from his faded office chair.

Professor Schiff asked if he could take the diving tour. He said he had a personal connection with the sunken ship. But the manager yawned indifferently. "Sorry, no diving today. The sea's too rough."

Professor Schiff explained that the ship had once belonged to his great-grandfather's great-grandfather.

Yellowbeard, assuming this was a joke, laughed politely. Then he said, "It's not diving season," and blinked his blue eyes irritably.

Gray waves pummeled the beach, crested in the northern wind, and sprayed salty shards into the diving club.

Duke and Professor Schiff drove to the famous snake farm, ate some tasteless yam burgers at a restaurant attached to a gas station, and continued on to the ruins of the Portuguese Mission. In the afternoon, on their way back to town, Duke suggested a stop at Shuffle Park. Professor Schiff had never heard of this tourist attraction, and as far as he could remember there was no such place recommended in *Lonely Planet*. He asked Duke to explain.

Shuffle Park, said Duke, was the biggest garbage dump in Africa (there was a tinge of pride in his customarily flat tone, as though he were describing a national treasure), and it was worth taking a look. Perhaps snapping a few photos. He added that he'd arranged to meet a man who traded spare parts there. But it would just be a quick visit, he promised, a few minutes at most. Besides, it was only a slight detour.

Professor Schiff agreed. He was in no hurry, after all. He didn't have any particular interest in garbage, but he was prepared to add this feature to his growing attachment to Africa.

They left the traffic jam at the western entrance to the city and drove onto a side road that passed perplexing concrete structures, huts, and tin shacks. And then, all of a sudden, like a lake emerging from among the hills, an enormous panorama of trash appeared before them.

The spare parts guy wasn't at his office (the skeleton of a burnt bus), nor did he answer the phone. "Maybe he's late," said Duke, "we'll wait for a while." He did not sound at all surprised.

The hum of trucks offloading cargo and the rattle of distant bulldozers blended with the noise of waves crashing against the piers. The ocean surrounding Shuffle Park on three sides was hidden behind the heaps of trash. Professor Schiff and Duke walked some distance along the central path bisecting the site, then stopped and stood silently observing.

The site was dotted with human figures gathering things from the trash heaps with a sort of gloomy precision, a listless perseverance, and no exchange of words. They pulled, dragged, broke, dug, rummaged, and filled sacks. There were women with babies' heads peeking out of cloth carriers tied to their bodies, and the baskets on their heads contained lengths of pipe, copper wires, and iron rods. There were scrawny men, white-haired elders, and children who sat in a circle diligently pulling out the innards of a giant electric appliance.

"Africa," declared Duke with a wave of his hand that encompassed the entire site.

Duke's bitter mockery sparked melancholy thoughts in Professor Schiff. Were the people of Shuffle Park a reincarnation of Africa's ancient hunter-gatherers? Was it here, at the national garbage dump, that tribal life had been reborn?

But even if he did not know much about this land, or this continent, or the traditions and customs of ancient times, one thing was clear to him: here in this drab savannah of garbage, engulfed in smoke and noxious fumes, there was no joy. Only bleak labor. These patient gatherers reminded Professor Schiff, ironically, of cotton-picking slaves. Yes, that was the image that came to his mind: a group of slaves in a misty field.

Professor Schiff's eyes began to pick out items in the trash heaps. Familiar items. Some of them were luxury brands: television screens, laptop computers, speakers, robotic vacuum cleaners, espresso machines, dryers. To his surprise, he spotted a multipurpose home exercise machine, the kind that incorporated a rower, stationary bike, and bench press. The machine was familiar to him from an advertising brochure he'd once found in his mailbox.

"Yes, this trash comes to us from all over the world, Europe, America," explained Duke in an amused tone, "in return for X dollars a ton. And don't ask whose pockets all that money ends up in . . . But as you can see, Professor, in the end everyone profits."

As they walked back to the car, their path was blocked by a group of gatherers. There were six or seven of them, maybe more, and at first glance they appeared to be a family. They were dressed in an identical uniform of rags, and their hair was covered with dust and ash.

One of the men grabbed Professor Schiff's arm and spoke in a language he could not identify. He longed to remove the dusty fingers from his arm. The man gave off a strange smell, an odor that made its cunning way through Shuffle Park's toxic fumes, straight into Professor Schiff's nostrils. A smell can be difficult to describe, but easy to remember. That smell—something like diesel mixed with canned sardines and dried urine—was extremely familiar to Professor Schiff. And as the man gripped him and mumbled, he suddenly remembered where he knew the smell from. Yes, it was from October 1973. It was the smell that had lingered on a coat he'd bought from a soldier who came back from the front at Sinai. A gray NATO coat with a little German flag sewn onto its left sleeve. Professor Schiff was certain of it. That was the smell. The coat from the Suez Canal.

That stench, which no amount of dry cleaning had been able to remove, had brought Professor Schiff closer to Africa than he'd ever been—until this trip, that is.

"He wants to sell you something," Duke translated the man's murmuring.

"Yes, yes, yes," said Professor Schiff, although he did not want to buy anything.

Then another member of the band, a thin, fragile man, approached Professor Schiff and held out his dusty hand.

"He wants a dollar for that thing," Duke translated.

Professor Schiff tried to focus on the object resting in the outstretched hand. It was a sort of tiny capsule, though it wasn't clear what it was made of. For a moment Professor

Schiff thought it was lipstick. Then it seemed like a thumb drive, the kind no one used anymore. "What is it?" he finally asked.

"He says this thing brings a lot of luck," Duke translated.

Duke took the object from the man's hand and held it up to his eyes. It was a mezuzah! A simple plastic mezuzah, the kind affixed to every doorframe in Professor Schiff's hometown. A common and fairly ordinary object.

Professor Schiff gave the man the sum he asked for. The story itself was well worth the price, and he knew he would find a way to work it into his new book. If and when he wrote it.

But though Professor Schiff was quite satisfied, the people who had just earned their daily pay showed no signs of happiness. They turned and walked away in gloomy silence. As if they'd understood that the new colonizer was not exploiting them for rubber or diamonds, but for stories. Stories of misery. Stories of sorrow. Stories of deprivation and poverty.

The man who had held Professor Schiff's arm finally released his grip and mumbled a few words, apparently saying goodbye. And yes, he smiled. A big, full smile. Professor Schiff took out his cellphone and took a picture of the man. Now the good story had a good picture to go with it.

11

There is nothing as generous as hospitality. Especially when the guests are complete strangers. Hospitality with no discrimination, no preferential treatment, no bias with regard to ethnicity, cultural background, gender, age, sexual preference, ideology, faith, socioeconomics, education level, social status . . . Oh yes, Professor Schiff would have gladly signed on to such a declaration. If only Lucile had been, in his eyes, a guest. But she was no guest. She was an intruder. An interloper who had infiltrated his thoughts and would not leave him in peace. Not even for a second. Which is why, despite his enchantment with Mrs. Lucile Tetteh-Ofosu, the constant reverberation of her presence between the walls of his home meant that by the end of the third day of her stay, he had plunged into a deep depression. It was a painful paradox, because Lucile Tetteh-Ofosu was now in his sphere, exactly as he'd wanted.

The more he considered the matter, the harder it was to avoid concluding that he had inadvertently positioned himself as a particularly shallow character in a silly romantic comedy. Not just silly, in fact, but the kind with a vague yet very present and very bitter taste of racism. Was it possible that the secret of his enchantment had to do with that ancient tension between a master and his subjects? And was that the reason for Lucile's forgivingly patient and clearly amused attitude toward him? Did she view him as a caricature of the white, Western, privileged man who was channeling his prejudices into a romantic entanglement?

"Something bad has come over you, Professor," she said to him, "you are very, very troubled."

Her hairstyle was different. Twenty-odd thin braids sprouted from square patches of black hair. She wore a printed fabric gown. There were tiny silver star-shaped studs in her earlobes.

Professor Schiff admitted to being troubled.

"But you're not a very happy person anyway, Professor, are you?"

"No, you're wrong, I'm actually quite happy sometimes."

"I'm not sure we're talking about the same thing."

Perhaps she was right. Either way, the last time Professor Schiff could pinpoint a definite sense of happiness was when Melchior had offered that he take Lucile. But he sure as hell couldn't tell her that. Particularly since it was now clear beyond any doubt that her very presence made him uncomfortable. This contradiction was inherently depressing.

"May I speak frankly?" asked Lucile.

"Yes."

"Something is enveloping you, Professor, like a sort of dirty sack over your head. Something is stopping you from breathing."

"There's nothing wrong with my breathing," he said with some alarm. She'd reminded him of his cardiovascular problem, which did little to add any cheer to this moment of reckoning.

"I'm not talking about oxygen."

"Meaning?"

"It's not just our lungs that breathe."

"I'm not sure I understand," said Professor Schiff.

"I didn't think you would, Professor," said Lucile, "but I know how to help you."

"How?"

"I have a feeling it's me who is burdening you."

He denied it. He told her he was very, very fond of her. *Fond*—that was the strongest word he allowed himself to use. He said he felt extremely close to her. He swore it was the truth. And it was. Although, of course, it was not the whole truth. And not the only truth.

She smiled and touched his arm. "I know you like me. But in these one hundred and twenty square meters around you, I take up far too much space. I could sense it before." Her fingertips left warm imprints on his forearm.

"No, no," Professor Schiff continued his desperate denial, "your presence here is very much welcome, and I completely agree with Tami that you can stay here until you find somewhere more suitable, and it even makes me happy. . ." He stammered a series of weightless, banal lines but could not squeeze out of his brain even a single idea that would prove his extreme sensitivity to human situations. It was a failure. A defeat, almost.

Yes, Professor Schiff was a very special person in his own

estimation. Very special. Yet also completely human. Meaning, entirely predictable. And that was disappointing.

Another day went by. And another. And one more. In the evening, when Professor Schiff heard Lucile walking in, he jumped up from his purposelessly open computer and watched her through the narrow gap between his study door and the frame. He saw only her silhouette, but what he was forced to complete in his imagination was infinitely more beautiful than the sweaty woman who kicked off her ridiculous high heels in the hallway.

Where was she coming from? What were her mysterious affairs? She certainly wasn't cleaning apartments.

Professor Schiff wanted to leave his room and greet her. He'd been waiting for her all day. Perhaps even longer than that.

But Tami beat him to it. "Hi, Lucile," she purred into the hallway in an overly saccharine voice. "How was your day?"

"Like this," said Lucile, and drew a heart shape in the air with her fingers.

"Oh, lovely," said Tami. "Come and sit with me for a while."

Professor Schiff listened intently. He knew Tami's melodies. He knew a plan was being hatched.

Lucile sat down on a dining chair. Her fingers stroked the edge of the table.

"Tea?" asked Tami. She filled the kettle and the hissing sound of boiling water began. "I don't know if I've already told you this, but you know I have a grandfather . . . Not exactly a grandfather, a step-grandfather, you could say . . . He's not a young man. A hundred and three, to be precise. Actually he'll be a hundred and four in January. He lives nearby . . . Perhaps you've run into him . . ."

"I haven't yet had the pleasure," said Lucile, shaking her head.

"We try to see a lot of him, actually. We're very close." She poured tea into three mugs and looked at the almost-closed door to the study and straight into her husband's spying eyes.

"He must love you," said Lucile indifferently.

"Yes, yes, very much so. Anyway, I was thinking today . . . You know, I just put two and two together, as they say, and it suddenly occurred to me that maybe, if you'd be interested, you might be able to help us with . . . What I'm saying, actually, is that perhaps you could spend some time with him, with Grandpa Morduch, for a little while, just to look after him."

"Oh, no, no," Lucile exclaimed. "I mean, your idea makes a lot of sense, Mrs. Kushner, and I'm flattered that you trust me that much, but . . ." A strange expression appeared on her face. Amusement? From afar, Professor Schiff had trouble reading it. She shook her head, and her thin braids danced this way and that.

"He just needs someone to be at home with him," Tami pressed on, "to talk to him a little. Someone very sensitive. Someone like you . . ."

"I don't know . . ." Lucile hesitated. She wasn't about to give in easily.

"It's not that Grandpa Morduch really needs care, he's not helpless or senile. . . He's in excellent health and a very happy, optimistic man, and he takes an interest in what's going on in the world, spends hours on the Internet. Apart from his hearing, which is a little . . . not perfect."

"I don't know. . . I'd have to take a look, you know, see what's going on there in this grandfather's apartment, what sort of forces are at play there."

Forces? What a strange thing to say, thought Professor Schiff.

But Tami, quick-witted as she was, replied immediately, "Oh, you have nothing to worry about, Lucile, there's excellent energy there. After all, it's not for nothing that Grandpa has reached a hundred and three in such good shape, upright and smiling."

At this point Professor Schiff finally emerged from his office. Slowly. Cautiously. Squeezing unobtrusively between the door and the lintel. But a sudden draft slammed the door behind his back.

"Ah, here's the professor," said Tami with feigned surprise. "Why don't we see what he has to say about my idea?"

"What idea?"

"For Lucile to live with Grandpa Morduch and look after him."

"But wait a minute, Tami," Professor Schiff mumbled. "I'm not sure that's . . . I mean, I don't know if . . ."

Tami always had the capacity to extricate him from the various tangles he got himself into. But, as on hundreds of previous occasions, her current project was born from a natural, almost insurmountable urge to matchmake, to forge connections, to initiate procedures, and to generally influence the movement of the universe. Professor Schiff hated this urge of his wife's, which was so opposed to his own personality—yet served his needs so well.

"He used to live in Africa," Tami said, keeping up the pressure, "so you'll have a lot to talk about."

12

What did this man of a hundred and three, almost a hundred and four, look like? Like this: His forehead was wrinkled and his blue eyes, which were as cloudy as a hazy heatwave in the summer sky, were buried among mounds of sagging skin. His cheeks were sunken, and five folds of skin drooped from his chin and filled his shirt collar like yeast dough rising in a pan. A glorious mane of white hair cascaded to his shoulders in a bohemian fashion. Sometimes he tied the mane back in a ponytail, and then his impressively large and hairy ears were exposed.

And how did this hundred-and-three-year-old (almost hundred and four) man's life proceed? That might be a superfluous question. A niggling one, even. A question that is only asked about people who have, allegedly, outlived their allotted years. Those who challenge the notion, "First to arrive, first to leave." Those who extend their retirement by forty years.

And yet, if one insists, it could be said that Morduch's days passed with monotonous speed, with the ease of a long drive that offers no views.

Until, that is, he encountered Mrs. Lucile Tetteh-Ofosu.

"Good evening, sir. How are you today?" asked Lucile, after transferring a kiss to the mezuzah with her fingertips.

Morduch stood in the doorway of his ground-floor apartment and looked at her in awe. This garrulous man was dumbstruck, and only after several moments of fiddling irritably with his hearing aid (pressing his thumb into his ear, pulling, twisting, with his head slightly tilted, then repeating the whole thing) did he manage to stutter, "Very well, very well, thank you."

"Excellent answer," said Lucile and held out her hand. "I'm Lucile, and I'm also very well."

A sand-colored cat covered with scars also stood in the doorway, looking at Lucile, though with no awe at all but rather with outright hostility. It blinked, grunted, then leaped resolutely onto a taxidermy crocodile, from there to a bureau crowded with wood and metal statuettes, then onto the windowsill and out the window.

"Oh, what happened to your kitty?" asked Lucile in a phony, childish voice, which disclosed no genuine sorrow at the departure of the blond lynx. She put her belongings down in the middle of the living room and ran a fast, circular look over the crowded space. Then she shut her eyes and motioned for the others to keep quiet. She listened. To what? Certainly not to the distant sounds of televised entertainment coming from the other apartments in the building and shaking the walls.

Morduch disappeared into the kitchen and Lucile opened her eyes.

"My diagnosis is that Mr. Murdock has grown used to being alone," she whispered to Tami and Professor Schiff, "and that is a very bad habit, if you know what I mean. If it goes on, he will live forever." Then she added loudly, although Morduch, returning with a copper tray of little glass cups, didn't really seem to hear, "I hope you won't miss the kitty very much, Mr. Murdock."

"The kitty?" Morduch wondered.

"He might have gone to look for another home, Mr. Murdock," Lucile explained, and then she flashed that smile, the one that Professor Schiff so looked forward to. "Because it's insulting when someone comes along to take your place." She gave a throaty giggle, and when Professor Schiff looked into Morduch's cloudy eyes, he thought he could see something briefly clarifying in them.

Lucile wandered languidly into the other room, and Morduch danced around her and tried to get her to show more interest in the enormous, endless collection of objects filling the apartment, or at least to linger, if only for a split second, on a particular item he happened to hold dear.

This collection, which Morduch referred to as "Congo," covered the walls, cluttered the shelves, filled display cabinets, squeezed into specially built recesses, hung from the ceiling, and tumbled to the floor. There was nothing it did not include. Masks, spears, leather shields, drums, necklaces, a mortar and pestle, a raffia skirt, a feather crown, taxidermy birds and reptiles, a cheetah skin, a zebra tail, countless wooden statuettes of thin-limbed human figures . . .

At the end of the tour, when Morduch ducked into the kitchen again, Lucile declared, "We'll need to make a few changes here . . ."

"Changes?" Tami asked.

"Yes, there's no choice. We must tidy things up."

"Tidy?" repeated Professor Schiff. "Tidy how?"

"I think we'll need to get rid of some things."

"Which things?" Tami asked.

"Everything, really."

"Everything?" Professor Schiff asked.

"Yes. Apart from the zebra tail perhaps."

"Is it urgent?" asked Tami.

"Extremely," Lucile decreed.

Tami and Professor Schiff were helpless. They assumed there would be no point in giving Morduch an ultimatum and that no form of persuasion would work. Because, after all, this collection had surrounded Morduch forever, more or less. At least since they could remember him.

Once again, it was Tami who had the solution. "I have yoga in an hour," she told her husband. "Could you please give me a ride to Redding?"

There is no clear account of what happened in that ground-floor apartment after Tami and Professor Schiff left. But the next day, all they were required to do was find a storage company and book a crew of movers and a truck.

Professor Schiff was surprised to discover that the entirety of the Congo collection fit into seven cardboard boxes. Only seven. And not even very large ones.

13

Professor Schiff claimed to know almost nothing about Africa, but this was somewhat dishonest. Mostly because in the past three decades, as a result of his family connections, he had had the opportunity to hear quite a number of tales about Africa from the former ambassador Mordechai Shtil, better known as Grandpa Morduch. Even if Professor Schiff was skeptical—and rightly so—of the factual solidity of these tales, they had unfortunately embedded an image of the continent and its inhabitants in his mind: a picture of comical fools surrounded by complacent wretchedness.

If one were to judge by these stories (which were more of a comic revue populated by pathetic characters), the African capital where Mordechai Shtil had been posted was a place of constant laughter.

Professor Schiff recalled, for example, the anecdote about a military band conductor who, at a reception for Secretary of Defense McNamara, conducted with one white-gloved hand while using the other to maneuver between the cap that kept falling over his eyes and the trousers that kept falling from his waist.

Or the lengthy tale about a respectable businessman and member of the local aristocracy who purchased from an

Israeli inventor a patent for manufacturing champagne concentrate, a miraculous extract that had only to be mixed with soda water. When this businessman racked up insurmountable debts, he tried to foment a military coup.

Or the story about the wife of a senior minister, an exceptionally large woman, whose chair collapsed under her weight at a festive Independence Day dinner. As she lay helplessly on the floor while the guests struggled to hoist her up, her husband, the senior minister, was fooling around with some floozy in one of the embassy rooms.

Oh, how funny! Such hilarity! So very hilarious and terrible was Africa.

After he resigned from the Foreign Ministry, Morduch stayed on in the entertaining arenas of Africa for about four more years. What did he do there, other than collect anecdotes and folklore artifacts? And even more intriguing: How exactly did he get rich? He had never told anyone how he made his fortune. He might not even have given away his secrets to his wife, Tami's grandmother. Was he an arms dealer? A pimp for the security industry? If so, it was no wonder that he called his collection of African artifacts "Congo." He must have wanted to remind himself, but only himself, that upon his return from the heart of darkness, he had inadvertently brought home, among other things, traces of Kurtz and the dictator Mobutu.

This, however, was mere conjecture. An educated guess. And since they'd found no evidence or clues, Tami and

Professor Schiff had concluded that if Morduch had been involved in arms dealing, he was just a small-time middleman. A minor transit station on a long and convoluted road. This conclusion put their minds at ease. Besides, their suspicions never got in the way of their love for him.

Nor his for them.

Professor Schiff tried to explain Morduch's status in the Schiff-Kushner family to Lucile. The relationship he sketched, with all its anomalies and appendixes, was not all that complicated. Certainly not compared to the Tetteh-Ofosu family, in which, as it later emerged, there was an extremely intricate web of ties between various fathers, previous wives, dynasties, religions, faiths, and traditions.

Mordechai "Morduch" Shtil's position was very clear. "After seven years," Professor Schiff told Lucile, "when Morduch came back from Africa, he had malaria, and that's how he met Tami's grandmother, the widow Dr. Dora Kushner, who was a hematologist."

"Tell me more," said Lucile Tetteh-Ofosu. "I like white people's love stories." She laughed generously. "Stories that always end in tragedy, even when there's a happy end."

"Morduch and Dr. Dora fell in love and got married, and she nursed him back to health, but then she herself fell ill, her condition deteriorated, and she died."

"In his arms," Lucile said.

"In his arms. More or less."

The rest of the story was fairly obvious, and Professor

Schiff saw no reason to spell it out. Thanks to his marriage to her doctor grandmother, Morduch became Tami's step-grandfather, and since he was a widower with no children of his own, he allowed himself to be generous with his adoptive family. This all seemed completely natural and obvious, at least to all parties concerned. He bought them an apartment. He bought them a car. Twice. He spoiled the kids with expensive gifts. He paid for music lessons and trips to Disney World. He covered the occasional bank loan.

And they repaid his generosity by calling him "Grandpa," took him to the hospital for periodic treatments on his right eye, which was losing its vision, went for walks in the park with him, invited him for dinner on weekends and served as an audience for his reminiscences, bought his groceries and picked up his prescriptions, and gave him a box of chocolates every holiday. Or a box of marzipan cookies. Or a selection of halva treats. Or a large tin of Turkish delight. Something sweet, in any case. Very sweet. As sweet as possible.

Because that was what the old man loved more than anything else: sugar.

14

Ladies and gentlemen, members of the Special Tribunal, distinguished Madam Attorney General, Head of the Investigation Team:

Do you really believe that human history can be turned inside out, like a sock, in the hope that the remedies of the present will dull the pains of the past? You are probably expecting that memory itself will be repaired. Or at least made more tolerable. Perhaps even that it will shrink down into a bittersweet yearning, or—I say this cautiously—into collective nostalgia. Because when the nightmares of the past fit into some sort of rational pattern, history—instead of serving as an indictment, as self-justification, or as an excuse for self-pity—will go back to being what it should have been to begin with: a story. Nothing more.

Honorable friends, please trust me: in the republic where *I* live, these dilemmas gnaw at us constantly, and have been doing so for more than seventy years. We have experience. But wait, do not misunderstand me. I am certainly not insinuating that the events did not occur. They absolutely did. Millions of human tragedies that left no trace. No documents, no photographs, no names, no numbers. Nothing. Millions of human beings torn from their families, their cultures, their lands. Innocent people doomed to a life of indescribable suffering and agonizing death. This happened. Of that there is no doubt.

And Klonimus Zelig Schiff? He lived and breathed, he walked the world with confident steps. Except that, unlike the wretched people he enslaved, he made sure to leave evidence of his existence and his deeds. I myself, as I stand here before you, constitute part of that evidence. How strange. Even though I never knew the man and did not benefit directly or indirectly from his estate—meaning, from the business he was engaged in—still you wish to see him in me. There is something confusing about that, isn't there?

Furthermore, if we apply this same logic, it's not at all clear what authorizes you to argue on behalf of previous generations. If you define yourselves as those enslaved people's heirs, what exactly did you inherit from them? The affront?

Well, I'm sure we'll have the opportunity to examine that issue, too.

Incidentally, my arrest was very dramatic. An event that certainly deserves to make it into my book. If I ever write it. And you, members of the Special Tribunal, Madam Attorney General, Head of the Investigation Team, you were arrested along with me, metaphorically speaking. Did you notice that? True, none of you were actually there, except perhaps in spirit. You preferred to watch the fantastic events unfold on television. I completely understand. There was no reason to leave your air-conditioned offices. But might I assume that some of you read, and perhaps even wrote, the arrest warrant, with its wonderfully precise wording, which the special officer read in a loud but trembling voice on camera?

"Agur Schiff, as authorized by the Law for Adjudicating Slave Traders and their Accomplices, Heirs, and Beneficiaries, 2018, Clause B, Subclauses One, Two, Three, and Four, as pertaining to the heirs and indirect beneficiaries of the profits obtained by lawbreakers, and according to Clause C as pertains to crimes against humanity, and Clause D as pertains to crimes committed against the African nation, and by the powers vested in me by the Minister of Justice and the Attorney General's Office, I hereby place you under arrest for a period of thirty days, subject to extension by the District Judge, until full clarification of your culpability in the Republic's Court . . ."

15

The special officer, wearing a blue suit and a tie—the sun had set, but it was still in the high eighties outside—tried to conduct the historic occasion in a respectful and ceremonious fashion. He was accompanied by two policemen in peculiar camouflage uniforms (blue and gray splotches) and black berets, and a camera crew backed up by a remote broadcast van. The hotel employees darted around trying to sneak into the frame.

When the police and the camera crew arrived, Professor Schiff was sitting peacefully by the pool, sipping a beer and daydreaming. The scene of relaxation in which he was captured was, of course, the perfect visual backdrop for the serious charges levied against him. Or at least those that pegged him as "a beneficiary of their profits." Wearing a swimsuit and an unbuttoned shirt, beer dribbling from his lips onto his beard, his bare feet almost touching the water, Professor Schiff undeniably looked like someone who's been handed a benefit or two in life. Profit or no profit. And the smirk on his face as he listened to the officer reading the arrest warrant (he was trying to decipher the heavy accent) merely added a comical dimension to the villain who later appeared on the evening news. The event was simply so unexpected that Professor Schiff was unable to treat it as anything other than a preposterous joke. Or a misunderstanding. Or perhaps another attempt to exploit his illegal purchase from the Museum of African Culture.

It took several minutes for the amused surprise to give way to dread. In fact, only when he was handcuffed and things suddenly felt very concrete did Professor Schiff understand that he was starring in a real-life drama—that is, completely fanciful but utterly real—at which point his brain began to transmit panic signals. His heart pounded, his stomach contracted, his mouth felt parched, and his legs turned into flaccid rubber sticks that could barely support his weight.

He kept repeating in a hoarse, trembling voice that he was innocent, this was a mistake, he wanted to see a lawyer immediately, he would not say a word until he was granted adequate representation as legally required, he demanded to meet with a representative of his country immediately, this whole affair was embarrassing and humiliating, he wished to express his unequivocal protest, he must let his wife know as soon as possible so she wouldn't worry, he loved Africa, he was sad to be treated this way by people he so treasured and admired, and various other declarative fragments that he tried unsuccessfully to string together into a sentence.

There is no need to replay the scene for you. You have seen it repeatedly on your screens. Even major international networks felt obliged to broadcast the moment when Professor Schiff turned into an international figure and household name. If not for the panic (which made Professor Schiff's hands tremble so badly that the handcuffs jangled), it would have been a dream come true. Granted, it was a warped version of things, but perhaps he hadn't been clear enough when he'd expressed his wish for fame and glory.

Professor Schiff had been handcuffed three times (such a perfect image!) before the cameraman was satisfied with the composition and timing. After the third attempt, he signaled his approval, and the handcuffs were thrown into a suitcase full of props. The officer gave Professor Schiff an envelope containing a copy of the arrest warrant, shook his still-trembling hand, thanked him for his cooperation, and said that he thought the professor had delivered a most respectable performance.

Professor Schiff hurried to his suite, where he proceeded to vomit repeatedly until he'd purged all the fear.

The day after the staged and videotaped arrest, Professor Schiff was asked to pack his suitcase, pay his hotel bill, and report—with no urgency and at his convenience—to a location where he would need to stay "until your case is clarified." A matter of a few days. And so it was that, on that overcast morning, Professor Schiff was picked up by Duke and delivered to Villa Clark.

The venue that was to serve as his private, exclusive detention facility—a former homestead built by a British gentleman farmer, which in the seventies had been the East German Embassy—was very much to Professor Schiff's liking. It was a modest but spacious two-story building, surrounded by a wilderness of tall grasses and flowering bushes (a poignant combination that reminded Professor Schiff of the long-vanished landscapes of his childhood). A boulevard lined with neem and mango trees led from the main gate to the villa, with occasional abrasions of red earth showing through cracks in the asphalt. At the distant edge of the former embassy compound stood a massive and extraordinarily beautiful wawa tree, a remnant of an ancient evergreen forest, surrounded by tulip and mahogany trees with the white flowers of a vine interwoven among their branches.

Ten stone steps climbed from the entry plaza to a columned veranda. On the plaza was a small pond with a mosaic floor (in a hammer-and-sickle pattern) on which dirty rainwater had formed a puddle. The pond's rim was wide enough to sit on comfortably and watch the hummingbirds and butterflies flit among the hibiscus flowers, but there was also a stone bench for those who preferred to sprawl under the branches of a yellow-flowered shrub whose name Professor Schiff did not know.

A true paradise, as he later wrote to his wife.

On the eastern horizon, dipped in a haze, stood the cubes of the capital's business district. In the north, the silhouette of a flat range of hills was visible. In the west, some ten kilometers away, was the national stadium, from which, when the wind blew in, one could hear the crowds roaring feebly like distant waves. The coastal highway was to the south.

16

Professor Schiff's first meeting with George Aboagye, the special investigator appointed by the Attorney General, took place in the villa's spacious living room, a few days after his arrest.

"Aboagye," said Aboagye by way of introduction.

"Abu . . . ?" Professor Schiff pondered unthinkingly and quickly stopped himself.

"Abo," Aboagye corrected him, "with an *o*, as in *abolition*."

George Aboagye was formal, polite, and eloquent. His job, he explained, was to prepare materials for an indictment, or, conversely, to recommend repealing the charges. Professor Schiff was cautious, angry, impatient, and stammering. But despite the title of Special Investigator printed on his business card, Aboagye was neither confrontational nor coercive. If he was engaged in any investigating or "gathering data," as he claimed, he went about it in a circuitous manner.

His first questions concerned Professor Schiff's impressions of the country and its people. Professor Schiff, naturally, replied with what had become his personal cliché: "Your country is a sad country, where people are always smiling."

Aboagye, though, was not always smiling. In fact, he never smiled at all. Nor was he particularly impressed with Professor Schiff's poetic commentary. He said, "That's exactly what I thought of Britain when I studied there, except that with the English, smiles are a sort of deception."

Professor Schiff had also studied in England, many years prior, and was eager to reminisce about London as a means of warming up the conversation, even if at this initial stage of their acquaintance, the rules of the game were not entirely clear. "What did you study?" he asked with feigned curiosity. "Law?"

"I specialized in the history of international law," replied Aboagye. "An M.A. at the LSE. I graduated in 2001. And you, Professor?"

"Art at Saint Martin's School of Art, from '79 till '81."

"So you're an artist?"

"In about the same way as you're a judge."

Aboagye made a sort of long *aaaah* sound, which Professor Schiff interpreted as confirmation that he had understood the crack.

"Yes," said Professor Schiff with a sigh, "in those days, studying art in London was a big deal."

Having discovered their shared memories of watching the electrical pipes rush by outside the Tube's windows, gloomy flats with a mildewy odor, hissing gas stoves, and the slippery flavor of tea with milk—could they now enter a more serious debate? Could they talk, for instance, about the empire that had given birth to both of their countries and its decisive impact on the joys and sorrows of its former subjects?

Aboagye said nothing, and his prominent eyes examined Professor Schiff as if he were waiting for an answer to an unasked question.

Was this his sly method of evaluating the detainee, or a sort of intimacy evolving in the comfortable, very slow pace at which things usually progressed in the host country?

"Pardon me," said Professor Schiff, "did you ask something?"

"No," said Special Investigator George Aboagye, "I didn't ask anything."

But then, of course, the questions came. When would the professor like to give an affidavit and begin his testimony for the newly established Special Tribunal? Would the professor be willing to take part in a press conference and answer the media's questions? When would the professor be amenable to meeting his country's ambassador? And, above all, was the professor pleased with the special conditions of his detention, and did he have any requests or complaints?

Well, no, Professor Schiff had no complaints. He was very pleased with Villa Clark, and in fact, he declared, he could not have dreamed of better arrest conditions. To bolster his assertion, lest the special investigator think he was just being polite, or, conversely, that he feared he might be hurt if he complained, he took Aboagye on a tour of the villa. Strangely, as Professor Schiff led the special investigator through the rooms and balconies, he felt as proud as he might if this were his own private estate.

He showed Aboagye the basement where the previous residents had left filing cabinets and a dusty battery of listening and recording devices; he revealed an abstract concrete sculpture covered with a patina, hidden among the bushes; he took him to the second-floor balcony, where a flag still hung (its colors were almost completely faded, but the East German hammer-and-compass emblem was clearly visible); he led him among rooms where countless mosquito nets hung (not only above the large bed, but also over the dining table, the desk, the bathtub, and the toilet—all signs that the authorities were very concerned with their prisoner's wellbeing).

Finally, the special investigator asked to meet the staff, who arranged themselves in a line along the columned vestibule, and Professor Schiff introduced them one by one, as if *he* were their employer rather than the Ministry of Justice and the Prison Authority. These people's jobs were to feed the distinguished prisoner, clean and launder for him, and of course keep an eye on him (to make sure he didn't escape? But to where? And for what purpose?) and protect the compound from stray dogs. But they answered to Major Addy, a retired Prison Authority official who specialized in running incarceration facilities.

Incidentally, the major had taken it upon himself to drive Schiff to the Holiday Inn's swimming pool every day, in return for a very reasonable fee. And for this, too, Professor Schiff was grateful. "Because without swimming, my life is no life," he explained to Aboagye.

It should be noted that the constant human presence swirling around Professor Schiff, who was jealous of his privacy, would ordinarily have been extremely bothersome to him. Fortunately, however, the gang worked slowly and a little sleepily, sometimes very sleepily, so sleepily as to actually fall into a deep slumber, head lolling back and legs splayed out. Even now, as these good people stood in a row before the special investigator, Professor Schiff thought they might be asleep, and he envied their ability to doze off while standing up with their eyes open. If he were to acquire this skill, thought Professor Schiff, he could put it to use at end-of-year faculty meetings. He made a note to himself about how important it was to learn.

One thing did bother Professor Schiff: the frequent power cuts.

"Yes, it's a problem," Special Investigator George Aboagye said and gave Professor Schiff a hollow stare. His gentle features were as impenetrable as a mask. "Especially now, during the harmattan, when there are lots of fires and infrastructure is damaged. We all suffer from it."

"But you're used to it."

"And you will get used to it, too. You're one of us now." He smiled, and then added, "For the time being." The smile was so unexpected that Professor Schiff was startled.

A few days later, at their second meeting, the power cuts came up again. Professor Schiff asked if a generator could be installed at the villa. Aboagye said that maintenance issues and logistics were not in the purview of the Attorney General's Office, and that Schiff should bring it up with Major Addy.

"I can't listen to music properly," Professor Schiff lamented.

"Music?" Aboagye repeated, his surprised tone tinged with a note of mockery.

"I can't live without music. Especially when I'm working."

"I believe you told me in our last meeting how much you love the quiet."

"Yes, that's true, I very much enjoy the quiet. That is to say, the sounds inside the quiet, if you know what I mean. The birds, the cicadas . . . But when I'm working. . ."

"When you're working?"

"Writing . . . My book."

Aboagye said nothing for a long time, then asked, "And what kind of music are we talking about?"

"Bach," said Professor Schiff.

"So that's your music," said Aboagye, nodding heavily, "Bach. That's what you like to listen to."

"Are you familiar with the music of Johann Sebastian Bach, your honor?" asked Professor Schiff cautiously. It was not condescension. Not at all. After all, he was in a foreign country. Foreign and distant. He was allowed to assume that the tastes of the people he met, including George Aboagye, a graduate of the LSE, were different than his own.

"A little," said Aboagye, and Professor Schiff thought he saw a hint of a smile.

"Bach," Professor Schiff explained, "is not just enjoyment. It is true sublimity."

"Sublimity. . ."

"Sublimity. Sometimes even . . . elation."

"Elation," Aboagye repeated with a nod. "In that case, allow me to turn your attention to an interesting fact, which is that Bach's music, which, as you say, gives rise to sublimity and elation, is an auxiliary product of the European economy in the eighteenth century." He paused for a moment to examine Professor Schiff's reaction. "And was that economy not, in that period of time, primarily based on the labor of hundreds of thousands of African slaves?"

Professor Schiff swallowed. "Yes. I suppose that would be fair to argue," he murmured awkwardly.

"Well then, Bach could not have composed his music were he not paid with money produced by slavery, could he? And naturally, he drank coffee. With lots of sugar. Perhaps he also smoked a pipe."

"I admit I've never thought of that."

"What did you not think of? That a good musician requires coffee, sugar, and tobacco?" Aboagye chuckled. "And by the way, I'm not entirely sure what his wig was made of. In the pictures it looks like cotton wool. So there might also be cotton in the story."

"What are you actually trying to say, Mr. Aboagye?" Professor Schiff asked tartly.

"That the legacy of European exploitation reaches every corner of refined taste," Aboagye barked. The sweat dripping from his forehead disclosed the effort this conversation was exacting.

"Fine, okay, and you have your own wonderful musicians, that's completely fine. I have a lot of respect for other cultures and other tastes."

"No, no, please don't condescend to me, Professor. There are people in Africa, here and there, who also listen to Bach.

Perhaps even the famous Coffee Cantata." A smile appeared on his face and vanished quickly. "And not just in Pretoria and Johannesburg. I'm talking about black people, in black Africa. *Negros* . . ." He looked at Professor Schiff out of the corner of his eye, as if to secretly examine what effect the forbidden word was having. "Negros," he repeated, "like me, for example."

"That's exactly my point!" Professor Schiff exclaimed, sounding a little choked up. "Bach belongs to all of humanity! Including Africa. Including the Africans. Like, like . . . like Leeuwenhoek's microscope . . . or like Newton's gravity. Yes, gravity! What would you do without it?"

"Bravo, Professor, you bring up excellent examples. I must say you would give your great-great-great-great-grandfather a run for his money with your racist patronizing."

"That was not at all my intention. Please believe me, Mr. Aboagye." But his startled tone divulged his defeat.

"I believe you," Special Investigator George Aboagye said and crossed his arms over his chest. "I certainly believe you." He wiped the sweat from his brow with his hand and then said very wearily, "And I'll see what I can do about a generator."

17

When Professor Schiff was planning his trip, he'd hoped to meet with the President of the Republic, His Excellency Vincent Matu Ayeh, so that he could sneak an interview with Ayeh into his book. The book he wanted to write. The book he was going to write.

As it turns out, getting an audience with a president is no trifling matter. Not even in West Africa. Not even in a country whose existence Professor Schiff had ignored for sixty-three years, a remote and humble country whose presidents are supposed to covet interviews with book-writing professors. Direct appeals to the presidential palace's press secretary and to the Ministry of Publicity and Communications yielded no results. Nor were phone calls returned. And that was more or less the end of the road for Professor Schiff's aspiration to meet the president.

But fate, ever the prankster, had other ideas, because instead of Professor Schiff asking to meet His Excellency, His Excellency asked to meet Professor Schiff. After all, this was no longer one more pestering tourist wanting to glimpse the esteemed dignitary (and, of course, to look down on him from his perch of intellectual pettiness). Now Professor Schiff himself had become a personage—someone worth a glimpse. President Vincent Ayeh wished to talk with the famous detainee, the first person officially suspected of committing crimes against the African nation under the new Law for Adjudicating Slave Traders and their Accomplices, Heirs, and Beneficiaries.

Since Professor Schiff was officially under arrest, the president's office preferred to hold the meeting at Ayeh's private home rather than at the official presidential residence. In other words, in the private palace instead of the public palace. Truth be told, Professor Schiff was a little disappointed not to visit the grandiose edifice (which, according to *Lonely Planet*, bore a likeness to a pair of elephant tusks). It stood on the edge of the capital, surrounded by two high fences and a concrete wall, lit up at night for the benefit of the few tourists who drove past on their way to or from the airport. But President Ayeh's private palace also provided Professor Schiff with some pomp and circumstance.

He walked through an exedra of columns, an inner courtyard, a long corridor, another courtyard, a foyer, an entry hall guarded by two mounted lions, a staircase with a glass ceiling, and another long corridor, at the end of which was the drawing room. There, Professor Schiff was met by the president's secretary, Mr. Luther, who instructed him to silence his cellphone, then briefed him on the etiquette of meeting the president: he must address the sovereign as "Your Excellency," and under no circumstances was he to sit before the Honorable President invited him to do so. He also gave Professor Schiff a list of topics that the president was unwilling to discuss: AIDS, the recent Amnesty International report, and the arrest of the opposition leader. The president would certainly be happy, said the secretary, to discuss soccer.

Professor Schiff, who had met a president or two in his life, but never an actual head of state, lost his confidence for a moment. "I was thinking of discussing a little history with him," he said.

"But only distant history, please," said Luther.

"The slave trade," said Professor Schiff.

"Slaves would be fine," said Luther.

"I thought that was why the Honorable President wanted to meet with me."

"No, the president heard that you teach something to do with film and animation. His Excellency and his wife are very fond of animated films. And cinema in general."

"I see."

"The main thing is not to go into anything too personal," Luther whispered. "His Excellency is extremely jealous of his privacy."

Just then, a large, broad-shouldered man entered the room, wearing a knee-length printed tunic, and marched toward Professor Schiff with a wide gait. "Mr. President!" Luther called out and removed himself to the corner of the room.

Professor Schiff bowed his head. But it occurred to him that this gesture might be too subtle for the occasion, so he quickly gave a deep bow that moved his face closer to the pattern of interlinked black stars on the green background of the carpeting.

"There's no need," Professor Schiff heard the president say above him in a deep, slightly hoarse, but surprisingly gentle voice.

Professor Schiff straightened up. His head was dizzy from the blood that had rushed to it when he'd forced himself to look at the stars. "Before anything else," he said, "I would like to express my deep gratitude to Your Excellency for the opportunity to meet Your Excellency. . ."

"Oh no, the honor is all mine, Prof," said the president, and he held out his large hand. "I'm the one who wanted to meet *you*, sir."

"Of course, Your Excellency," Professor Schiff mumbled. "I'm flattered, Your Excellency."

"I wanted to hear from you personally, Prof, how it feels to be given the chance to play such a significant role in history."

He was not especially tall, President Ayeh, but his massive shoulders and thick neck reminded Professor Schiff of Picasso's minotaur drawings, right down to the sparse, gray beard that joined his frizzy hair in straight lines.

"Your Excellency," Professor Schiff murmured, "I confess that until this moment I had a slightly different view of the affair."

The president removed his dark glasses and fiddled with them as he wondered, "Different? What do you mean, Prof?"

"Well, it's not exactly pleasant to be accused of a crime."

"Yes, but your crime is an important crime, a principled one. You're not just some rapist or murderer."

"I understand your logic, Your Excellency, but still, up to now I've always considered myself a decent, honest man, or at least a law-abiding one, more or less, and I came to your country with plenty of goodwill and a lot of appreciation . . ."

"Yes, and precisely because you are an honest man, Prof, you understand the meaning of criminal accountability."

"Your Excellency," said Professor Schiff bitterly, "I am known as a man of principles, however—"

"Sometimes you have to pay a personal price in order to uphold your principles, do you not?" President Ayeh gestured at one of two green-velvet armchairs. The chairs' carved frames depicted hunters with spears chasing antelope. He sat down first, followed by Professor Schiff, who perched rigidly on the edge of the seat, ready to stand up abruptly. "But either way," President Ayeh continued, "you can always make a movie about it when the whole affair is over."

"In all honesty, Your Excellency, I'm more of a writer than a filmmaker."

"A writer? Oh . . . that's a pity. You know, I once considered making movies myself. It was my plan B, after I retired from soccer." The president waved his hand dismissively, and a contemplative, melancholy look came over his face. "But as you can see, Prof, I channeled my energy into public service. I absolutely could not turn my back on my calling." He stood up abruptly, took out a handkerchief, wiped the sweat from his brow, sat down heavily, sighed, and said, "All right, then you'll write a book. That's better than nothing."

"Yes, I'll write a book . . ." murmured Professor Schiff. "In fact, I already have my opening line."

President Ayeh's narrow eyes hung on Professor Schiff with a look of amused anticipation.

"This is my opening line: 'Yes, it's true: my grandfather's grandfather's grandfather was a slave trader.'"

"Excellent first line," said Ayeh, "although not particularly commercial, I think."

A servant in livery wheeled a trolly into the room, placed a silver platter and gilded floral cups on the low table between them, and poured coffee with an expert flourish. "Sugar?" he asked.

"No thank you," said Professor Schiff and shook his head vigorously.

His thoughts wandered. He remembered his conversation with Special Investigator Aboagye about Bach's coffee-drinking habits. And suddenly, as he distractedly put a silver teaspoon into the cup and stirred indifferently, for no reason at all, as if his hand were experiencing a spasm, the melody of Bach's Chorale Prelude 639, which he so loved, came into his mind, so alien to the palms bowing in the wind and the soldiers in red berets outside the enormous window, patrolling the path with cocked rifles. Professor Schiff found himself momentarily unable to explain to himself why or how he had come to be here, in this dusty, colorful, noisy capital on the shores of the Atlantic Ocean, a republic that answered to a president in a flamboyant tunic, a country in which he, Professor Schiff, stood accused of crimes against the African nation. Was he supposed to find solace in the fact that J.S. Bach shared the dock with him?

Ayeh gaped at the teaspoon aimlessly circling Professor Schiff's cup. "You're right, Prof. You're absolutely right. Growing old demands concessions. And when I look at pictures of myself from back when I was the Bundesliga's king of goals . . . You know, Prof, there was one year when I was named Europe's Player of the Year." He pointed to a series of blown-up newspaper photos on the wall, all of which showed a young Vincent Ayeh in typical center forward poses: head-butting the ball, dribbling it between another player's feet, leaping through the air with his legs scissored, charging the goal with his body slanted sharply toward the field, slipping away from a group of players . . .

The second part of the meeting between the president and the man suspected of committing crimes against the African nation began with a long silence, the rhythmic sounds of sipping (wonderfully synchronized) from their gold-rimmed coffee cups, which were refilled again and again by an unobtrusive servant who knew exactly when to appear, and the clamor of a lawnmower driven by an elderly man in military garb, which drove back and forth outside the large window.

Chorale Prelude 639 quieted down in Professor Schiff's brain. He began to wonder when he would be permitted to move to the next stage, when *he* would interview Vincent Matu Ayeh, as he had planned to do once upon a time, before everything had been turned upside down. Which words would he choose to breach the silence? Or, rather, what would be his first question to the president? Something shrewd, probably. Something like, "So, which of the skills you acquired as a center forward in the Bundesliga serve you as president, Your Excellency?" The president would probably not bat an eyelid and would answer with an impenetrable expression, saying something along the lines of, "Quick reflexes, especially when it comes to the latest Jaguar models," and they would both laugh, and Professor Schiff would put the exchange in his book and the president would deny saying it, and Professor Schiff would never reveal that he'd made the whole thing up.

But the first to break the silence was the president, who suddenly said, "So tell me, Prof, what are your plans for afterward?"

Professor Schiff was roused from his fantasies. "Afterward . . . ?"

"After this whole affair ends," said President Ayeh, examining Professor Schiff with a sideways look. "Assuming, of course, that you don't go to prison for thirty years."

"Afterward? Afterward I'd like to travel to the waterfalls and hike in the jungle."

The president's face lit up. "Ah, yes, the waterfalls! You must see them. Only someone who has beheld our massive waterfalls can understand the African soul . . ." His soccer player's muscles jostled his feet. "But why would you go hiking in the bush? What's of interest to you there?"

"It has to do with my family story, Your Excellency."

"Ah, yes, your grandfather. The one it all begins with."

"My grandfather's grandfather's grandfather," Professor Schiff corrected him.

"Whoever it was," said the president with an impatient wave of his hand. Then he grinned. "Yes, Prof, our country is astonishingly beautiful."

"But is it completely safe to travel there?" asked Professor Schiff cautiously. "Rumor has it there are still groups of rebels in the north—"

"Those are lies spread by enemies of the state, my dear professor. The civil war is distant history; it ended long ago. Now there is peace. You have nothing to fear. There is not even one corner of my republic where there is any danger to anyone. The only thing you must watch out for is snakes. Snakes and hippopotamuses. Did you know, Prof, that the hippo is the most dangerous animal in Africa?" He laughed. "Yes, those fatties have a lousy temper."

President Ayeh sighed, pulled his cuff back to glance at his watch, then stood up. Professor Schiff leaped off his seat and also stood, erect and tense.

"It was very interesting talking with you, Prof. I'm certain we will meet again." The president tugged on his tunic, held out his massive hand, and briskly strode across the room and out through one of the doorways.

Just as the minotaur in the colorful tunic vanished, as if on cue, a thin man in a suit reappeared. It was Luther. "Your taxi is waiting in the parking bay, Professor Schiff. Please follow me."

When they arrived back at Villa Clark, Duke and Professor Schiff sat silently watching the gray sky through the dusty windshield. They both sensed this would be their final drive together.

Finally, Duke broke the long silence. "I wanted to ask you for a souvenir, Professor." He opened the glove compartment full of treasures and took out a square piece of cardboard, which he placed in Professor Schiff's lap.

"What's this?"

A newspaper clipping was glued to the cardboard. It was an article cut from the front page of the *West African Star*, with a photograph of Professor Schiff. The headline read: "Cleaning Up History—Settling the Score with Slave Trade Criminals."

"It's for a scrapbook I've been making," said Duke, and he offered a pen. "Could you please autograph it, Professor?" He pointed to a space at the bottom of the clipping.

"You're asking for my autograph?" Professor Schiff had only ever been asked to sign his books. And not very often.

"Yes, I collect famous people's autographs," Duke explained, "so I'll have something to leave my children."

Professor Schiff signed his name on the margin and handed the souvenir back to Duke. "How many children do you have, Duke, my friend?"

"Several. But I've already collected quite a lot of autographs. Bishop Desmond Tutu, Muhammad Ali, Komla Dumor, Michelle Obama, Vincent Matu Ayeh, Graça Machel, Binyavanga Wainaina, Naomi Campbell, Jerry John Rawlings . . . All good people."

Professor Schiff felt proud to have been asked to join such distinguished company. But then Duke added, with an awkward smile, "And you, Professor, will be the first bad person in our collection."

Only extreme embarrassment could effect such pure honesty.

When he got out of the car and walked to the villa, Professor Schiff pondered his arrogance, this desire of his for fame and glory, a desire that tortured and troubled him, a desire he could not get rid of, or conquer, or fulfill. He turned back to look at the Toyota driving away in a cloud of red dust and tried to imagine Duke's heirs splitting up the collection. *And here's an autograph from some guy named Professor Schiff*, says one of them. *Anyone interested?*

18

Ladies and gentlemen, members of the Special Tribunal, Madam Attorney General, Head of the Investigation Team:

I think it is time to tell you what I managed to find out about my notorious great-great-great-great-grandfather, Klonimus Zelig Schiff. But I must warn you: if up until now you weren't particularly fond of my dear ancestor but were willing to grant him the benefit of doubt, or at least find a few feeble arguments in his favor, I have a feeling that from this point onward you will loathe him with your whole being. Even partial forgiveness, I fear, will no longer be in any way feasible.

Ostensibly, the next episode in the slave trader's story is illuminated by a ray of light. Because the elderly Klonimus Zelig Schiff fell in love. And this unexpected, glorious, mad love that was ignited in his aging heart was what drove him to execute the plan that had been simmering in his mind since his wife's death. It is what made him renounce his status, give away his assets, part with his daughters and his beloved son, and set sail with six families of freed slaves to an unknown destination across the ocean.

Wonderful, you may say. The man had a heart. Trader or not. Slaves or not. He was human. He was just like us.

Besides, you must be anticipating a measure of sweetness with which to console yourselves after all the bitterness and sourness I've showered upon you, are you not?

Well, please forgive me, but I must ruin the romantic mood by informing you that the object of Klonimus Schiff's ardor was a fourteen-and-a-half-year-old slave girl.

Yes. I thought so. Just as I expected, I see before me a row of faces turning white.

But what are we so upset about, ladies and gentlemen? Is it that the young lady had not yet reached the age of consent we currently subscribe to? Or the inherently coercive power relations between a master and his young slave? Or is it that a withered, wrinkled old man dared to yearn for a healthy young creature not yet spoiled by time? Indeed, whichever angle we examine the matter from, it will disgust us. But I am committed to the truth, ladies and gentlemen, and so I shall continue.

With your permission, I should like to be more specific: Klonimus Schiff was sixty-three, an age that in the early nineteenth century was considered old. Very old. At the extreme end of average life expectancy. But it's not that anyone was bothered by this age difference of almost fifty years. No, that was something no one could have known (with the possible exception of the trader who sold her to Schiff, and he would likely have only guessed at the commodity's age based on the condition of her teeth). The troubling thing is that the girl . . . Oh, this is very embarrassing . . . She became pregnant. Yes, the girl whom Klonimus Schiff purchased, adopted, loved, and, as they say, *knew*, carried his child in her womb.

Distinguished tribunal members, I do not report this pedophilic relationship in order to shock you. Nor to amuse you with a clever parable. My English, after all, is not eloquent enough to compete with the classics. But I must inform you of what I learned from the diary in my possession. I must do so if only because, as my ancestor's representative, I have an obligation to explain his motives as best I can, even if his chances of gaining any sympathy from you, citizens of the present, are slim at best.

I'm sure you recall the papers I purchased from the Museum of African Culture. Ultimately, I was able to photograph only three sides of two pages, which were translated for me by my Dutch friend Margo.

I don't know why my great-great-great-great-grandfather kept that diary. Why does anyone keep a diary? He must have been hoping that someone would someday read his words. Because not only did he write them, he also did his best to make sure they were preserved. For whom? Was it for me? His descendent who must now answer for his misdeeds? Or perhaps it was for you, ladies and gentlemen, so that you can get to know him and perhaps thereby gain a better understanding of his motives?

Either way, as befitting a personal diary, it blends reports on the marine journey (weather, sea conditions, encounters with other vessels) with descriptions of the passengers' daily routines (joys, sorrows, celebrations, quarrels, troubles, and moments of euphoria). There are also declarations of love for the girl who became his wife. I will get to that soon.

But I must confess that even after I touched the papers, repeatedly peered at them through a magnifying glass, caressed them, smelled them, even tasted them with the tip of my tongue, then reread the translation over and over—still I harbored doubts about their authenticity. It is true that the ship from whose rotting wooden innards the documents were extricated was identified conclusively years ago. No one disputes that it is the *Esperanza* lodged in the seabed, fourteen meters down, three kilometers from shore. No one disputes that the sealed copper-lead-wax crate (a marvel of nineteenth-century marine technology, remember?) pulled out from among the crumbling beams was used by Klonimus Schiff as a safe. And yet I remained suspicious. The circumstances under which the pages had come into my possession left a bitter taste of fraudulence and deception, and after what happened, I could no longer trust Dr. Baidoo, the director and chief curator of the museum.

What convinced me of the diary's veracity was one single page. It was a page on which the writer does not describe the voyage, the sailors, the sails in the wind, the waves, or the flying fish. It contains no documentation. It was not written out of a commitment to any particular facts, nor from an unexplained need to leave behind a historical remembrance.

On this lone page—and I assume it is one of many that were lost—there are nothing but declarations of longing and passion for the young girl with whom the writer was in love.

And there is another surprising fact about this page: it is written entirely in Hebrew!

Hebrew, ladies and gentlemen, is a language in which I am extremely proficient. And so, unsurprisingly, despite the florid awkwardness, the biblical vocabulary, and the antiquated grammar, the contents are absolutely clear to me.

Incidentally, I had no trouble explaining to myself why this man who was desperately in love, whose whole being was bursting with passion, chose to express his feelings in the holy tongue. This mad love, which he was apparently experiencing for the first time in his life, brought him spiritual elevation. He did not dare involve the Holy One in the matter, of course, but he undoubtedly drew inspiration from another smitten Jew: King Solomon, poet of the sequence of love poems collected under the title "Song of Songs."

Ladies and gentlemen, imagine, if you will, Klonimus Schiff on a summer day in 1831, in the heart of the Atlantic Ocean, surrounded by a gang of freed slaves for whom he was omniscient leader, caring father, and benevolent master, and beside him a girl with whom—so he had decided—he was about to start a new family. No—a new tribe. More than that, even—a new nation. There he sits, in his swaying chamber, copying verses from "Song of Songs" into his diary, committing them to memory, and teaching his young lover to recite them in the ancient, foreign tongue:

I am black, but comely... Look not upon me, that I am swarthy, that the sun hath tanned me... Behold, thou art fair, my love; behold, thou art fair; thine eyes are as doves... Thy teeth are like a flock of ewes all shaped alike, which are come up from the washing... Thy lips are like a thread of scarlet... Thou art all fair, my love; and there is no spot in thee . . . Thy stature is like to a palm tree, and thy breasts to clusters of grapes . . .

Up on deck, as the *Esperanza* slowly nears the shores of Africa—your shores—he watches his beloved as she stands before him, leaning on the railing with the smooth tropical waters behind her, and he writes in his diary, "*Many waters cannot quench love, neither can the floods drown it . . .*" And those are also the words he wrote, transliterated in Latin characters, beneath her portrait, which was painted by the most loyal and gifted of his protégés, a freed slave by the name of Ajax Witte Voetjes. It is a watercolor of extraordinary precision and subtle detail, which was tucked among the pages of the diary. I present it here for your review.

As you can see—if we are to trust the skills of this amateur artist, Witte Voetjes—Klonimus's beloved was not exactly a tall and beautiful goddess. Or rather, she did not have the appearance that fools like us, cowed by the stereotypes of romantic movies, might have imagined. Nor did she suit King Solomon's imagery. There are visible scars from smallpox on her cheeks and deep burn wounds on her arms. It is plain to see that her left foot, which protrudes from beneath her white dress, has no toes. No, that is no artist's error. On the contrary: he must have wanted to direct the observers' attention to this defect. And I would like to believe that he did so according to the explicit request of the man who commissioned the painting, the man in love with its subject: Klonimus Schiff. Why?

Because Klonimus Schiff demanded that the portrait be as accurate as possible. Faithful to the original. Had the journey taken place twenty years later, he would probably have brought along a photographer with a daguerreotype. He wanted the girl's exact likeness to be preserved in his safe along with other paintings by Witte Voetjes. Along with his diary. Along with the ship's logbook. Along with the love poems.

And yes, we may now confirm the assumption we made earlier: Klonimus Zelig Schiff kept those documents for me. For all of you. For this tribunal. He did this so that when those who came after him judged his conduct, they could rely upon the documentation of his last great adventure, the one he embarked on with a delegation of six families, a captain, a small crew of sailors, a painter, and a black girl who was about to give birth to his fifth child.

He named his beloved Ruth, which is customarily the name given to women who convert to Judaism. And he gave her the middle name of Zipporah, after Moses's black wife. There is no record of the name she was given by her parents.

Her handicap must have caused her pain. She clearly had trouble walking: in the painting, she leans on a cane. Her gaze is full of sorrow. Her lovely smile hints at resignation.

When I looked at the painting for the first time, I immediately understood why this elderly man had fallen in love with her and how he became so attached to her.

Oh, Grandpa Klonimus!

19

Special Investigator George Aboagye moved the empty beer bottles aside and placed a small recording device next to the wet circles they'd left on the table. He spoke into the microphone, first looking at the floor before peering around the room as he announced the time and date. Then he stopped recording and attached the microphone to Professor Schiff's shirt. "Ready?" he asked.

Professor Schiff shifted in his wicker armchair until he felt he'd found the right position. "Yes, ready," he said, crossing his arms.

Aboagye turned the recorder back on. "Professor Schiff, I would like to begin our conversation with a direct and possibly somewhat provocative question: To what extent do you identify with your great-great-grandfather?"

"Great-great-*great-great*-grandfather," said Professor Schiff.

"Excuse me, your great-great-great-great-grandfather. How many generations are we actually talking about? Or, to put it otherwise, when did this man live?"

"He was born in 1765."

"Meaning . . . there are roughly two centuries between you. And so, to what extent do you identify with this slave trader?"

"I find the word *identification* extremely problematic. Klonimus lived in a very different time. It's hard for us to imagine how people lived back then, what motivated them, which values they leaned on, what their aspirations were . . . Not only how they dressed, what they ate and drank. That, too, of course. But the biggest challenge is to try to reconstruct their emotional world. We would like to assume, of course, that people have not changed over the generations. That is an assumption that enables us to dig up archeological sites and think that what we're finding under all that earth are ancient duplicates of ourselves. It's a useful assumption that allows us to investigate the past comfortably, unburdened by attempts to decipher incomprehensible codes. But is it a correct assumption?"

"Meaning, this man, for whose deeds we are now demanding that you accept responsibility, is not completely alien to you?"

"I try to imagine him, as much as I am able . . ."

"If I understand correctly, you came here hoping to acquire articles that apparently belonged to him, and over which you claim ownership—correct me if I'm mistaken—by virtue of your being his legal heir, is that correct?"

"I came here because of research I'm conducting into the man's life. As to your question, that man, my grandfather's grandfather's grandfather, is both a stranger and a relative. Identification, if there is any, seems to be primarily with an invented character. A sort of crumbling skeleton on which I hang a body. In the archives there is quite a bit of information about his life, yet still I am forced to fill in the gaps with my imagination."

"I agree that the moral and legal frameworks within which our ancestors' lives were conducted, the principles that directed their lives, have changed completely. That does not, however, absolve us of responsibility for acts committed in the past. Don't you agree, Professor?"

"But perhaps first we need to define what that responsibility is, and I'm not entirely convinced we will succeed."

"It's not that complicated. If you read the letter of the new law, the law under which you were arrested, you can see how this responsibility is defined. It is phrased in a clear and precise fashion. But there are also straightforward examples that everyone knows. For instance, the Germans, or the German political entity that was founded after the war, took full responsibility for the crimes of the previous regime. They even managed to translate that responsibility into financial reparations. To weigh it on a scale. There are other cases, too. The modern world tends to judge people who lived in the past, and even if we pardon them due to so-called extenuating circumstances, we try to compensate for the injustices and damages caused."

"If that's the case, Mr. Aboagye, allow me to ask you a question that surely has come up before regarding this new law of yours. What gives you, of all people, the authority to represent the victims? And not only to ask for an apology and an acknowledgement of the crimes, but to demand compensation and even punishment in the name of millions of people who were removed from this continent centuries ago, with whom you essentially have no real connection?"

"I disagree with you, Professor. We do have very close connections with them, and that is precisely what validates the demands made on those who bear responsibility."

"Well, you were born here, into the same ancient traditions . . . or what's left of them."

"No, Professor, no. The bond between us and those miserable people is rooted in the fact that the coerced, massive, prolonged migration is what made this continent what it is today: a depleted, exploited, desolate place. A place whose inhabitants do not like it. A place that people only want to leave. To flee. The exploitation wrought irreversible destruction, and the kidnapping of those millions and their transportation over the sea created a space, a black hole—forgive the pun—from which everyone runs. It is a momentum that cannot be stopped. And that, Professor Schiff, is the bond. It's true that Africa has bad publicity. But corruption, coups, civil wars, deranged dictators, famine, and genocide—those are things you can find anywhere on Earth. What you will not see is a departure on such a grand scale. Thousands of desperate people trying to cross the Mediterranean in rickety fishing boats, gathering at Lampedusa or Lesbos, climbing fences, walking across the snowy Alps, and yes, suffocating to death in freight trucks. It suggests a poetic equivalence, of course, with the slave ships—a provocative one, perhaps, but still valid, don't you agree?

"People began migrating from here a hundred and fifty millennia ago, the original Homo sapiens . . ."

"You will not succeed in consoling me with nostalgia for the Stone Age, Professor."

"Still, it's a source of pride, isn't it? After all, to think that humanity began here, on this continent, then dispersed across the entire planet . . . And if we take the future into account, then the entire universe . . . who knows . . ."

"Oh, you are most generous, Professor," said Aboagye, and a fleeting tinge of a smile twitched on his cheeks.

"Yes, how easy it is to be generous when you have nothing to lose."

Aboagye pressed a button on the device and stopped recording. "Well, thank you very much, Professor. I think we're done for today." He removed the microphone from Professor Schiff's shirt, wrapped the thin cord around the recorder, and placed it in a smart leather case. On his way to the door, he turned as if having remembered something trivial. "Professor, I was asked to let you know that the prison service has agreed to your request and will soon be installing a generator at Villa Clark."

Professor Schiff gave a theatrical sigh of relief.

"But, if I understand correctly, they will need to cut down on other expenses," Aboagye continued, "and so they're considering housing other detainees in the villa. How would that be, Professor?"

Professor Schiff hesitated briefly, then said, "Of course, why not," although the idea of relinquishing total control over his territory bothered him deeply. Still, he was only a guest here. Or rather, a prisoner for an indeterminate length of time.

"It'll only be another one or two people," said Aboagye with a blank expression, "but they might not be European."

"Why are you telling me that, Mr. Aboagye?" Professor Schiff asked indignantly.

"Oh, just because I fear you may not be able to share Bach with them, Professor. The sublimity, the elation . . ." He scanned Professor Schiff with an amused look. "But then again, once the generator is clattering, you won't be able to hear much anyway."

20

It would be a stretch to argue that the route from the Schiff-Kushners' home to Mordechai Shtil's apartment—not a third of a mile down the road—was particularly interesting. Brown stains left by bats on car roofs, a pile of crushed cardboard boxes and polystyrene packaging, a prismatic oil stain on the asphalt, an ad for guitar lessons pinned to the ficus tree—all these barely offered a reason to move one's eyes. Still, Professor Schiff found himself walking the route frequently, very frequently, two or three times a day, morning, noon, and night.

It's not that he was one of those people who enjoy wandering aimlessly. Quite the opposite: on ordinary days, meaning pre-Lucile days, Professor Schiff preferred his relationship with public spaces to be mediated through double-glazed windows. (There were, however, a few destinations he wanted or needed to reach. Like the pool, the university, the hospital where he periodically took Morduch for treatments.) But the new situation engendered a new routine. A wandering routine. And whether or not he had an excuse—walking the dogs, "getting some fresh air," sampling the weather, taking in any changes that might have occurred in the world in the past few hours, or picking something up at the grocery store—his feet always carried him in the same direction, along the same route, to the same destination: Morduch's apartment.

And what happened in Morduch's apartment? Not much, really. As soon as Professor Schiff walked in (his heart pounding in the hope that Grandpa Morduch would be fast asleep, or that his hearing aid would be off), Lucile would welcome him with a long—if slightly reticent—touch on the arm, lead him to the living room, and offer him cold water. Always only cold water. Professor Schiff would sit down on the couch and Lucile would sit next to him, though at a safe distance, near the wall now unadorned by the Congo collection. It was all a little embarrassing for the first few minutes, but then Professor Schiff would come up with some airy question about life and fate, and Lucile would answer at ponderous length, regaling him with the doctrine of the believers, of those who try as hard as they can to elbow their way into a rosy future. She also told him about Africa and about the royal dynasty to which she belonged, about the family's extreme wealth (by way of which it transpired that in earlier times a few of them had engaged in kidnapping and transporting human beings—yes, her people had also been in on the orgy—didn't you know, Professor Schiff?), about unimaginably grand palaces of gold and ivory, about their dispossession by the colonialist bureaucrats, and about how they were deposed from their aristocratic status and turned into a family of peddlers and fabric traders. And now refugees.

She spoke slowly and calmly, as if singing the chorus of a lullaby, talking on and on, until in the dark horizon over the ridge of her lips there glistened a few beads of sweat, which she dabbed at with her long finger.

But when it came time for Professor Schiff to speak, he fell silent. Instead of repaying her by relating what he had discovered in the archives—the remnants of the sunken ship on the shores of her homeland—and about his great-great-great-great-grandfather, visionary of the slave state, he simply stared at her mutely. But, predictably, precisely when he should have orchestrated an intersection between her biography and his, he lost his capacity for speech. He would then allow Lucile's voice to fade, stand up on his tired feet, gulp down the rest of his water, say goodbye (receiving another touch on the arm, no more), and walk back home.

"You're making a fool of yourself," said Tami with that not-really-a-smile of hers. She monitored his activity with the patience and composure of a bird-watcher.

"I know," said Professor Schiff.

"Besides, you have a wife you're supposed to be living happily with. There's a bit of a problem here, don't you think?"

"You're right. So what do you want me to do? Leave home and stay in a hotel, like in the movies?"

"No," said Tami, "but I just want you to know, Aguri, that I'm very, *very* disappointed in you."

Her black hair, which refused to go gray, falling on either side of her forehead, gave her a boyish look, even if there was very little youthfulness left in her face. Of course, Professor

Schiff could still easily see all the features that had won him over three and a half decades ago: the sardonic smile, the sharp nose (which had perhaps grown slightly over time), the faded freckles, the eyes (just slightly crossed in a most charming way) always accentuated by black eyeliner. Over the course of those long years, though, all her social justice values had seeped away, moving from her mind to the outer layers, altering her expression of playful sweetness into one of a forgiving pedagogue.

She had lovely hands, tan arms, athletic legs, and when her back wasn't out, she always had good posture. Her small, thin body, which was usually clad in shades of gray and light blue, bore a pair of large breasts that once, long ago, she had allowed herself to delight and take pride in. Now she blamed them for her back problems. The excess weight on her chest, she claimed, was unequivocal proof that the Creator was a male chauvinist. And she wasn't joking.

Professor Schiff was not to voice an opinion on the matter. In general, he was wise to avoid blurting out any comment of the type that men, including professors, sometimes tended to make. Because the rules of political correctness were strictly enforced in the Schiff-Kushner household. It hadn't always been that way. There was a time when Tami Kushner had treated words—even the very bad ones, even the ugly ones—forgivingly, fearlessly, and had not given preference to the weaker, more transparent or euphemistic ones. She herself sometimes used to curse and swear, and was even quite good at it, especially when she was arguing with her husband. But she'd lost that skill. Now instead of cursing she would harden her face and growl, "Aguri, I am very, *very* disappointed in you."

But *he* was disappointed in *her*, too. In that ordinary, banal way so typical of long marriages—namely, of situations in which disappointment is the default state. She knew that. He knew she knew that. They both knew. Because they were both people with plenty of awareness and understanding. And this was why they found the disappointment itself so disappointing.

"I asked Lucile to come with me to the meeting at Alissa's on Tuesday evening," Tami said.

"So you're bringing her into the gang?"

"The gang" was what Professor Schiff called the group of Tami's friends, all women, who met once a week to discuss social activism issues.

"We're discussing sexual harassment in the asylum-seeker community," Tami explained. "It'll be interesting to hear what she has to say."

Although Professor Schiff never missed an opportunity to mock these meetings, he envied them. He secretly longed to belong to a salon where important issues were discussed, or where one could simply chatter and drink herbal tea and munch on homemade baked goods. But he knew very well that a prerequisite for joining such a group, even one of weekend cyclists, was to give up two things: cynicism and self-importance. And this was too big a sacrifice for a lost cause.

Be that as it may, the expropriation of Lucile for the benefit of the gang irked him.

"What about Morduch?" he asked.

"What about him?"

"Lucile is supposed to take care of him, isn't she?"

"You'll fill in for her," Tami stated.

And so it turned out that Professor Schiff's wife had her own interest in Mrs. Lucile Tetteh-Ofosu. Hers was of a different nature, of course. She might not have been enchanted by the princess-like personality, but she certainly was enthusiastic about her refugee status, her condition as a penniless immigrant, and her belonging to a persecuted community of the downtrodden and the wretched.

When Tuesday arrived, however, and Professor Schiff went to Morduch's to relieve Lucile so that she could attend the meeting, it turned out that things weren't going exactly according to Tami's plan.

"No, no, no!" Morduch protested, vigorously shaking his white mane of hair, "Mrs. Lucile isn't going anywhere!"

"But . . . " Professor Schiff tried.

"No buts," Morduch cut him off, "Mrs. Lucile is staying here with me." To underscore his resolve, he blocked the front door with his body and spread his arms out theatrically, like a Goya figure. "Absolutely not!"

Lucile was clearly embarrassed. She said softly, almost in a whisper, "Please, Mr. Murdock, don't get so upset. Everything will be fine, I'll be back before midnight . . . "

Morduch didn't hear her. He couldn't hear her. His finger was fiddling with his hearing aid. His right eye, the bad one, almost popped out of its socket, fleeing the heap of wrinkles like a marble.

"And if something happens to me?" he screeched wildly in English. "If I fall down? Who will help me up?"

How strange, thought Professor Schiff. For years this ancient man had fought for his independence, insisted on living alone without any supervision, and now all of a sudden he refused to let Lucile go for one evening. His possessiveness might have been amusing had it not reminded Professor Schiff of that other embarrassing scene (oh, how he wished he could erase it from his memory) at Attorney Melchior's.

"Grandpa Morduch!" Professor Schiff yelled into the old man's ear. "Let's find out what Lucile wants."

Morduch fell silent. He backed away from the door and collapsed breathlessly onto an armchair.

"I'll stay with Mr. Murdock this time," said Lucile.

21

The stadium was overflowing. Dozens of people sat in the aisles, on the scaffolding of unfinished fencing, on the light poles, on cellular antennas, and on trucks parked outside. The crowd of twenty-five thousand was awaiting His Excellency, the Honorable President Vincent Matu Ayeh, who would be kicking off the major international match.

As it turned out, the Schiff affair was not the only exciting event going on in the Republic. A principle apparently instilled by past potentates, and notably internalized here, was that there's nothing like a packed stadium, a parade, a festival, or some other entertainment broadcast on giant screens to feed the weary soul of the nation, lift its mood (which naturally and perpetually tended downward), distract from civil wars, numb the pains of an ill economy, beautify the landscapes of dirt and mud, and alleviate the oppressive heat.

The villa's staff—Kweku, head of the security detail; his wife, Esther Efua, the cook and overseer of supplies; Nana, the gardener and pest exterminator; Ali, the maintenance guy; his wife, Fatimatu, in charge of laundry and cleaning; and three tots of unclear parentage—were all lounging in front of the television in the back room. Kweku, Nana, and

Ali were arguing about the national team's chances of beating Burkina Faso in the African Cup's qualifying rounds.

Professor Schiff lounged on a wicker armchair, though he wasn't very interested in the match. He'd never cared much for soccer.

"What do you say, Prof?" asked Esther Efua. "Which team are you betting on? Us or them?"

Professor Schiff considered his answer. He wanted to support "us," because he did in fact feel, by now, that he belonged to this "us," albeit perhaps involuntarily. But the raucous scenes on television reminded him of his status as an enemy of the African nation, an enemy soon to be tried in front of that very same riled-up mob. On his own. With no team.

Meanwhile, in the stadium, fences were breached and people ran across the yellow field. Police fired shots in the air to prod the hoodlums back to the bleachers. The game was supposed to start at four. It was almost five. Through the whistling, applause, drumming, horns, and noisemakers, a brass band played a very slow rendition of the national anthem over and over again. Fans waved tattered cloths in green-red-yellow-and-black. Vendors walked up and down the aisles with baskets full of meat dumplings and baked delicacies.

Heavy clouds were amassing to the south, slowly darkening the stadium.

At five o'clock, the crowds suddenly quieted down, and after a few seconds of absolute silence, they burst into rhythmic calls, "*A-yeh! A-yeh!*" followed by boisterous applause.

A heavyset man in a batik shirt and white trousers strode onto the field and waved both hands at the crowds. It was the President of the Republic, Vincent Matu Ayeh, former center forward in the Bundesliga. He shook the referee's hand, walked to the ball waiting in the center of the field, and kicked at it lazily. Then he waved at the roaring crowd again, looked at his watch, and hurried off the field. The game kicked off.

"Us," said Professor Schiff all of a sudden, "I mean, you."

"I hope so," said Kweku. He held the cross hanging around his neck up to his lips. So did his wife.

"*Inshallah*," said Ali.

Professor Schiff remembered the plastic mezuzah in his pocket. As soon as he got the chance, he decided, he would hang it up on the front door of Villa Clark. It couldn't do any harm. And if one day, when Lucile Tetteh-Ofosu turned up (miraculously, magically, regally), she would be glad to find the sacred object welcoming her.

Fifteen minutes and two goals later, a cavalcade of official black cars rolled into the villa compound with horns blaring and headlights flashing. Even before the assembled residents could get up, the car doors flung open and a roiling gang of perspiring men in suits poured out onto the front plaza, marched into the villa, and milled around in the vestibule and the foyer. Standing out in the hubbub was a man in a colorful batik shirt.

Indeed, it was a presidential visit. Except that instead of being pleased by the honor, Professor Schiff, who had always loathed surprise parties, was angry at how casually his privacy had been invaded. Yes, despite the fact that, officially, he was a "detainee" and the villa a "special detention facility."

He tried to slip away through the kitchen into the courtyard and up the exterior staircase to his room, but the people crowding the foyer blocked his path and surrounded him. And just as the president stood out among the dark suits, so did Professor Schiff among the dark faces.

As if acting on an invisible command, the security and press entourage split in two, opening up a passageway, at one end of which stood President Ayeh and at the other end Professor Schiff.

"I was in the neighborhood, Prof, so I decided to stop by and personally check in on our famous prisoner," declared Ayeh. "I also want to introduce you to the wisest, most beautiful woman in the world." He indicated the tall beauty standing next to him. "Professor Schiff—my wife, Clementine Ayeh."

The first lady, in a tight-fitting white suit, her straightened hair adorned with a headscarf that seemed to have been cut from the same colorful fabric as her husband's shirt, balanced expertly on a pair of stilettos.

The cameras flashed and clicked.

"I'm sure you're not angry at the spontaneous visit, Professor Schiff?" said Mrs. Ayeh. She came closer and placed a long-fingered, long-nailed hand on his arm in a gesture of patronizing friendliness. "I only hope we're not disturbing you in the midst of your important work."

Professor Schiff mumbled a few niceties. Of course, he said, he was delighted to host the Honorable President and his wife at his villa.

His villa. That is what he said. Yes, he allowed himself to use the possessive pronoun for this site, in which he felt as if he were the only guest at a luxurious writers' retreat. With all the requisite symptoms, naturally: claustrophobia, self-pity, and total creative drought.

"How is the book coming along?" asked the president.

"Very well, Your Excellency. Full steam ahead."

This was a lie, of course. Since arriving at the villa, Professor Schiff had written no more than a few barely cohesive lines. But he felt he should report something. Something that would convince himself—yes, mainly himself—that he was still worthy of the title *author*.

"You've certainly aroused my curiosity, Professor," said Mrs. Clementine Ayeh. "What is the book about?"

"I usually . . . I mean, in most cases, I don't talk about a book . . . " Professor Schiff stammered awkwardly. "I mean, not before it's finished . . . Completely finished. It's a matter of principle for me."

"Ah, yes, you are a man of principles, I remember," said the president. "It's a shame. Clementine and I so wanted to hear about it."

Professor Schiff had no choice but to improvise and, remarkably, he managed to deliver an extremely articulate narrative, or rather a sort of tale disguised as the synopsis of a convoluted plot. "It's a science fiction novel," he held forth confidently, "that takes place in the third millennium and tells the history of the first Jewish settlement on a distant planet in Alpha Centauri . . ."

The First Couple listened intently. After the brief lecture and a short pause, Mrs. Ayeh grinned delightedly, clapped her hands, and announced, "Wonderful! Simply wonderful. Extraordinary." She pondered, then added, "Do you know what I think, Professor? I think it must be made into a movie."

"I agree," President Ayeh quickly offered, "Mrs. Ayeh is absolutely right. It should be a movie."

"And it'll be even better than *Planet of the Apes*," said Mrs. Ayeh. "Remember *Planet of the Apes*, Vince?"

The honorable President of the Republic nodded with a dreamy look in his eyes, and chuckled. "Of course, honey, how could I forget *Planet of the Apes*?"

Professor Schiff remembered it, too. At least the ending. Yes, that final scene on the beach, when Charlton Heston kneels in the foamy waves in front of the ruins of the Statue of Liberty and cries out in anguish, "God damn you all to hell!" Or something like that. Yes, there was definitely a *God* in there somewhere, and there was a *hell*, but they both played a decidedly secular role—as befitting a nuclear holocaust.

Anyway, Mrs. Ayeh's acuity greatly impressed Professor Schiff. Because in the plot he had outlined—which was, admittedly, total hogwash—one could indeed identify the potential for a special-effect-laden cinematic epic. Except that the comparison between *Planet of the Jews* and *Planet of the Apes* aroused a certain discomfort in him, even though it was clear that the president and his wife hadn't meant to offend, and that the analogy had only come up because of the sci-fi context, which in both cases was amusing in its utter implausibility.

"You know, Clemi," said the president, tugging the hem of his long shirt, "the professor and I have already met. Yes, and I've already heard a few details of his literary endeavor."

Indeed, during that first meeting, when Professor Schiff had tried to explain to the president what had brought him to Africa, he had said he was doing research for a book. But he had absolutely not insinuated that it was a ridiculous sci-fi caper. The book was in its embryonic stage, and the research in its early phases, but Professor Schiff knew exactly what he wanted to write about: things that had really happened. Facts. He wanted to write about Great-Great-Great-Great-Grandfather Schiff and the real events that had occurred right here, on the African coast, almost two centuries ago.

"You met without me?" said Mrs. Ayeh. She giggled and made an exaggerated expression of anger. "Why wasn't I invited?"

"You were in Brussels, honey, at the European Union's conference on immigration."

"Are you certain?"

"Or was it Milan Fashion Week? I can't recall."

"Either way, I'm happy we're meeting now, Professor," said Mrs. Ayeh, "and I'm especially happy to have been able to hear about your project. I find it very, very interesting."

Professor Schiff murmured, "I must say, madam, that I am flattered, and extremely glad that my preliminary concept is so . . ."

". . . challenging," Mrs. Ayeh completed Professor Schiff's mumbled reply. Then she quickly added, "But in a good way."

"And moving," said the president. He put his hand on his wife's shoulder—which was not easy in light of their significant height difference—and she stroked his thick fingers. "Mrs. Ayeh has a great interest in film, not only as a talented and sought-after actress, but also as a director and designer." He surveyed his entourage as if to solicit confirmation.

Mrs. Ayeh giggled. "The president is exaggerating. I've been in a few films, and even won a few awards, but I'm really not such a big star . . ."

"She's wonderful," insisted the president, "and besides, you might be interested to know, Prof, that Mrs. Ayeh is not only my wife but also our minister of culture."

A long pause provided a photo-op: Professor Schiff on the left, the president on the right, and between them the tall, handsome first lady. Professor Schiff smiled effortlessly. Had he managed to adopt the quality so typical of the locals: smiling?

"Allow me to ask you something, Professor Schiff," said Mrs. Ayeh. "What does this planet look like? I mean, how did you imagine it in your story?"

"To tell you the truth, it's something like . . . like . . . this country. Like your country . . ."

"Incredible!" she cried and clapped her hands together. "Incredible. What a coincidence."

The sun set quickly, and then it began to rain abruptly and very powerfully. The noise of the car engines revving joined the sound of rain lashing the villa's roof. Walkie-talkies rustled. Umbrellas snapped open. Security guards rushed the president and his wife into a car whose wheels were kicking up a whirlwind of mud and bits of grass. The headlights cut through a cascade of water.

The speed with which they had to depart made the presidential couple abandon all etiquette. Without even waving goodbye to Professor Schiff, they simply vanished as quickly as they had appeared.

Later, when the clouds made way for a swath of clear night sky, Professor Schiff reclined on the balcony, gazed at the wet garden teeming with nocturnal activity, and tried to process his impressions of the presidential visit. Could he allow himself to presume that these people liked him? Did he like them? Would the visit lead to anything else? How would he describe it in his book, the book he might write, the book he had in fact already begun to write?

Kweku joined him with a bottle of Akpeteshie and a pair of glasses, and they silently sipped the spirit.

Finally, Professor Schiff asked, "So who won, Kweku?"

"The match was rained out."

"But still, someone must have been declared the winner?"

"Professor," said Kweku, "here we like to say, 'What you don't know—didn't happen.'"

Professor Schiff burst out laughing. Kweku stared at him in astonishment, then joined in.

22

Professor Schiff was not at all surprised to find himself standing on an improvised stage in the white fort. The enormous wooden door, the hexagonal paved courtyard, the rusty cannons, the double staircase, the shadowy vestibules, the crashing waves beyond the crumbling walls, the small doorway leading down to the slaves' dungeon—it all seemed a very appropriate setting for a press conference with the man about to become the first defendant under the newly legislated Law for Adjudicating Slave Traders and Their Accomplices, Heirs, and Beneficiaries.

His impressions from his first visit to this fort, back when he'd been a mere tourist, were still fresh. The intense horror he'd felt while touring the dungeon had been utterly detached from any knowledge, any understanding, any capacity to connect the injustices to his own life. He had observed, filled his lungs with the damp air, touched the walls, and even knelt down and dug his fingernails into the slippery film covering the floor stones. And when he'd walked through the "point of no return" to the beach, he'd thought—and he remembered this well—that the greatest villains produced by humanity had never paid a price for their deeds. True, it was a childish observation. Not the sort of contemplation befitting a professor. But in light of all this naked horror, thoughts, too, become bare. Devoid of any intellectual guise. Now it was he himself who was the villain, or rather the representative of all those other villains, and it was in this capacity, thrust upon him unbidden, that he answered the journalists' questions.

Sitting on his right, at a table covered with a green tablecloth, was Special Investigator George Aboagye. A huddle of journalists and camera crews faced them.

"Professor Schiff, what do you think of our country?"

"I like it very much."

"Are you being treated fairly? Are they treating you well?"

"Yes, very well. I have no complaints. On the contrary."

"It was reported that in one of the tribunal meetings you said there was no need to mention the horrors of the slave trade. Do you still believe that?"

"I said that the horrors were in the background all the time anyway, of course, but if the accusation against me is a matter of principle—because, after all, I personally haven't done anything to anyone—then the discussions should also remain on a principled level."

"What did you know about the transatlantic slave trade before coming here?"

"Very little. More or less what everyone knows. I'd read a few books."

"Professor Schiff, would you define yourself as a liberal?"

"In my country I'm considered a leftist, but that pertains to opinions about local politics. I abhor nationalism, xenophobia—"

"What about racism?"

"Racism, too, of course."

"Professor, are you worried about the investigation's results, and the trial it might lead to?"

"I'm sixty-three. This is the time to stop worrying and start being fatalistic, isn't it?"

"How did your family respond to the affair? A while ago it was reported that your wife refuses to come here because she's afraid of vaccinations, especially the yellow fever vaccine . . . "

"No, that's not true. My wife is a very busy woman. We agreed that there's no reason for her to come here, for now."

"In that television interview, when she was asked about the reason for your trip to Africa, she said, and I quote, '*cherchez la femme*.' Can you explain what she meant?"

"I don't always understand my wife. That's the beauty of our relationship."

"And does she always understand you . . . ?"

"No comment."

"It was reported that you've started writing a new book and have already interviewed His Excellency President Ayeh. Is the book connected with this affair?"

"Only partially. But I don't wish to talk about the book. I don't discuss books before I've finished writing them."

"Do you think this affair will influence Africa's relations with the West?"

"No, I don't think so."

"Professor Schiff, what message would you like to send the descendants of your great-great-great-great-grandfather's victims?"

"I'm sorry, but I don't have any message. Honestly. I wish them what I wish all of you, ladies and gentlemen: happiness, serenity, and much health."

The press conference finally came to an end. Tripods were folded up, cables bundled, spotlights turned off, cameras packed in cases, and the reporters began thronging to the exits.

Now Professor Schiff noticed three white faces in the crowd. Even from sixty feet away, he immediately recognized them as his compatriots, fellow speakers of his language. Perhaps because of how they elbowed their way against the current, forging forward with breathless determination. Aboagye motioned for them to approach.

"These are representatives from your embassy, Professor Schiff," he said, "as the minister of justice promised the ambassador. We just had to find the right timing." He stood up and slipped away.

Professor Schiff's compatriots—or perhaps it would be more accurate to say, his fellow tribe members—comprised a bulky, broad-shouldered man who blew on his glasses and wiped them with a tissue; a freckled young woman with her red hair braided and coiled atop her head; and a tall man with a boyish face, several pens poking out of his pocket, and a small, metal, blue-and-white flag pinned to his lapel. They came up to Professor Schiff and shook his hand, one by one.

"Do you have everything you need, Professor Schiff?" asked the redhead. "Any complaints or requests?"

Professor Schiff said he had no complaints and was perfectly satisfied. Well, apart from the power cuts perhaps.

"You'll have to get used to those," she said.

"We will soon convene the whole legal team we've assembled for you," said the tall man with the pens and flag, "outstanding individuals. And a series of expert witnesses who are the finest minds in their fields. We're bringing in a historian who is an authority on the eighteenth-century transatlantic slave trade, and a very well-known legal scholar, an international figure, who is well-versed in all the relevant areas, from liability limits when it comes to crimes against humanity, to retroactive implementation of the law, slavery statutes, and so forth."

"Of course, this is not exactly in accordance with diplomatic protocols, Professor, but we view your case as a matter of national importance," said the redhead.

"And by the way, we're also working behind the scenes, of course," whispered the bespectacled heavyset man, "through unofficial channels."

The redhead shoved a business card into Professor Schiff's hand and said, "If you have any questions or requests, don't hesitate to call. Leave a message and someone will get back to you as soon as possible."

From the card, Professor Schiff learned that her name was Ilana Sasson and that she held the title of deputy consul. The other two remained anonymous for the time being, which added an aura of mystery yet also professionalism to the brief, unilateral conversation.

It was like doctors stopping to see a terminal patient on their morning rounds.

23

"Three things determine what sort of life a person lives," said Lucile, "his desires, his mistakes, and various external forces that control him." What these forces were, she did not explain. She was probably trying to spare Professor Schiff from having to study a rather complicated system of spirits, souls, divinities, and a plethora of other hybrid entities fusing physicality and spirituality.

It is worth noting that Professor Schiff treated all supreme forces equally and indiscriminately. He scorned both private spirits and anonymous deities, just as he spurned the best-selling gods who had achieved fame and seniority. He was suspicious of any whispered prayer or blessing that included a direct or indirect address to celestial management. He was hostile to sanctified objects. Yes, like mezuzahs, for example, which Lucile was actually rather fond of. Even on this matter, though, he was willing to forgive her. Just as he now listened to her spiritual pontifications with great interest.

"Success and failure are not only dependent on us," Lucile explained, "and in fact, most of the things that happen to human beings aren't up to them at all. Not their birth and not their final departure. Not disease, not accidents, and not a woman you meet one day and take a liking to without having any idea why."

She elaborated on the tenets of her faith with seemingly no desire to persuade Professor Schiff. And indeed, despite his great affection, he maintained his stance as an amused onlooker. (So, too, incidentally, did Tami, who actually attributed considerable significance to black cats, broken mirrors, and knives passed from hand to hand.)

And then Morduch's complaints began.

Strange noises echoed through his apartment, noises that reminded him of sound effects in a cartoon. A few days later he claimed to have heard a male voice singing, or perhaps reciting, and from time to time tapping metallic fingers on the living room table. Then he said his reading glasses had disappeared, and only after a whole day of searching did he find them—in the fridge. Furniture shifted places. A dusty half-eaten apple suddenly rolled out from under the wardrobe as if an invisible hand had pushed it. And in the middle of the night a desperate bird, perhaps a turtledove, somehow got into the apartment and proceeded to bump into the windows and leave droppings on the television.

There was no rational explanation for all this. Professor Schiff and Tami Kushner, of course—perhaps because of their damned prejudices—were inclined to dismiss all these reports as an old man's delusions. After all, Morduch would be turning a hundred and four soon, and it was widely known that an aged brain was susceptible to erosion over the years.

Some say paranoia is a symptom of this degeneration. Oh, how easy it is to accuse old age.

"Grandpa Morduch," said Tami in a very loud voice, right into his ear, "I don't think it's a burglar."

"I know, I know," Morduch shushed her impatiently, "burglars don't sing and recite and drum on tables."

"They also don't eat apples, hide glasses, and let birds in," added Tami in a murmur that he likely did not hear.

"So if it's not a burglar, who is it? Who could it be?" said Morduch bitterly. "Are you saying I'm hallucinating? Senile? Muddled?"

"No, no, we never said that, God forbid. Everything has a rational explanation."

"I don't need explanations, Tami dear," Morduch snapped. "You know me, you know how sensitive I am to the thin line between fantasy and reality."

Professor Schiff and Tami Kushner assumed if they let the matter go, it would fade away. But the phenomena grew worse and the complaints more frequent. Daily.

Finally, when one morning Morduch found himself standing in the stairwell outside the apartment after, as he claimed, someone—again, through an invisible hand—had dragged and pushed him out and slammed the door shut, the Schiff-Kushners had no choice but to get to the bottom of things. And this required, despite the unpleasantness of it, questioning Lucile. With the requisite tact.

They told her about Morduch's complaints, hinted that of course it might all be a figment of his imagination, but perhaps—they suggested cautiously—she could offer her own guess.

She replied immediately and decisively: "Toga."

"Toga?" Tami Kushner repeated. "Who is Toga?"

Whoever this Toga was—please let it not be a husband or partner or male friend, Professor Schiff begged his own private Providence. He prayed. He was willing to take an oath. To start kissing mezuzahs, even.

But there was another possibility—one he was absolutely incapable of considering.

Well, explained Lucile Tetteh-Ofosu, Toga was a spirit. Yes, a spirit that had been with her, protecting her, since childhood. This invisible, ethereal bodyguard had been hired for the job by Lucile's grandmother (may she rest in peace), who, though not an accredited professional in folk medicine (a shaman, in Professor Schiff's limited knowledge of the lingo), was sufficiently skilled to be able to help in cases that could not be resolved by science. Or the law. Or common sense. And Toga performed his duties admirably. For example, he'd once stood between Lucile and a wicked neighbor waiting to ambush her on her way to school. Another time he'd removed her from a bus moments before it crashed. Except that over the years, Toga had become controlling, Lucile went on to explain. Intolerably controlling and extremely jealous, especially whenever a man came into her life.

The facts spoke for themselves: her first marriage came to a premature end when her husband, a decent, kind man but also a devout Muslim, decided he had to perform the haj, set off on his pilgrimage to Mecca, and never returned.

Her second marriage, though never formalized in a civil or religious agreement, was quite successful and even resulted in three wonderful children. It ended when the man became enslaved to alcohol. First palm wine and beer, then drinks with higher alcohol content: whiskey, Akpeteshie, and finally wood varnish. He became an embarrassing nuisance, and there was no choice but to return him to his mother, who would care for him until he died of liver cirrhosis.

And the third husband—the one with whom Lucile had crossed barbed wire fences and arrived here—wasn't worth mentioning at all. And it was all Toga's fault.

Ostensibly, of course. The evidence for the spirit's interference in Lucile's love life was, for the time being, circumstantial.

At the usual gathering place around the dining table, in the dusk of a summer evening, Professor Schiff and Tami Kushner heard Lucile's confessions while, outside the window, the heavy branches of the mulberry tree grew dark, and the shade of blue glimpsed through the leaves turned deep and black. They did not believe in spirits. But the depths of that sky, which the large tree tried to hide from them, reminded them that disbelief never solves riddles.

"Let's assume that everything you say is true—and I'm definitely not insinuating that it is," said Tami. "Why would this spirit—what did you say its name was? Toga . . . Why would this Toga suddenly care?"

Despite trying very hard, Tami and Professor Schiff found it difficult to take Lucile's account seriously. They certainly preferred the previous explanation, the one that attributed the mysterious occurrences to the imaginings of a man with dementia. And in fact, even if they had replaced their stubborn agnosticism for a moment, just one brief moment, with the tenets of Lucile Tetteh-Ofosu's faith, and even if they had conceded that an invisible entity with a fanatical male ego was orbiting Lucile, they still would have been completely unable to grasp how Mordechai Shtil, their very own Grandpa Morduch, had anything to do with it.

As it turned out, all they needed was to use a little common sense.

"I'm sure you don't know this," Lucile said, "and the truth is, it's supposed to be a secret for now, but perhaps it's time to let it out. I hope Mr. Murdock won't be angry." Her lovely lips smiled delightedly and her eyes glazed over dreamily. "A week ago, Mr. Murdock asked me to marry him. I said I needed time to consider his proposal, and this morning I decided to accept."

24

Professor Schiff privately summed up the salient points:

Mrs. Lucile Tetteh-Ofosu—a forty-seven-year-old woman from a small West African country who had a hazy biography involving an unproved affiliation with a royal dynasty, a philosopher with some knowledge of mysticism, a fan of hairdos, owner of a diverse wardrobe, a woman possessed of captivating beauty, musical locution, and a throaty laugh, the woman with whom he was enthralled—was going to marry Mr. Mordechai Shtil, also known as Morduch, an affluent man of a hundred and four who alone had held the title of Grandpa in the Kushner-Schiff family for many years.

She would, in doing so, become Tami Kushner's step-grandmother. Grandma Lucile.

As if this melodrama were not grotesque enough, it was now invaded by an element of greed that played a modest yet bothersome role. To put the dilemma subtly: Professor Schiff, Tami Kushner, and their children had grown accustomed to enjoying Morduch's generosity, and at this juncture they did not feel prepared to relinquish it. Being spoiled, of course, is something that one can and perhaps should give up. But is it possible to hand over a sizeable inheritance to a waif who happens to appear out of nowhere? And not just that but . . . an African one? In other words, a woman whose motives might (and only might, at this point) arouse some shadow of suspicion?

Oh, such shameful thoughts. Thoughts one should certainly repress, since they are not worthy at all of discussion. Certainly not out loud.

"I know what you're *not* thinking about," said Tami to Professor Schiff, "what you refuse to think about."

"What am I *not* thinking about?"

"You're *not* thinking about the money. The inheritance."

"That's right, I'm *not* thinking about money at all."

"That's very good, I'm glad you're also *not* thinking about money. But if you *do* happen to have any concerns about that topic, then I can put your mind at rest. I've spoken with Morduch. It turns out he doesn't have much left. Almost nothing, actually. That's what he told me and I believe him."

"What did he say?"

"He said he knows we're worried about the money. He said he thinks we're angry at ourselves because we're ashamed of our greediness and hate ourselves for being suspicious. He said that since he loves us so much and feels so close to us, he wants us to stop being angry. Because he registered the title to his apartment in our names ages ago anyway. And that we shouldn't forget how all these years he was lavish with us and never spared a penny and supported us endlessly. And most importantly, there's no point in grieving because there's very little left of his fortune. Almost nothing. Enough to support him and Lucile for a year or two."

"That's what he said?"

"Yes, and he also said that falling in love is a mysterious and surprising business that can't be explained, and he's certain we'll understand and be happy for him."

"So what did you say?"

"What could I say? That Professor Schiff is jealous? That what angers him isn't the money, but something entirely different?"

Oy, what a lousy story, said Professor Schiff to himself. A pathetic story. A laughable story. But he found no comfort in his attempt to merely observe the events unfolding around him, nor could he cool his injured pride. He felt betrayed. Yes, betrayed! And a slight nausea mounted in him when he imagined Grandpa Morduch stuffing himself with a glossy piece of wedding cake.

Considering the groom's advanced age, the couple felt a certain urgency. And since these sorts of events demand a series of preparations (in a country where you can't just walk into an office, pay a fee, and get a permit to tie an everlasting bond), the entire Schiff-Kushner family—including Professor Schiff, as he stewed in the juices of his affront, disappointment, and jealousy—was about to enlist in the project.

But first, there was an urgent need to solve the biggest and most challenging obstacle: Toga, the bodyguard spirit.

"I suppose this time there's no choice but to get rid of Toga once and for all," said Lucile Tetteh-Ofosu. Tami and Professor Schiff had never heard her sound so strident.

"Maybe we can just talk to him," Tami suggested, and quickly added, "whoever or whatever it is." She advocated solving conflict through dialogue, and Professor Schiff wondered if she would volunteer to conduct the negotiations. But how could one reach an understanding with an entity whose very existence was in doubt?

"No!" Lucile retorted. "It's over." She shook her head and the glorious tower of curls swayed left and right. "This time he must leave, disappear, cease to exist."

Tami was horrified. "That sounds very drastic. Shouldn't we try a gradual approach?"

"Trust me, Mrs. Kushner, I know what I need to do."

"Are you sure it's the only way?" Tami insisted.

"Yes. Yes, there is only one option." She got up and started moving around the dining area, her arms crossed and her eyes staring into space, as if she were a poet summoning her muse. Professor Schiff and Tami Kushner watched her tensely. Finally, she stopped and said, "Yes, I know what I have to do, and you will help me." Then she symbolically rolled up the sleeves of her colorful shirt and said, "Right. First thing: a rooster."

Professor Schiff was startled. In his mind's eye he saw a horrifying voodoo ritual: faces painted white, rattling gourds, brandished scepters, bone necklaces, dances with rhythmic drumming, masks, colorful capes, fire, and smoke . . . And now, a slaughtered rooster with its innards spilling out.

"I don't know . . ." he said hoarsely, "I just don't know."

But it wasn't only the poor rooster. The scene he envisioned did not fit into any locale he knew. He struggled to imagine an appropriate site for such a ritual. Their backyard? The park? The beach in the evening?

"Don't worry, Professor," said Lucile, "I just need you and Mrs. Kushner as witnesses. You won't have to do anything. Just be with me while I banish Toga."

"Is it dangerous?" Tami asked.

"Only if you're inexperienced. It's like messing with electricity."

Where did she find the handsome fowl, whose feathers shone in metallic green and whose scarlet comb wobbled like a jester's hat? They did not ask, and she did not say. She only requested that they try to keep things secret, especially from Morduch. Because that was how spirits preferred it. Any contact between the human and celestial worlds required the utmost caution.

As instructed by Lucile, Professor Schiff moved the furniture up against the living room walls, rolled up the rug, and lowered the blinds until the room was partially dark.

The glorious rooster was let out of his crate, jumped onto the floor with an angry crow, and promptly began roaming around the room, stretching his neck out and bouncing his head from side to side irritably. Lucile Tetteh-Ofosu, barefoot and wearing her familiar cleaner's outfit, sagging gym shorts and a faded T-shirt, joined the rooster, trying to adapt to his confident gait, in what might be described as a circular dance in which the rooster led and the woman followed. During the course of this lengthy spectacle, her lips moved constantly.

It had to be a spell, thought Professor Schiff.

After half an hour of aimless marching, the rooster suddenly called out a weary *cock-a-doodle-do*, flapped its wings, and squeezed into a corner of the room.

"That's it, it's over," declared Lucile.

"Toga's gone?" asked Tami, with a slight note of bereavement in her voice.

"Yes, he's gone." Lucile's forehead was covered in beads of sweat. Her shirt clung to her damp back.

"Where did he go?" Tami wanted to know.

"What do you mean? He passed into the rooster," Lucile replied.

Professor Schiff breathed a sigh of relief. In the end, not a drop of the rooster's blood had been spilled, not a single feather from his grand tail plucked. He was merely worn out by the ritual he'd been forced to participate in. Much like Professor Schiff and Tami Kushner, who had expected a folklore spectacle and instead been given a slow and extremely tedious parody of the Jewish atonement ceremony.

25

Honorable members of the Special Tribunal, Madam Attorney General, Head of the Investigation Team:

Allow me to present you with two pages from Klonimus Schiff's travel diary. I am convinced that based on the limited materials I have here, you will be able to form an impression of the man's unique personality and understand something of his motives.

I should note, for good measure, that because of the fragility and brittleness of the original papers, I am providing you with copies, along with the English translation (and here I must thank my friend Margo for her excellent work).

And now, the text:

Sunday, 4 Tishrei, 5592 since the creation—
September 11, 1831

Smooth sea. Standing air. The slow currents insist on pushing the Esperanza *back west, and like the righteous Elijah the Prophet atop Mount Carmel, I, too, look to the sky and await the wind.*

Thursday, 8 Tishrei, 5592 since the creation—
September 15, 1831

Faint southern wind, almost imperceptible. Very slow progress.

Captain de Groot decided to veer 12 degrees northward. The wind changed at half past five in the evening, a little before sundown. Toward seven, it picked up and the sea became extremely turbulent.

Monday, 12 Tishrei, 5592, before dawn—
September 19, 1831

Yom Kippur was observed, down to the last commandment and law. I served as the cantor. The congregation, being as of yet unschooled in the prayers, answered me with sounds alone yet with great intention. But what did they have to ask forgiveness for? What were they to atone for? Unlike me, they are all as innocent as babes. Only I carry a heavy load. And they, who have repented and found faith—their wounds are scarlet red, their skin black, but their souls snowy white. Indeed the storm tormented us greatly on that holy day, but the fast only aided us in overcoming our bodily pains. It is possible that I erred in determining the beginning and end times of the holy day. It is hard to see the sky through the clouds.

Sunday, 18 Tishrei, 5592—September 25, 1831

Early in the morning we saw to the southwest a fleet of three English frigates sailing one half a mile from each other. Within two hours, the first of His Majesty's ships, The HMS Dryad, *had caught up with us. An officer with the rank of commodore, wearing a tricorn adorned with feathers, surveyed us through his telescope. Then he waved and tried to talk to us through a sound-amplifying tube, but we could not hear his words because he was speaking into the wind. The soldiers next to him raised their rifles and fired warning shots in the air. The British commodore must have noticed the* Esperanza's *dark-skinned passengers, and wished to find out if the ship was conveying a cargo of slaves. I instructed the congregation to come on deck, and they all crowded around by the port-side railing, wearing their fine clothes, and waved at the British frigate. Mr. and Mrs. Zwart broke into song and the whole chorus quickly joined in. They sang the ancient hymn I had taught them,* "Adon Olam," *and when they had finished the last verse they remembered, they kept humming the tune, with the customary accompaniment of rhythmic body movements and hand-clapping. I myself stood on the bridge with my beloved Zipporah in my arms. Because of her handicap, as well as being with child, she has trouble steadying herself. The singers made me extremely proud. The English frigate lowered a raft and dispatched an officer accompanied by three soldiers. Much to my surprise, one of the soldiers was a—*

(I shall not, of course, repeat the illicit word that was in common use at the time the diary was written. Margo translated it accurately. Still, I allow myself to omit it. Either way, it is interesting that Klonimus viewed the juxtaposition of the soldier's red uniform and his dark skin as sensational, or at the very least, noteworthy.)

The officer boarded the Esperanza. *At his demand, I allowed him to review the ship's logbook. Then he questioned the crew and spoke with a few members of the congregation, and when he'd put his mind at ease, he paid us the honor of drinking tea with Captain de Groot and myself. The Englishman told us that they were in pursuit of a pirates' ship.*

Thursday, 29 Tishrei, 5592 since the creation—October 6, 1831

The western wind has grown very harsh, and the Esperanza *sailed through heavy rains and a thunderstorm. De Groot ordered all sails dropped. On the seventh night of Sukkot, a candle was knocked over in one of the women's chambers and set fire to the floorboards. The fire was quickly extinguished and the damage was negligible. Unfortunately, however, Mrs. Nelly Suiker's medicine box was burnt. Mrs. Suiker had taken on the duties of Dr. Martin, may he rest in peace (he died only one week after we set sail), and she seems to have done an excellent job thus far. Apart from the doctor, two children (the twins Joseph and Benjamin Zwart, may God protect their pure souls), and a baby (Esther Met-Zonder, may her memory be for a blessing), we did not, praise Hashem, lose anyone. The storm did not abate until the next morning.*

Wednesday, 5 Marcheshvan, 5592—October 12, 1831

Another storm. The sea appears to be constantly roiling. De Groot has trouble steering the Esperanza. *I gathered everyone and we prayed. I told them the story of Jonah the Prophet. Mrs. Van der Moeder and Mrs. Knoflook were extremely frightened and burst into bitter tears. They thought I was about to draw lots to decide which of them would be thrown into the sea. I was very disappointed by this response. I thought they had managed to overcome the miserable hindrance imposed upon them for so many years. I have tried so hard to bring them to the level of understanding and sensitivity required of cultured people. A few of them, it seems, are doomed to remain children forever. Others, like Ajax Witte Voetjes, my trusted aide, will one day inherit my position. My beloved Zipporah reassured the frightened ladies. She explained that none of the ship's passengers is a prophet, and therefore everyone is safe.*

Monday, 10 Marcheshvan, 5592—October 17, 1831

I once again recalled Jonah the righteous. Yesterday afternoon there was smoke visible on the horizon. When we got closer, we realized the source of the smoke was the deck of a ship anchored at sea. It was a whale-hunting vessel. Tied to the length of the ship was a gigantic carcass of a creature the likes of which none of us had ever seen, either alive or dead. It was, of course, the famous fish known as the cachalot, from whose head oil is produced. A few men suspended from the deck on ropes butchered the corpse, and the pieces were carried up to the deck on pulleys. Despite the distance, the horrible stench clung to our clothing. We quickly sailed as far as the wind would permit.

Sunday, 17 Marcheshvan, 5592 since the creation—October 23, 1831

A lone albatross dropped upon the deck a cap that had been lost by one of the sailors in last week's storm. I heard someone comment, "The Lord works in mysterious ways." Others, in whom the soul of an idolator still resides, said it was a sign. A sign of what? And from whom? Could it be that the Almighty squanders His infinite greatness on retrieving hats? We who have entered into the covenant of Abraham do not question the ways of Hashem, for everything that is created was created by His word, for Him, and that is its entire purpose. And yet, sometimes——

(And here, at the end of the page, the text is cut off.)

26

I thought about my great-great-great-great-grandfather a lot. And about those pages, written in such neat, uniform handwriting, with only a slight variance in the thickness of the ink lines reflecting the goose-feather nib that had imprinted them on the paper. He had a very steady hand, this sixty-three-year-old man. A hand that was able—in the midst of a howling storm—to police the alphabet as if the letters were field workers under his command. Was it the hand of a clerk or a slave trader? Was that hand trained to whip? To beat? Was it crude and malicious like the heart that pumped blood into it? Or was it a limp and delicate hand, a hand accustomed to counting gold coins, patting sacks of sugar, touching cotton, filling out columns in account ledgers?

You should know, my distinguished friends, that since the moment I acquired those pages, there has been no diminishment in the magic of the ink marks that lead back to the writer's fingers, to his pupils, to the furrowed brow and the tongue protruding with effort, like a child's, as he scratches in his notebook. Blue faded lines that lead right into the soul of Klonimus Zelig Schiff, my grandfather's grandfather's grandfather.

But I will not pretend. I do take a great interest in him, and I wish to study him not only as a distant relative but also as a model of the period. Mostly, though, I find myself delving, and delving again, into the story of mad passion between an elderly man and a disabled young girl. In that sense, at least, I resemble (too closely, I fear) any other pulp writer: just give me a peek (I suppose I haven't changed all that much since buying that quick glimpse between the popular girl's legs in third grade) and I'll run to write about it. In fact, I'll write about it even if I don't get a peek, simply using my imagination, which aims to burrow down and expose the deepest, darkest regions, and there is nothing that can stop it. Like the shaft dug out in an underground railroad.

Oh, ancient forefather! When I dig you up from the past, when I invent you, reconstruct your life, create you from my imagination, am I not in fact yearning to take your place on Earth?

I was with him in the grand bedroom of Schiff Villa, in Paramaribo, when he woke suddenly at dawn and found himself sprawled in the armchair next to the bed, wearing his wrinkled and sweat-soaked Sabbath suit, as his ashen wife Esperanza lay in the bed beneath the netting. Her mouth was open, her chin turned up, as if in her final moments she'd tried to swallow back her soul as it took flight. She had died while he slept, and he had not heard her utter her last words, or say goodbye to him—her husband of thirty-five years—and to the whole world.

Only a few hours later, when they began preparing for the funeral procession, did Rosetta, the mulatta slave, tell him that at the very last moment Esperanza had opened her eyes and said in a loud, lucid voice, "My dear husband, it is time to make old Rosetta a free woman; that is my will and my final request." And indeed, Rosetta added, what was the point of keeping an elderly slave whose mistress had passed on? Liberty and death lived under the same roof. Especially in the slavery regions.

"You're lying!" Klonimus said, and struck her cheek. And that was more or less the first thing he did after his wife Esperanza died.

I was with him in the synagogue on Sabbath morning, when his youngest child, Solomon, read from the Torah on the occasion of his bar mitzvah. I say *youngest* though I know that a short while later, in the womb of the girl Zipporah, a new descendent was created. But wait. All that will become clear soon, ladies and gentlemen. For now, let us return to the synagogue, where Master Klonimus, one of the congregation's wealthiest and most distinguished members, is standing behind his son, scanning the crowd of people come to celebrate with him. Among them he sees his best friends, all landowners, manufacturers of sugar and rum, self-satisfied men with their beards neatly combed and perfumed, wearing suits and felt tricorns. In the front row he sees his own empty chair, a glorious piece of furniture adorned with silver leaf, on whose velvet cushion one can clearly see the indentation left by his body, a topography that has evolved over more than two decades. And in the gallery, where the women sit, he sees his three vain daughters fluttering silk fans to cool their flushed cheeks. Yes, the heat in Suriname is intolerable. And I feel the hatred tingling in the elderly Klonimus's gut. I sense the repulsion mounting inside him. The resentment, the nausea . . .

I was with him when, in the dead of night, after a four-hour ride, he reached the slaves' living quarters. This crowded village, arranged in a grid of dirt paths as straight as soldiers' barracks, was lost in deep sleep. Functional sleep. The sleep of worn-out machines.

The place aroused great distress in Klonimus, perhaps even sadness. Yes, sadness. The moon appeared and disappeared in the overcast sky. Snores, sighs, and the murmurs of tormented dreamers accompanied Schiff as he roamed among the shacks. At first he tried to tread quietly and not make any noise with his boot spurs, but then he realized nothing could wake these sleepers. Not the bite of a flea, not the gnawing of a rat, and certainly not the sound of footsteps. None of them would tear themselves away from their dreams until the painful chime of the gong, followed by the foremen's wakeup calls ("God's blessings upon hardworking people!" was what they shouted out in Dutch) and the lashings of their whips, an hour before sunrise.

Who were these people? How did their days unfold? For decades, they'd been nothing but columns in the account ledgers for Klonimus, alongside sums of rum and sugar yields. Now, wandering among the shacks, he suddenly had the absurd notion—extremely absurd—that he was one of them, a partner to their terrible fate, afraid, helpless, and deadly exhausted.

When Schiff walked into the shack he'd been looking for—it's unclear how he'd found it, since they all looked the same, faceless, address-less—he saw in the thick shadows a pair of white eyes looking at him and a single tooth glistening in a smiling mouth.

"I am Klonimus Zelig Schiff," said Klonimus.

"I know who you are, sir, and I know what you want." The man was old. Very, very old, older than Mr. Schiff by many years, or at least so he appeared. Because a slave's years are not counted by the same calendar that tallies the lives of free people.

The man lit a small fire in the middle of the shack. An orange light danced across his wrinkled face.

"You know?" Klonimus asked in surprise.

"I know, sir. You want me to summon your wife from the dead."

"And can you?"

"Yes, sir, I can."

27

Ladies and gentlemen, members of the Special Tribunal, Madam Attorney General, Head of the Investigation Team:

The Ministry of Justice's representative, Special Investigator George Aboagye, visited me a few days ago. He came to ask my opinion on an idea concocted by the attorney general's office. The idea is this: in the trial—if indeed I am put on trial—the accused—namely, me—shall be seated in a booth made of reinforced glass. Aboagye explained that the glass booth was intended primarily for the defendant's safety—meaning, my safety. The attorney general holds that we should not underestimate the strong feelings that the trial, if it occurs, might arouse in the public.

But I ask you, ladies and gentlemen: Is this glass booth truly intended for my safety? Because I suspect that although you may be genuinely concerned with the defendant's survival and good health throughout the spectacle, what is more important for you is to set the stage properly. It's very clear that the trial, if there is one, will be—let's be bold enough to say it plainly—a show trial.

I completely understand the historical importance of such an event, however, and so I can accept the theatricality: here is a man who reaps the profits of the transatlantic slave trade, trapped before us in a glass booth, day after day, week after week, unable to sit comfortably or stretch his limbs. Do you really think the spectators will pick up on the ironic subtleties of the metaphor? Do you honestly think a defendant squeezed into a glass box will suggest the image of people crowded into the belly of the *Brookes* slave ship? How many of the viewers will even know that infamous illustration? Without any intent to disparage the local crowd's imagination and abstraction skills, I'm afraid quite a few of them will confuse the glass booth with a shower stall in a three-star hotel (the likes of which, unfortunately, most of them will never have the chance to use). Others will see a resemblance to the glass cases that house rare displays in natural history museums. Do you think I am a rare display?

That, incidentally, is also what I asked Special Investigator Aboagye. I'm sure you can guess his answer. What he said was, "Professor Schiff, not only are you not rare, there are many others like you. Far too many. That is why you are here." He then suggested his own metaphor for the glass booth. "You won't be the first to be presented in a glass booth in our country," he said. "Before you came another European who carried the guilt of the Western world upon his shoulders."

"And you put him in a glass booth, too?" I asked.

"He put himself in it," answered Mr. Aboagye. "He was here roughly a decade ago. He toured the main streets while seated in a bulletproof glass cell. You know, a custom-built vehicle . . . A one-of-a-kind Mercedes." Mr. Aboagye's expression remained inscrutable. "This distinguished guest needed the glass to protect him from mud sprayed by the motorcycle cavalcade. So that his white robe should not be soiled, God forbid, by specks of African earth."

I got the hint. "The pope?" I asked cautiously.

"You said it," he replied.

You know Aboagye and his unique style. This was no joke. It was an ideological argument. "So you understand, Professor," he added, "white people in glass cells are a tradition for us."

By the way, what exactly are Mr. George Aboagye's duties? He claims his job is to assemble the indictment materials, or, alternatively, to recommend that the procedures be repealed. But what exactly is the nature of this "assembling"? Which incriminating details is he trying to expose through our conversations?

On his last visit, he brought me a gift wrapped in colorful paper and tied with a gold ribbon. The wrapping paper had a pattern of Christmas trees, red scarves, and snowflakes. It was a book. But not a light detective novel, the kind that might provide me with a few hours of entertainment. It wasn't even a representative work of West African literature. No, it was Frantz Fanon's *The Wretched of the Earth*, no less.

Well, I said to myself, the special investigator must be trying to test my reputation as a man with broad horizons and a thirst for knowledge, who also boasts the title of professor. As I leafed through the oh-so-familiar and endlessly quoted book, I struggled to remove the expression of disappointment from my face. It took a few moments for me to understand that the key to Aboagye's gesture was the colorful Christmas wrapping he had chosen to envelop Fanon's bitter, angry, anti-colonialist essay.

It was an amusing provocation, yet I didn't even crack a smile. After all, any response I gave might be used against me in court. When I sit in the glass booth.

28

The barrage of fireworks that launched Independence Day celebrations startled Professor Schiff terribly. The stories he'd heard about coups, civil wars, and extremists' attacks had left an impression. But perhaps there was nothing unusual about Professor Schiff's anxiety? Perhaps the fear of calamity smolders in everyone who visits Africa? Because—let's admit it—there is a certain factual basis for the violent imagery that has adhered to this continent.

Either way, Professor Schiff was startled. But later, when he realized it was a holiday, and spectacular blooms of fire burst over the horizon in yellow, red, and green, he joined in the national merriment and deigned to raise a toast with the staff before they all went out onto the streets to party.

All of them except Kweku, that is. He had to stay in the villa with Professor Schiff. That was his job, and he performed it with integrity, albeit with an absolute lack of desire. In his opinion—which he voiced bitterly—it would have made more sense "to shut the professor up in one of the rooms and lock the door."

Esther Efua had prepared heaps of dumplings for them, and set out bowls of plantain chips, sugar cubes, and lots of beer. But for her husband, Kweku, this was small consolation.

He and his prisoner were about to spend a boring, quiet independence eve together at the villa. "See?" said Kweku. "Look how your grandpa is ruining Kweku's fun."

They watched the special programming on TV, went out to look at the second round of fireworks, listened to the dim sounds of celebration that reached them from the stadium, and when they'd exhausted all possible topics of conversation (dogs, women, family, illness, Jesus, and other gods), they moved on to playing checkers. The gambling method was simple: the loser paid the winner five dollars. Two straight losses—ten dollars. Third loss in a row—fifteen. And so forth.

Kweku was a skilled and fast player. Within half an hour, Professor Schiff gave in and asked to stop. He'd lost a lot of money. But of course, as befitting a detainee, his wallet was empty. Kweku was furious and demanded his winnings immediately. Professor Schiff promised to pay his debt as soon as he possibly could, but that wasn't good enough for Kweku. He didn't think spoiled white professors could be trusted, since, as he said, they'd been "brought up to live at other people's expense." Not to mention that the professor would soon be going to prison—a real one this time, not a resort for celebrities—and then there'd be no chance of him paying his debt because he'd have to spend everything he had to buy "food without worms and maggots."

Kweku pulled a Bible out of somewhere (which came as no surprise to Professor Schiff, who'd noticed that his hosts always seemed to have a Bible within arm's reach) and forced Professor Schiff to put one hand on the holy book, raise the other hand, and repeat after him: "I, Professor Schiff, hereby solemnly swear to pay Kweku Kingsley Okuro the sum of one hundred and fifty dollars as soon as possible." But after giving it some more thought—though briefly—Kweku decided that the oath was not enough, because Professor Schiff wasn't even Christian. And so at midnight, the two men could be found edging their way through the crowds in the prison service's green Land Rover, blowing their horn and flashing their lights.

They were looking for an ATM. Kweku knew of three such devices he believed to be operational. One, he claimed, was at the central branch of United Bank of Africa, on Patrice Lumumba Street, which was where he was now trying to get.

Of all Professor Schiff's fears—and there were quite a few—the worst was the one he felt at the sight of a horde of people celebrating. His mother, a refugee from Germany, had taught him that every jubilant parade is trailed by a potential pogrom. Professor Schiff had internalized this message thoroughly and tried all his life to stay away from excited crowds.

This time, he failed. Torrents of people flowed from February Fifth Boulevard to Liberty Square, where vendors had set up makeshift food stands. On a stage decorated with the Republic's flags, a band was accompanying a full-bodied singer in a very tight gold-sequined dress and a man in traditional garb drumming on a djembe. A group of women, also in traditional dress, danced, with wonderful agility but without moving from their spots, to the rhythm of a melancholic chorus.

Kweku drove the Land Rover onto the cracked sidewalk and slowly snaked through the crowd. The vehicle filled with echoes of fist punches and kicks. Furious faces were glued to the windows. Kweku pulled up outside United Bank of Africa's marble exterior and pointed at the machine embedded in a recess. "There it is! There's our darling."

Professor Schiff refused to get out, but Kweku leaned over, opened the door, and said, "Don't worry, Kweku is watching. Kweku is protecting you."

His habit of referring to himself in the third person, like a grown-up prodding a child to take his medicine, only increased the terror that had completely taken over Professor Schiff. He gripped the door handle.

"Okay," said Kweku, "then I'll do it. Just give me your card and tell me the PIN."

Professor Schiff realized his fate was sealed, and had to quickly deliberate between two options: risk being abducted by the mob, or lose the plastic card that was his lifeline to his bank account—namely, to the world beyond the ocean. He opted for the former.

The second he opened the Land Rover's door and leaped out, he was promptly carried away by the river of humanity. The marble wall was getting farther and farther away, and when he turned around, he could barely make out the Land Rover's lights flickering among the heads. He put his hands over his face to protect his glasses—his most precious possession at this time of crisis—and as he half-rocked, half-danced with the crowds screaming along with the electric guitars and djembes blaring from the loudspeakers, he suddenly saw himself as he must have looked through the Land Rover's window: an aging white man, dripping with sweat, being tossed from hand to hand like a ragdoll.

It was a ridiculous sight. Truly comical. He snickered softly, then chuckled, and finally let out a loud, hearty, rolling laugh. "Happy Independence Day!" he shouted at the top of his lungs. "Happy Independence Day!"

And then something odd happened. The people around him retreated. At first hesitantly, then quickly, with panicked shrieks. He kept standing there, sweating, in what was now an island surrounded by an empty ring some twenty meters wide. He heard a horn blowing behind him: it was Kweku in the Land Rover. The door swung open and Professor Schiff climbed in.

"But just because the machine is out of order doesn't mean Kweku's letting you off the hook," said Kweku. He opened the glove compartment and took out a bag of sugarcane pieces. He handed one to Professor Schiff, put another in his mouth, and sucked on it. He turned the car around and drove against the flow of people thronging into the square. After chewing and sucking for a few minutes, he said, "You got lucky, Professor."

"What happened?"

"The people were scared. They thought you were putting a spell on them."

"But why?"

"Because you put your hands on your eyes and laughed, and you made strange movements, and you looked altogether very dangerous."

29

Most distinguished members of the Special Tribunal, Madam Attorney General, Head of the Investigation Team:

Allow me to wish you a happy Independence Day. I have prepared a few words for the occasion. May I read them to you? Well, then:

Fifty-two years ago, the empire to which you belonged announced that it would amputate you from its aging, vile body and spit you out into the world. At that moment you turned from an atrophied limb into a vibrant, independent entity. It was the moment you'd longed for. It was what you'd fought for. To be masters of your own destiny; to own your land and its resources; to educate your children in your own language (or rather, in the five languages spoken here) and according to your own cultural values; to legislate laws (at times puzzling and far-reaching, but that, too, is part of the matter); to maintain a department of justice, an attorney general's office, and a prison service; to set your own economic policies; to maintain an army, an air force, and a coast guard; to operate a police force that boasts a rich variety of uniforms, hats, symbols, and badges—and is remarkably profligate when it comes to highway roadblocks; to send a delegation to the Olympic Games every four years and a film to the Academy Awards every twenty years; to raise an international soccer player and elect him president; to produce ten millionaires from the oil and mining industry; to establish a space agency, a stock exchange, a tropical forest research school, and let us not forget the Institute for African Culture with its fine museum; to operate tourist sites at the slavery fort with no maintenance budget; to print money; to fly a flag (though, in my in opinion, one that is too similar to other flags in the region); to play a national anthem; to set off fireworks on Independence Day. . . . What else does a small but happy nation need?

I remember how, on one of the trips I took with Duke—I can't recall where or when—we drove over a bridge and saw, down below in the stream, women doing their laundry. I asked Duke to stop and I got out to take pictures. I stood on the bridge and gazed down at the bare-chested women standing knee-deep in the water, beating their laundry on a rock and singing.

In those days, I was a tourist through and through, with a tourist's unthinking and rather idiotic desire—one might say compulsion—to preserve everything the eye sees and the brain experiences. And so, naturally, I took out my cellphone to snap pictures of the women. They smiled up at me, of course—that, too, is an instinct of people captured in a tourist's camera lens—and continued their tiring work, as if encouraging me to persist with my pointless documentation.

All of a sudden, I woke up, and like a sleepwalker roused from his slumber, I stopped myself. I stopped being a white, privileged tourist busy collecting souvenirs. I don't know what shook me out of it. Perhaps it was Duke's comment: "You know, Professor, my mother was a washerwoman."

I put my camera back in my pocket. Instead of taking photos, I said to Duke, "If no one has done it yet, then it's time someone wrote an ode to the African woman's back. The back supports the head that lugs cargo, the back carries babies, it bends over to sweep paths, it arches so that wet cloths can be beaten on a rock."

"Maybe you'll write that ode," said Duke.

We continued on our way, and the literary task assigned to me by Duke was forgotten. Only now, as I stand before you, do I remember it. Because it occurs to me that the back—the African woman's back, subject of the ode I never wrote—is you, ladies and gentlemen. You are that strong yet supple spine. And I do not mean that entirely as a metaphor. Not in the conventional literary sense. Because although I did not photograph the washerwomen in the creek that day, for a brief moment I saw Africa's survival skills in plain sight.

Distinguished members of the Special Tribunal, Madam General Attorney, Head of the Investigation Team:

I wish you a happy Independence Day, and may you celebrate many more such days.

30

Yes, I talk with my wife, Tami, every so often. Am I supposed to thank technology for allowing me to view the person I'm talking to on a little screen? Or should I yearn for bygone eras, when, in order to conduct a dialogue, human beings had to collect their ideas and formulate them in coherent sentences?

Distinguished members of the Special Tribunal, Madam Attorney General, Head of the Investigation Team:

What do you think? What is your opinion about the fact that in this age of instant communication, when thousands of miles can be narrowed down into an almost imperceptible electronic flicker, a pair of spouses can find nothing to say, reduced to staring at each other's familiar faces on a screen and yawning?

It's no wonder that I contemplate my forefather, Klonimus Zelig Schiff, who asked the old slave to raise his wife Esperanza from the dead. It was a big risk. They might have found themselves staring at each other without knowing what to say, as Tami and I do on either end of the intercontinental line. True, the task of communicating with the world of the dead was assigned to a skilled artisan with a reputation in his vocation, rather than to a nameless Internet service provider. But the dialogue itself depended solely on the speakers and their ability to exchange meaningful content. At least so it seemed.

I shall mention only that Klonimus Schiff, given his faith, was extremely skeptical of the elderly slave's area of expertise. He was familiar with the story of King Saul (which I'm sure you remember: Saul asked the Witch of Endor to raise the spirit of the prophet Samuel so that he could consult with him), but the laws of Judaism, which Klonimus followed dutifully and unquestioningly, strictly forbade any dealings with sorcery, witchcraft, or any sort of spirit world. In fact, Klonimus Schiff had expressly forbidden these practices in his jurisdiction, under threat of severe punishment.

Still, being a modern man, and what was called in those days "a man of the world," he could not turn his back on a metaphysical experiment that might allow him to visit the other side of reality. Once he'd decided to do it, he knew exactly where to find the old slave, who was apparently not the only sorcerer in the area, but the finest one, according to Klonimus's informants.

A moment or two after Schiff walked into the hut, once his eyes had adjusted to the dark and his nostrils to the odor (a dense mixture of smoke, cornmeal porridge, and sour sweat), he introduced himself. "I am Klonimus Zelig Schiff," he said.

"I know who you are, sir. And I know what you want," answered the old man, and without delay, as if he had been planning the task for some time, lit a fire in the middle of the hut.

“You know?” Klonimus was surprised.

“I know, sir. You want me to summon your wife from the dead.”

“And can you?”

The flame leaped up suddenly. It was as sharp as a cypress tree and reached as high as Klonimus’s face, lighting it in an orange glow.

“Yes, sir, I can,” the old man replied. Then he added with an apologetic smile, “But the dead do not like to be disturbed without a reason, sir.”

“The reason is my personal business,” said Klonimus firmly. It was too late to change his mind, but his curiosity was wearing thin. He felt humiliated. “Just do what you have to do,” he grumbled imposingly.

Not only did the old slave feel no amity for Schiff—which was understandable—he also made no effort to fawn over him or make a show of obedience. “People think the dead know things about the future, but the dead know nothing,” he said.

“Nothing?” asked Klonimus wanly. He felt his muscles weaken and his strength drain. The flame turned blue and then translucent. “Nothing?” he repeated.

“They know everything about death, sir. But only about death.”

A figure suddenly appeared in the flame. It was a young woman. She wore a white veil.

“Esperanza?” Klonimus asked hoarsely.

The young woman lifted the veil from her face. Yes, it

was Esperanza. She was really there. He could see her. She was so young. Was he young, too?

"Can you see me, Esperanza?" asked Klonimus. She nodded and smiled at him. He did not remember her that young. "Can you see me?"

She nodded again, then held up her thin hand over her face. She waved at him slowly, shyly, the farewell of a little girl setting off on an excursion, then she turned her back.

"Wait, Esperanza, wait!" Klonimus cried out desperately. He knew she was about to return to the great abyss, into the timeless void where she belonged. "Wait a minute, just one more moment, we haven't even talked yet . . ."

"What do you want us to talk about?" a voice asked. But it was not Esperanza's. It was a different, raspy voice. Certainly not the voice of the young woman whose figure still flickered in the fire.

"I want . . . I want . . ." said Klonimus, "I want . . ." His words came out with great difficulty.

"What, what do you want?" grumbled the hoarse voice.

"For you to talk to me . . . Talk to me, Esperanza."

"What do you want me to tell you?" the hoarse voice said impatiently.

It was not Esperanza. It could not have been. His wife had never spoken to him that way, in such an irritated tone. But who knows? Perhaps the cold of the Underworld, the loss of corporeality, the absence of time, had affected her temperament? They had certainly affected her vocal cords.

The figure in the flame began to fade until it had

completely vanished. Only an outline of the back, the neck, the white veil still hovered in Klonimus's pupils. The flame shrank down abruptly and resumed its orange hue, and finally the fire died out until only glowing embers remained. Klonimus girded his remaining strength and whispered, "Rest in peace, Esperanza. Rest in peace, my wife."

The old slave lay on the pile of dried weeds that served as his bed. His eyes were closed, his toothless mouth open, and his breath heavy. He looked fast asleep.

Klonimus took a gold coin from his pocket and placed it in the slave's limp hand. Then he walked to the doorway. He was wobbling. His knees shook. He felt terribly weary.

And so that conversation, too, had come to naught, just like the technologically sophisticated calls between a husband and wife centuries later. Or so it seemed. But on his long way home, as he dozed on the back of his mare (both man and beast were close to utter exhaustion), there suddenly appeared in Klonimus Schiff's mind the question he had planned to ask Esperanza in their astonishing meeting, which due to his great excitement and the effects of the magic, he had forgotten to ask. The question was a simple, prosaic one: "My dear wife, where did you hide the key to the safe in the bedroom?" Klonimus did not know what was in the little steel safe, and perhaps even after his wife's death he had no right to dig through her belongings and uncover whatever secrets she had hidden. Because secrets are supposed to die with the person who kept them. But miraculously, no sooner had he remembered the unasked question than he recalled its answer, just as if Esperanza herself had whispered it in his ear: "In the pantry, in the drawer where the flour for matzo is stored, in a linen bag."

Ladies and gentlemen, allow me to skip ahead a little. As it is, I've been making too many digressions and adding too much detail to this testimony. Let us allow the determined widower to retrieve the key from its hiding place, to fetch the safe, and to open it with trembling hands. Much like us, he could not have guessed what might have been hidden by a Jewish matron of fifty, wife to one of the wealthiest merchants in Paramaribo, who had been bedridden for five years and eventually died in great torment.

Well, the safe was empty.

No, wait. Something fluttered inside it. Klonimus's heavy breaths breathed life into a folded sheet of paper on the bottom of the steel box. A letter? He unfolded the paper and read:

With Heaven's Grace

These are my last words and this is my will:

My beloved husband,

It is not with any joy that I take my leave from this world. But you know that my suffering is too great to bear, and I am certain, my beloved husband, that you, too, would wish that I be released from my pains so that I may rest in peace in the other world to which I depart.

But how may I find redemption? How can I rest in absolute peace, knowing that the community of black people whom

Hashem, blessed be He, has delivered unto you so that they may work for you and that you may care for all their needs, continue to be afflicted with ignorance and fatuity?

And so, I hereby ask you, my kind and good-hearted husband, that upon my redemption, redeem them, too. Upon my departure, give them their freedom. Release them from their ignorance. Bring them salvation. Teach them the Torah of Moses. And like Moses, lead them. Be their shepherd. Gather the innocent black sheep and take them with you to the Promised Land.

For only then shall my eternal sleep be sweet, and my rest everlasting.

Bless you, my husband, and may your days bring light,
Your faithful wife,
Esperanza Schiff
Daughter of Don Meyuchas Levi and Esther née Berdugo
Tuesday, 28 Shevat

Ladies and gentlemen, if you think this letter is more laughable than touching—I agree. And yet even if we acknowledge that the words were written by a woman whose severe illness and pain had somewhat addled her brain, we may nevertheless find in them a certain notion. It's not easy. Nor was it easy for Klonimus Schiff. He had already begun to free his chosen slaves and convert them to Judaism, building a sort of congregation around himself, yet he did not see himself in the role conceived by Esperanza: namely, a popular leader of biblical proportions.

The pathos-laden style was fitting for the era in which she lived. The righteousness suited her character. Only the vision was something new and surprising. For in her life, until those final moments, Esperanza was known as a practical, unsentimental woman (which I believe is evident from her expression in the couple's portrait that hangs in the museum in Paramaribo). But who knows what a person undergoes in her final moments? Or perhaps the destiny she determined for Klonimus in that strange letter-cum-will was not a revelation at all, but one last prank she allowed herself to play on her tyrannical husband?

31

On the streets they walked, Lucile Tetteh-Ofosu was a familiar figure. Passersby said hello, stopped to exchange a few words, waved or called out, came over to touch her. Professor Schiff felt he was in the company of an important personage of high esteem. They were on their way to return the rooster, which Lucile had borrowed for three days from an Eritrean poultry vendor. The rooster, now a surrogate for Toga the bodyguard spirit (and having possibly, therefore, gained a few ounces), was crammed into a cat carrier. Professor Schiff, devoted porter that he was, switched the carrier from one hand to the other. His arms felt like they were about to drop out of their sockets. But he was happy to accompany Lucile, of course. In fact, he was positively thrilled to be spending the morning with her, and he sensed it had some surprises in store.

He was right.

"When was the last time you prayed, Professor?" asked Lucile suddenly, without turning to look at him.

The question was direct and unambiguous. There was no point in concocting a clever retort. Nevertheless, Professor Schiff found it very difficult to answer. He shifted the carrier with the rooster to his other hand again. "Maybe when I was a boy," he said.

"That's exactly what I thought," said Lucile. And then, when they could detect the aromas of the market around the corner, they turned onto a side street that Professor Schiff had never noticed before, and she said, "Here's our cathedral." She pointed at a particularly dilapidated apartment building.

"Cathedral?" Professor Schiff could see no double-spired Gothic structure peeking out from among the crumbling walls of the nameless south Tel Aviv street.

"Our place," she explained, "the place where we clean off the dirt." She pulled his hand and dragged him into the building. The crate with the rooster knocked the peeling whitewashed wall. "Come on, Professor, there's a chance that a few minutes with God will be good for you."

The church Lucile insisted on calling "our cathedral" was in a ground-floor apartment. A mezuzah was nailed to the doorway, much like the doorways of all the apartments in the building, but here in "our cathedral" someone had taken pains to hand-paint the mezuzah in turquoise and add a gold contour around it.

Lucile knew the place well. She moved a loose brick in the wall next to the door, took a key out of the cavity behind it, and opened the door.

The apartment was empty. Professor Schiff put the carrier containing the rooster on the floor and looked around in amazement. Instead of stained-glass windows, there were plastic blinds. A table covered with shiny velvet was the altar. Opposite it were rows of folding chairs. On the wall hung a large wooden cross decorated with colorful glass pieces and mirror shards, and next to it a sign said, in fluorescent letters: "Blessed are those who are persecuted, for theirs is the kingdom of heaven."

Lucile kneeled at a chair, rested her folded hands on it, closed her eyes, and put her forehead to her forearms. Her lips moved as Professor Schiff watched, enrapt. Finally she raised her head, opened her eyes, looked at him, and smiled. "I prayed for you, Professor," she said.

He remembered how the first time he'd met her she had kissed the mezuza "for him," and the day before yesterday her lips had murmured an incantation when she'd been busy banishing the dybbuk. She was, without a doubt, indiscriminately fond of all beliefs and willing to zigzag among them, jumble them together, and reinvent them at every opportunity. Religious rituals of the world, unite! thought Professor Schiff to himself with a chuckle.

"Do you feel a little better now?"

"Yes," he said, "much, much better." And perhaps he really did. There seemed to be, in this quiet apartment with its pungent smell of disinfectant, a calming presence. Or was it Lucile's prayer?

The rooster started making angry sounds. Professor Schiff bent over, peeked into the carrier, opened the grate, and reached in to help the bird, which was lying on its side, turn over. The furious rooster pecked at his hand and Professor Schiff pulled back, bumped into a chair, and fell on the floor, hitting his head. His glasses flew off and landed next to Lucile.

"The revenge of Toga?" asked Professor Schiff, groaning in pain.

"No, not Toga," Lucile replied gravely. "This time it's to do with Peter."

"Who's Peter?"

"Peter, Jesus's apostle. Don't you know the story of Peter and the rooster, Professor? Didn't you learn any Bible?"

"I was taught a different Bible, Lucile," Professor Schiff explained apologetically.

But now, watched over by the sparkling wooden cross, Lucile set aside the holy book and took on the role of caretaker. She instructed Professor Schiff to stretch out on the floor and rest his aching head on her lap. She cradled the back of his neck with one hand, and covered his eyes with the other. Then she bent over and put her lips to his bruised forehead.

They returned the rooster to the Eritrean poultry man (who was obviously proud of his virile protégé, whom he assumed had been borrowed for breeding purposes), paid the exorbitant loan fee, and Lucile was given back the cellphone she'd left as collateral. Then they took the same narrow streets back to the parking lot, where they walked up and down until they finally found Professor Schiff's Honda among the other blazing hot metal boxes.

A few minutes later, when the car had cooled down a little, Lucile said, "You know, Professor, there's something we need to discuss."

Professor Schiff could feel the moment of intimacy they'd shared dissipating. They drove silently until they found their way out of the maze of alleys encircling the market.

"You want me," said Lucile, "right?"

Professor Schiff swallowed and locked his eyes on the road. He did not dare look at her.

"I know you want me. That's the truth, Professor, isn't it?"

"You might be right, Lucile," Professor Schiff murmured. "I don't know. I really don't know." Was he in denial, or did he truly find it hard to articulate his feelings?

There was heavy traffic. They snaked their way among the cars, switching from lane to lane, speeding up and slowing down. A red light finally stopped them. Professor Schiff's hands let go of the steering wheel. He was suffocating, and even though the air-conditioning was at full blast, he opened the window to gulp in some hot air.

Lucile asked, "What were you thinking that day at Attorney Melchior's?"

"I don't remember, Lucile. I really don't."

"You liked me, didn't you?"

Professor Schiff hesitated slightly. But then, wanting to confess without sounding anemic, he said, "You know, there are those moments . . . Moments that break through the monotonous flatness of life like a wellspring in the middle of a desert."

"Every moment in life is a wellspring of water," said Lucile.

He immediately regretted the artful metaphor. "I suppose you're right," he said, and then stammered awkwardly,

"But back then, on that day... Yes, I admit, there was something about you."

"There was something about you, too, Professor," Lucile said with a laugh, "and I immediately knew what it was. It was that desert you just spoke of... the boredom. No, there was no chance of you not falling in love with me, Professor. I could see it on your face."

Had she really seen all that on his face? Had she seen the fear of all the seemingly predictable tomorrows awaiting him? Coupled with the fear of any change that might disrupt the proper course of things? And if so, was there really any chance of him not falling in love with this woman who had happened into his horizonless desert?

The people waiting at the light next to them gave them curious looks. The light changed to green. The Honda lurched.

"By the way, Professor, you never told me what Attorney Melchior owed you money for."

The breeze from the open window rustled her frizzy hair and rummaged in her plunging neckline.

"Is it important?"

"No, it's not important," said Lucile.

32

But perhaps it is important. Perhaps it's important to recall how things unfolded. At least for the sake of the historiographic record.

It was approximately two years before that fateful meeting with Lucile Tetteh-Ofosu that Professor Schiff was contacted by Attorney Yoel Melchior. They did not know each other, and Professor Schiff was unsure why, and upon whose recommendation, Melchior had decided to turn to him, of all people, nor how he located him.

Melchior said he was leading a group of businesspeople who had started a production company that "aimed to launch original, groundbreaking cinematic projects." And when one of these people (probably Melchior himself, though he did not explicitly say so) got the idea for a groundbreaking and original cinematic project, they'd decided to come to him, to Professor A. Schiff, and ask him to develop the idea, which "embodied incredible potential." They wanted him to write a first draft of the screenplay.

It was an odd request. Professor Schiff was neither a scriptwriter nor aspiring to be one. His first response, therefore, was to say no. Attorney Melchior promptly added twenty percent to his proposed fee.

It can be assumed that even two years ago there was a stack of unpaid bills on the Schiff-Kushners' kitchen table. Their daughter might have been having expensive orthodontia at the time, and their son—who was twenty-three—must surely have needed a bass guitar and an amplifier. It was probably also the right time to buy a robot vacuum and/or a new computer. Except that money had always been a very minor temptation for a finicky and slightly lazy snob such as Professor Schiff. Furthermore, he had Morduch. And at the time there was no reason to suspect that the generous benefactor would relinquish his grandfatherly role and stop financing the spoiled family's whims.

No, it was not the four thousand dollars that persuaded Professor Schiff. What made him eventually agree, and even enthusiastically throw himself into the work, was the idea's complete absurdity.

"It's a romantic adventure story," Yoel Melchior explained, with glazed eyes and the expression of a man who has experienced an epiphany. "It takes place in the third millennium, and tells the history of the first Jewish settlement on a planet in Alpha Centauri . . ."

The preposterous sci-fi invention, so simplistic as to be genius—either that or utterly idiotic, bordering on nonsensical—immediately captivated Professor Schiff. But Melchior was not only a fast-talking, slippery lawyer. He also knew how to tease out Professor Schiff's secret dreams of fame and glory. "This is your opportunity to produce a masterpiece," he gushed, "on the scale of . . ." He reached for a fitting example but lacked the proficiency to find one, so Professor Schiff took a few stabs in his own mind: Swift? Vonnegut? Huxley? Theodor Herzl? Then inspiration struck: "I know what we'll call it! *Planet of the Jews*."

"Wonderful!" exclaimed Yoel Melchior, and he shook Professor Schiff's hand. "Wonderful! *Planet of the Jews*!"

And so Professor Schiff went to work. He did not work too hard, but he made some progress and even met his deadlines. Every few weeks he sent a stack of printed pages to Melchior's office, and in return Melchior would send back a few words on office letterhead, always using more or less the same phrases: "Schiff, you've really moved me this time. You're an absolute genius. I salute you. Admiringly, Yoel."

Four months went by in this way, until one evening the envelope Professor Schiff had sent to Melchior was returned unopened with a letter—an actual letter, with a beginning, a middle, and an end (as they say in the vocation Professor Schiff had temporarily adopted)—in which he was regretfully informed that *Planet of the Jews* had been put on hold.

Professor Schiff demanded clarification, in phone messages and through every other medium. Meanwhile, he continued to work, though with a heavy heart. But just as Attorney Melchior had appeared out of nowhere a few months earlier and convinced Professor Schiff to take the job, he now suddenly, with no warning, tried to do the opposite—namely, to make him resign. He gave Professor Schiff a brief lecture, perfectly articulated and extremely persuasive, about the project's lack of purpose and about how cinema was on the decline and its days were numbered, and so there was no sense, economical or otherwise, in producing a film. Any film. Especially one that takes place in a different world and a different time. "Gone are the days when people went to the drive-in to neck in the back seat while *Planet of the Apes* played on a giant screen," Melchior lamented. "Remember *Planet of the Apes*?" And that was the end of his speech.

Professor Schiff said he was very sorry to hear this, and Melchior said dolefully that he was happy Professor Schiff understood, and that perhaps one day they would have another chance to collaborate.

At this point things became clearer. The reference to "one day" as a possible source of consolation was an obvious clue.

"But I did my part," said Professor Schiff.

"Yes, and as I said, I'm sure this is not the end. Things are yet to happen in the future."

In the future. That's what he said. Professor Schiff could not help being outraged, given that the project had been defined from the get-go as "futuristic." This was a cynicism he was unwilling to tolerate. "But what about my work?" he yelled.

"You did wonderful work, Schiff. I admire your talent. And I truly am sorry the initiative fell through."

"You'll have to pay me, as we agreed."

"I fear that will not be possible," said Melchior, giving Professor Schiff a friendly squeeze on his shoulder. "But, as compensation, we will consider allowing you to use our idea without acquiring copyright." He was apparently perfectly sincere. He truly believed in the poetic force of this tale.

Professor Schiff was furious. But his response, of course—which included yelling into the phone, pounding his fist on the terrified secretary's desk, and sending threatening letters—was nothing but a fruitless emotional outburst that had no practical consequences.

The business group that had employed Professor Schiff ceased its entertainment activities. Or, more accurately, ceased to exist and declared bankruptcy. *Planet of the Jews* was dead. Professor Schiff's labors went down the drain and his fee became a number quoted in a lawsuit that he filed against Attorney Melchior. But, as happens on rare occasions—too rare—what began as an accident led to a fascinating adventure. Because, on balance, his meeting with Lucile Tetteh-Ofosu was no less than "a wellspring of water in a barren desert."

Or something like that.

33

Distinguished members of the Special Tribunal, Madam Attorney General, Head of the Investigation Team:

I assume that, like me, you must be wondering about the daily comforts of a Jewish magnate living at the edge of the Caribbean in the early nineteenth century. What was the nature of the pleasures he might have derived while surrounded by ugliness and misery? And, more generally, can the endless accumulation of capital and property in and of itself compensate for a slow decline into tropical decay, amid continuous exploitation and sadism? What is the point? What is the purpose?

These questions arose of course, in the mind of Klonimus Zelig Schiff himself. True, one has to ask why they did not arise sooner. Much sooner. Before his beloved wife fell incurably ill. Before he witnessed his decadent daughters become addicted to luxuries. Before he grew disgusted with his loathsome avocation. Before he began converting his own private chosen people to Judaism. Back when he could have left that terrible, remote, tropical country—perhaps with no wealth, but with a clear conscience.

These troubling questions did eventually surface, however. And once they did, Klonimus could no longer brush them away or suppress them. Wherefore had time passed this way? What were those sixty-three years about? Was it solely to grow rich—to double, triple, and quadruple his profits, to rake in piles of gold—that Klonimus Zelig had sprung from his mother's womb? True, he still had the prayers and the mitzvahs to bolster him (and, of course, he had the holy Bible, especially Exodus, which helped him justify his own deeds and slightly quieted his increasing sense of guilt), and he found some comfort in the fact that God glanced at him every so often. Nevertheless, his days had grown bland. Desolate. Dark. And instead of lamenting their loss, Klonimus found himself delighting in how swiftly they slipped away from him.

He lost all interest in the trade business. His passion for buying and selling, the joy of tallying profits, the huge satisfaction he had derived from watching his ships unload their cargo and from studying his accounting ledgers—all these vanished. (In fact, transporting human beings had stopped being a respectable business. And yes, it was now also illegal, at least officially. Because of course the plantations still produced sugar, coffee, and cotton for the addicts across the ocean, and of course people found circuitous ways to provide working hands. But the world still managed to change.)

As if to darken Klonimus Schiff's mood even further, Paramaribo was beset by a series of disasters: a devastating hurricane, a fire that destroyed a quarter of the city's homes, a tsunami caused by an earthquake far out in the Caribbean, a murderous attack by the jungle Maroons, a slave uprising . . .

And now, suddenly, his eyes were opened to the misery and horrors around him. It was not necessarily the images of slavery he saw. He was accustomed to that. But now he noticed sailors begging, sick seafarers who'd been abandoned by their captains and left to die on the piers by the reeking river water, mulatta prostitutes hiding faces eaten away by syphilis beneath coats of white makeup, drunk soldiers murdering each other in street fights.

At this point, I suppose, the idea of leaving began to gnaw at Klonimus. Was it not time to sell his holdings in the plantations, get rid of the slaves, lease out his ships, take his leave from the small community of converts under his patronage, pack up the silver vessels and teak furniture, clean the headstone on Esperanza's grave one last time, kiss the warm stone that the tall grasses would soon cover, take his young son, Solomon (he had given up on his three debauched daughters), and sail to Rotterdam—return to his homeland in Old Europe, whose cool tranquility stood protected by screens of progress and culture? Indeed, at least in terms of the climate and the cultural offerings across the sea—the chance to watch a fine opera instead of a public hanging—my great-great-great-great-grandfather could count on improvements.

But as so often happens with plans, doubts intervened.

Yes, ladies and gentlemen, that was Klonimus Zelig Schiff's state of mind in the spring of 1829. But then, out of the deepening gloom, there emerged a moment of grace. One of those moments that one cannot—and, in fact, must not—await, because they always arrive unexpectedly.

The moment I am about to describe to you was one of infatuation. There is no need to explain. No need for a soundtrack. You can all remember such an occurrence, or at least claim to. That moment when your heart is caught in a magnetic field from which no power in the world can extricate it.

Please forgive me if I seem to be sliding into sentimentality.

Try to imagine, ladies and gentlemen, a late afternoon on a hot and humid day (one not dissimilar to ours) in the city of Paramaribo. Beginning at Fort Zeelandia and stretching to the southwest, the famous Waterkant—a platform lined with storehouses, cafes, public houses, and supply shops—fills with people emerging from their afternoon siestas. Klonimus Schiff is among those strolling along the promenade, hurrying to a business meeting in a cafe near De Heiligenweg—or rather, to a meeting in which a business is about to be terminated. Because Schiff, in accordance with the mood described above, is already taking steps to curtail his business. To complete the picture, I will only add that behind Klonimus Schiff in his blue suit and top hat (just imagine, in that oppressive heat, but status has its requirements) walks a black boy whose sole but vital job on this excursion is to carry a parasol and provide shade for his master.

Schiff and his chaperone pass a pavilion sheltered by old sails: the public auction plaza. Schiff turns and walks in. It's an unplanned stop. Just a quick nostalgic glance at the place where, in better days, his agents used to put his imports up for sale. But in recent years activity here has come to a standstill. The pavilion is deserted. A sour smell of old beer rises from the floorboards.

At the far end stands the old sales platform. Next to it, sacks of coal are piled up alongside bundles of burnt tiles. On the edge of the platform sits a hunched figure whose silhouette merges with the outline of the pole next to it. Schiff goes closer. It is a young girl. Her eyes are closed. She seems to be asleep, and when he approaches her he can see her eyeballs moving under their lids. Schiff stands before the girl and watches her, enchanted, waiting with serene patience to enter her dream. A strange quiet prevails in the pavilion, as if soundwaves have suddenly frozen. The voices outside fall silent, too. The seagulls do not screech. The wind stops rattling the ships' ropes. The foremen do not yell. Whips do not lash. Sacks do not land on decks with a thud. Wheelbarrows do not squeak on the piers. Barrels do not clatter down the ramps.

From within this auditory vacuum there comes a raspy voice: "Interested?" Pipe smoke curls up lazily behind the pole. "You can have her for the cost of the clothes she's wearing."

The temptation to buy a commodity for almost nothing is huge, although Klonimus Schiff doesn't seem to have any use for her. But he is interested. Very interested. To the point of excitement. He cannot explain to himself what it is about this girl that he finds so attractive, yet he knows that he will not continue on his way without her.

The owner of the raspy voice, a brawny man in shoddy clothes—he is clearly not a trader, perhaps a lowly captain who transports goods between the islands—comes up to Klonimus with his hand outstretched. "She's about fourteen. Speaks English, reads and writes, sings like an angel."

"An angel?" murmurs the astonished Schiff.

"I know, she doesn't look like an angel," says the large man, sticking the pipe back in his mouth, "but . . ."

The girl opens her eyes and looks around with the surprise of someone discovering a new landscape.

"But . . . ?" wonders Klonimus Schiff expectantly.

"A virgin. Guaranteed."

Schiff smiles at the girl, and she smiles back. He holds out a hand to help her off the platform. Only now does he notice her handicap. He shoots a reproachful look at the man, who shrugs his shoulders and mutters through his pipe: "Yes, well . . . She won't run away from you, sir. Just let her sing . . ."

Schiff takes a few gold coins out of his purse and throws them in the big man's dirty hand. His heart is pounding. He knows this is a moment of grace.

"Shall we go?" he asks the girl.

She leans on his arm and limps away with him, onto the noisy pier bustling with people and carriages.

34

Apart from the pilot and copilot, the group that took off in a helicopter to tour the waterfalls included five passengers: Professor Schiff, as the special guest of the president and, in fact, the person for whom the trip was being held; the host, His Excellency the President of the Republic, Vincent Ayeh; Luther, the president's secretary; and two bodyguards in camouflage and red berets, armed with submachine rifles. The reason for the excursion was simple, or at least so Vincent Ayeh presented it: "As long as you haven't seen our momentous waterfalls, you cannot understand the might of the African soul."

Professor Schiff—who had always wanted to visit the waterfalls, or at least since reading the West Africa guidebook (nineteen countries, three hundred and eighty million inhabitants, five million square kilometers, four hundred and ninety six pages including color illustrations) on the flight from Paris—was very happy when the president invited him. And he could not have dreamed of finer travel arrangements. The airborne living room was not only as magnificent as a cinematic version of the Orient Express, but it was also remarkably spacious.

The president and Professor Schiff reclined in side-by-side white leather armchairs. There was a coffee table bolted to the floor between them, on which, in addition to an elegant computer and three cellphones, there was a wooden bowl full of chocolates and candy.

While Professor Schiff took in all this grandeur and tried to come up with a description for the book—yes, the book he would one day write—the president leaned over and said secretively, "When we get to the waterfalls, Prof, remind me to tell you a nice story with a moral."

"Does it have to do with the waterfalls?"

"Of course."

"Your Excellency," said Professor Schiff, "perhaps instead of me reminding you, you could tell me now?"

"No, no!" the president shouted into the increasingly loud rattle of the propellor, which was becoming a deafening screech. He shook his head vigorously to indicate that this was a patently absurd suggestion. "I'll tell you when we get there," he yelled. "Please remind me!"

And then, minutes after they lifted off from the helicopter pad at the presidential palace, the president took off his shoes, shut his eyes, and fell fast asleep.

Professor Schiff put his nose up against the window and watched the metropolis receding beneath him: neighborhoods of stocky houses in gray and black, scattered haphazardly; a sprawling urban market in a circular flow of colorful spots; office buildings made of steel and glass sprouting up from clustered shanties like giant plants in beds of mushrooms; winding alleyways, streets bustling with vendors, roads clogged with traffic, a desolate beach . . .

Luther, who sat trapped between the two armed giants in the front row, turned around and motioned for Professor Schiff to put on his headphones. It wouldn't be a long flight, he said through the radio, but it might be a bit bumpy. Nothing to worry about.

The views changed. Now the helicopter cast its shadow on rows of banana trees and oil palms. Fields of millet were spread out among the plantations. Red dirt roads bisected massive plains of burnt growth. Close to a worn asphalt road stood termite hills, acacia and neem trees, and the occasional shriveled baobab and withering palm. Children waved up at them from a crowded rural market. One tried to chase the helicopter's shadow on his bike. Fires burned in a dry cornfield. Stray dogs scurried around the slopes of an abandoned mine.

Farther ahead, the brush grew thicker. The trees were denser, creating a thick mass of tropical forest. The forest climbed up the side of a mountain range, and the helicopter rose above it and turned north. The glimmer of a giant river appeared in the jungle, rounded a bend, and disappeared into the green mass.

And then, suddenly, the helicopter swerved and dropped quickly at a sharp angle, straight into the middle of a small village that appeared below, in a clearing in the evergreen forest.

"What happened?" asked the president, who opened his eyes when the wheels hit the ground. The engine noise gradually died down until it stopped.

"We've been informed there's a bomb on the helicopter," said the copilot. His chocolate-hued forehead was covered with beads of sweat.

"Informed by whom?"

"The security officer of the presidential guard, Your Excellency. We've also had word from the police and from special forces HQ."

"I suggest you quickly exit the helicopter, Your Excellency," Luther spluttered. "We'll follow you."

The whole gang stared at the president in tense anticipation, but he returned an amused look and asked, "Do you really believe that nonsense?" Then he spoke to the pilot: "Do you believe this drivel, too, Flight Lieutenant?"

The pilot ran his tongue over his parched lips. His fingers trembled. He nodded hesitantly.

"Fine, fine," President Ayeh finally acquiesced, "but I'm not getting out without my shoes."

He bent over to put his shoes back on, and Luther quickly kneeled before him on the floor and helped him tie the laces.

"It's the opposition playing tricks. Public relations stunt," muttered the president, "but you don't worry, Prof, there's no bomb on this helicopter. There might be people who want to finish me off. Yes, that's quite likely. But you? You? The famous descendent of the slave trader? No! That is completely implausible! After all, you're our most precious asset." He snickered into the folds in his neck.

Professor Schiff actually thought *he* was the prime target. Hadn't the attorney general considered putting him in a glass booth for his own protection? Either way, he wished the president would hurry.

Outside the helicopter, through a ray of sun refracted in the windowpane, he could see a clump of huts built from clay bricks and covered with thatched roofs. Next to them was a larger structure, apparently a school, which unlike the huts had windows, a blue door, and a roof made of corrugated tin. A large mango tree shaded a pump surrounded by a concrete water trough. Beside it a few plastic containers floated in a muddy puddle.

"What is this place?" asked President Ayeh.

"We're not sure, Your Excellency," said the copilot. "According to the navigation system we're in a place with no name, and according to the map we're nowhere."

"Ask the control tower at the airport," Luther suggested.

"They call this place 9 degrees, 31, 57 north on 0 degrees, 0, 14, west," said the copilot.

By now, a few curious onlookers had gathered around the helicopter, showing no fear of the propellor blades, which were still slowly rotating. President Ayeh waved at them through the window, but none of them waved back. And worse—not a single one of the curious faces showed any indication that they recognized the man waving.

"But maybe the people who live here know what their home is called," Professor Schiff murmured.

"Yes, yes, that would make sense," Luther concurred. "After all, if they get bills, they must have an address."

The leader rubbed his forehead to accelerate his thoughts.

"What about the bomb, Your Excellency?" asked the pilot, in a screech as hoarse as shrapnel scratching a steel board. "What about all those people?" He pointed at the faces glued to the windows. "What about us?"

"Gentlemen, you are free to go," said Ayeh. "Whoever wants to can run away. Especially you, Flight Lieutenant." He furrowed his brow, evinced a sternly authoritative expression, and then stood up, fastened the top buttons of his colorful shirt, put his dark sunglasses on, and said, "Well, let's go and meet the people."

What were the feelings of Professor Schiff during these long moments while he was trapped in the presidential helicopter, waiting helplessly for a lethal bomb to go off? He was afraid, of course, and the fear activated all the familiar bodily symptoms. But this time the terror was accompanied by a sense of great sadness. A sense of missing out. Because of the gaze. Because of his last intense, dizzying gaze through the helicopter window.

And this is what Professor Schiff saw: women wearing ankle-length dresses, their hair cropped almost to their scalps, some pregnant, others carrying babies on their backs; boys and girls in school uniforms (brown skirts or trousers, pale-green shirts—the colors of the surrounding forest), most barefoot; elderly people as skinny and crumpled as pieces of paper, sprawled on mats in the shade of the lone mango tree; a group of men who all had the same smile that flashed on and off (were they related?), some wearing T-shirts with faded international company logos; a rusty motorcycle lying on its side; wet cloths hanging from a low tree that had lost most of its branches; a pot bubbling over smoldering ashes; palm branches laid out on the ground to dry; clay pots for fermenting sugarcane syrup buried halfway in the earth; chickens and chicks scurrying among the clay huts; dirty dwarf goats butting horns; a bitch passed out from the heat with a litter of puppies dozing off on her teats . . .

But President Ayeh was right, it seemed. At least for now. Because nothing had exploded. And as the minutes ticked by, the group of men managed to persuade themselves that it was a false alarm. Or a mistake. Or a welcome malfunction.

Professor Schiff's pulse returned to normal and the panic became an embarrassing memory. He shook out his legs and followed the president toward the villagers. He was trailed by Luther, the copilot, and one of the two bodyguards.

"You see, Prof, it's all for the best," said the president. "This emergency landing is an excellent opportunity to get to know the people intimately." He marched ahead, seemingly unaware of the crowd circling him. "Unfortunately, it's not often that the president of the Republic gets the chance to meet his constituents so directly and spontaneously."

Professor Schiff found the nameless village beautiful. Yes, the place was astoundingly impoverished, yet extremely serene. It emanated the serenity of those who have nothing, those whose sole fortune is the narrowness of their horizons, which prevents them from comparing their lot to that of Professor Schiff and people like him. They lived, undoubtedly, in deprivation of a scale Professor Schiff could scarcely conceive.

The crowd was swelling quickly. It now seemed as if the entire village had assembled. One might have thought it was an organized welcome party for a long-awaited delegation. A long-limbed man whose left eye was as white as a pebble, wearing a dusty fedora, grabbed Professor Schiff's hand and led him into the crowd while talking excitedly. He must have thought Professor Schiff was the head of the delegation (presumably not because of his flushed face, but due to his graying curls), but Luther, who spoke the man's language, quickly corrected his mistake and all attention switched, appropriately, to the president, who strolled assuredly, king of his domain, greeting the crowd with a nod of the head and a wordless smile.

It turned out that the man with the fedora was a figure of authority. A sort of village elder, judge, or representative of the tribal chief. Luther translated his incessant chatter. His salutations included a promise that the local spirits would behave themselves with the guests. The president replied with his own suitably hyperbolic flattery, and Luther interpreted.

"What would we do without Luther?" the president wondered. "The man is fluent in four local languages, in addition to English, French, and Portuguese. And just so you know, Prof, despite his name, he prays in Latin."

The helicopter, where one of the bodyguards and the pilot had remained, disappeared behind the huts. Professor Schiff walked alongside the president. Behind them straggled the copilot and the second brute in fatigues, his rifle slung clumsily over his shoulder.

Professor Schiff touched Ayeh's sleeve. "Where are they taking us, Your Excellency?"

"We are guests, Prof, they're showing us their home."

They walked slowly, surrounded on all sides, without knowing what itinerary their hosts had planned for them.

"Do you think we're safe here, Your Excellency?"

"You can never be safe in Africa," said the president. He lifted his dark glasses and winked mischievously at Professor Schiff. "First a bomb almost killed you, and now you're about to be cooked in a pot."

A few moments later they reached the village center, which consisted of a dirt square covered with footprints. The president stopped, took off his glasses and looked around. The crowd stopped and waited, too. In the tense silence, a few murmurs and whispers were passed around, as the assembled tried to guess what the important man in the colorful shirt was plotting.

The president whispered into Luther's ear. Luther conveyed his words to the man in the fedora, and the man in the fedora shouted the announcement to the crowd. The murmurs and whispers turned into vocal debates. Then Luther walked away through the crowd and vanished.

"Please, Prof," said the president, "I'd be happy if you would help me until Luther gets back.

A gaunt boy ran over and handed the president a bundle of branches and some bamboo canes of various lengths and widths. The president examined the bundle gravely, then picked out two reeds. He motioned for the crowd to make way, and the two of them, the president and the professor—the former with regal resolve, the latter with the awkwardness of an adjutant—walked to the edge of the square. The president lodged one bamboo reed in the ground, and Professor Schiff, at the president's instruction, staked the other one some seven steps away from the first. A shadow marked a straight line between the two reeds.

Meanwhile, Luther returned, and a hum of excitement rose from the crowd. Under his arm he carried a shiny, brand-new soccer ball with a colorful swirling pattern. Luther bent over and rolled the ball to the president's feet.

"I never travel without a ball," explained President Ayeh to Professor Schiff, "and usually two or three, just in case."

He easily toed the ball onto his shoe, bounced it twice, kicked it up, caught it on his knee, returned it to the tip of his shoe, kicked it up again, spun on his axis twice, then bent over, caught the ball on his back, let it slide down to his behind and from there to the ground, then toed it again, bounced it twice, and finally stopped the ball and stepped on it so it wouldn't move, as though it were a living creature bending to his will.

The crowd applauded. Ayeh put both hands up and signaled for the villagers to clear the square. They huddled around the edges and waited in obedient silence.

Professor Schiff also moved aside. He wondered if the president would continue to juggle the ball, or if he would now deliver a rousing speech explaining to these hardworking, hungry people that ball tricks were a worthy consolation for those whose very survival was in question. He was the president. They were his citizens. The ball, air trapped inside a container of synthetic leather, was a banal allegory for life and destiny.

But President Ayeh had other ideas. He took off his sweat-drenched shirt, handed it to Luther, and with his watermelon paunch exposed, stood between the two sticks and informed the onlookers that they were about to watch a soccer match in which he, President of the Republic Vincent Matu Ayeh, would compete, alone, against the village team.

The crowd went wild. After several moments of frantically dashing around, some thirty men, teenagers, and boys walked onto the square, all barefoot, and huddled around the president. It took a few more minutes of loud consultations, a short argument, and a few shoves until the gang managed to filter out eleven team members. The others trudged back, crestfallen, to stand with the spectators.

Luther gave the kick-off signal by clapping his hand, and the match started. Started—and ended. Within seconds. The president threaded the ball with dizzying speed among ten pairs of bare feet that tried to stop it, then kicked it straight through the bamboo goalposts. One-zero to the president.

The crowd—at first stunned, then overcome with disappointment—responded as any soccer crowd would, with boos addressed mostly at the goalie. After some loud arguments, the goalie was forced to resign and make way for a replacement.

The second round also ended with a lightning victory for the president, and once again the spectators and the team had a shouting match. A few opinionated men poured onto the field and analyzed the brief match by reconstructing moves, marking lines in the sand, and arguing with the players and one another. Things would undoubtedly have devolved into a melee had the man in the fedora not intervened and dispersed the group with shouts.

In the third round, which was even faster than the first two, the president once again triumphed over the locals. Succumbing to audience pressure, a few of the players were switched ahead of the fourth round. But the new team was defeated just as swiftly.

For the fifth round, the president allowed himself to defer his expected victory just a little, in order to demonstrate a series of spectacular tricks. He traveled back and forth between his adversaries with the ball appearing to be glued to his shoe, wove in and out of a cloud of dust, wriggled, jumped aside, and finally kicked the ball into the goal and set the final score: five-zero for His Excellency the President of the Republic.

The crowd cheered enthusiastically when Ayeh did a victory lap around the square, his arms spread out and his large belly swaying, as if he were reliving a moment of triumph in the Bundesliga. Breathless, he shook the barefoot players' hands, gave each of them a bill from a stack of money handed to him by Luther, and finally signed the ball with a permanent marker and gave it to the fedora wearer.

The entire village—women, children, and men—accompanied their president, His Excellency Vincent Matu Ayeh, to his helicopter. Now that they finally knew him, they were able to love him.

The women's dresses swirled in the eddy created by the propellor, and as the helicopter took off, the dozens of waving hands looked to Professor Schiff like swaying black wheat stalks.

Once the village huts were out of sight, the president, on his way to the washroom to freshen up and change his clothes, asked, "So what was that place called, Luther?"

But Luther had no answer. He'd forgotten to find out, and no one had volunteered the information.

"Copilot? Do you know?" asked the president.

But the copilot had also forgotten to ask.

That afternoon, they hovered above the waterfalls, and the sight was indeed spectacular. The chopper circled twice; flew low toward the center of the frothy falls until thin shards of water, like spring raindrops, covered its windows; then climbed up again and turned its nose south.

"Your Excellency? You asked me to remind you to tell me a story," said Professor Schiff.

"A story? Oh yes, yes. The story is this: during the dictatorship, in the nineties, the army's special forces used to capture opposition members, or anyone suspected of resisting the regime, put them on a helicopter—no, not this one—and fly out here, to the waterfalls, where they'd throw them out." He lounged back in his seat, reached for the bowl of sweets, and pulled out two candies wrapped in gold paper. He handed one to Professor Schiff, unwrapped the second, and put it in his mouth. "And then," he continued, chewing thickly, "in '97, when the dictator Jacobs was deposed, they put him through a grueling interrogation. Asked lots of questions. There were many things they wanted to know. And when they'd finished, just out of curiosity, they asked him why he'd had opposition members thrown into the waterfalls. Why hadn't he just shot them? Easier, faster, cheaper . . . Do you know what he said?" The president looked at Professor Schiff and waited. Luther, in the front row, turned around to hear the answer.

Professor Schiff shook his head.

The president sucked the rest of the chocolate from between his teeth, took another candy from the bowl, and slowly unwrapped it. "He said that throwing people into the waterfalls is the noblest way an African can send another African to the spirit world. Nice, don't you think?"

35

There are certain situations that one knows from the very first moment will not end well.

Besides, how did Lucile Tetteh-Ofosu end up at a dinner organized by the Schiff-Kushners' good friends, Assi and Alissa? What was Professor Schiff thinking when he invited her to join them? Was he longing to show her off (as a man in love does), or did he want to display his enlightenment (as a man concerned about his progressive image does)? Or was it all Grandpa Morduch's fault, when he was suddenly beset by pangs of conscience about his bossiness and urged Lucile to take a few hours off and "go out to have some fun with people your age."

Whatever the reason, she was now sitting with them, ostensibly an equal among equals, but the polite smile frozen on her lips made it clear—especially to Professor Schiff—that she did not belong. The occasion was forced, uncomfortable, stupid.

The restaurant was filling up, and the diners' chatter and clanging silverware mingled with the violent bass lines emitted by hidden speakers.

". . . so why are we so opposed to all those people we call migrant workers?" Alissa was asking. She was a pale-faced woman with stretched wrinkles, who liked to cover her freckles with sunscreen even at night. Since she was sitting next to Lucile, Professor Schiff thought her face helped illuminate the table. "What's wrong with being a migrant worker?" she added in a whiny tone.

"I'll tell you what's wrong," answered Assi, her husband, "they're taking jobs from people who live here." He looked up and shook the ponytail that hung at the back of his neck, thick and gray, as if it had been yanked off the rear-end of a young colt. "Look at that guy in the kitchen, for example. I mean, one of our people could have been working there, no?"

A dark-skinned man was zipping around the open kitchen, moving in and out of a screen of steam, slamming plates piled high on the stainless steel counter, and wiping the sweat from his glistening brow.

"That's just it, Assi—none of our people are interested in those jobs. There's no one to do them," said Tami.

"And what do you say, Lucile?" Alissa asked.

But Lucile said nothing. Her gaze was fixed on the man in the kitchen.

"We call them migrant workers," Alissa went on, "but I'm sorry, aren't all human beings in this day and age migrant workers? No, really, isn't all of humanity in a constant search for a better life?"

"You're talking a load of rubbish, Lissi," said Assi. "You're always such a bleeding heart. Come on, there's hardly space for our kids here, so why do we need tens of thousands more people polluting the environment?"

"Humanity these days is frenetic," Tami offered, "competition . . . everyone wants more . . . greediness . . . Yes, it's the neoliberalism . . . consumerism . . . that's what makes everyone crazy."

The dark man in the white chef's clothes disappeared into the steam and then emerged again to place new dishes on the counter. Lucile did not take her eyes off him.

"I agree with Tami," said Professor Schiff, "humanity is in a constant search for a better life . . ." But he wasn't interested in the conversation. He already knew what was going to be said and by whom. He was following Lucile's gaze.

"Those migrant workers, they're just like us," Tami said. "We also roam from job to job, go up the ranks, change places, skip between the floors, get better terms, add another few pennies to our salaries, clutch at things with our nails until they're bloody, just to get a title . . . Professor, for example . . ."

"And what do you say, Lucile?" Alissa asked again.

Assi flicked a credit card between his fingers. He signaled for the waitress. "What rubbish," he muttered, "total rubbish."

In fact, it was his fault. Assi. He was the one who'd dragged them to this restaurant. He'd insisted. Literally begged. Over the past few years he'd completely given up on reading academic texts, and all he did now was flood his once-brilliant mind with food and restaurant reviews. "Take that man over there, for example," he repeated, "that one, there, in the kitchen."

"You mean the chef?" asked Professor Schiff. Now he noticed the cook's reaction to Lucile's stare. He was signing something to her. Yes, signing. With his fingers. He touched his left eye. Then he pointed at his wristwatch. They were communicating!

"That guy in the kitchen, he probably came from somewhere in Africa, God knows where, maybe Sudan . . ."

Fifteen yards from their table, in the open kitchen where a tropical storm was brewing, the dark-skinned chef was twirling and banging down dish after dish on the counter at a murderous pace. He was doing a dance. The speakers provided the drumbeat. His dark face was beaded with sweat.

"Does anyone even check them?" Assi went on. "Does anyone care if they're bringing in diseases? I wouldn't trust them."

The conversation was irking Professor Schiff. It was filling him with boredom. Actual fatigue. This happened to him sometimes when he talked with his few friends, especially Alissa and Assi, with whom he'd been dragging out a friendship since his London days, in the late seventies of the previous century.

Assi waved at the waitress with both hands.

"Lucile, what do you think?" Alissa nagged. "What's your opinion? We're interested in hearing it. What do you have to say, Lucile, on this topic of migration?"

But Lucile still did not speak. Her eyes were conversing with the cook.

When the little group finally stood up and shook the crumbs off their clothes, Professor Schiff plucked up the courage and asked, "Hey, Lucile, do you know that man in the kitchen?"

"Of course," she replied simply, "that's Felix Ofosu. My third husband."

36

And so, she had a husband. A real man. Flesh and blood.

And why shouldn't she? It was completely logical and absolutely reasonable, even if Professor Schiff had chosen not to investigate the matter. People usually pair off, after all, and they frequently do so in the early stages of their existence. Moreover, very often—more often than one tends to believe—couples stay together for many years. Professor Schiff and Tami Kushner, for instance, had been sharing their lives for over three decades, and they continued to do so even after their two children had left home and each gone their adult ways.

In fact, Professor Schiff had known of this man for some time. If he was surprised, it was only because in his mind he had chosen to preserve Lucile as a figure with no real biography.

He said nothing. Neither did Tami, who examined Felix Ofosu with a sideways, penetrating look. Only Alissa commented, "We didn't know your husband cooked."

Assi grumbled, "But at some point we really should say something to him about the spiciness. Far too much chili. Far too much."

To Professor Schiff's relief, Lucile quickly slipped out of the restaurant, and the party soon followed.

They were already at the blue Honda in the underground parking lot when they heard Felix Ofosu, the third husband, yelling after them.

"Hello? Is that you there, friends?" his hoarse voice echoed between the parking lot columns, a split second before the car beeped to signal its doors unlocking. He appeared beside them, perspiring and grinning, wearing a blazer and a purple shirt. "I can't sit in the back, I get nauseous," he said, out of breath.

"There's no room for you, Felix," Lucile said firmly. "There are five of us." To prove the veracity of her statement, she proceeded to count the party out loud, pointing at each person and assigning them a number.

"We'll manage," said Felix with a chuckle. "I'm sure it's not a long drive."

But Lucile was adamant. "It's long. Long enough."

"Four can fit in the back seat easily," Felix insisted, in meticulous English and a deep, raspy voice. "I know Hondas, these things are a marvel of design." He was a very tall man with a square jaw and a fashionable haircut, temples shaved.

"Where do you want to go anyway?" asked Professor Schiff, barely concealing his hostility.

"What do you mean? Wherever Lucile's going."

"Stop your nonsense, man," Lucile grumbled, "there's no room for you. I'm going to my work and you go back to yours."

"I can tell you're not all that happy to see me, woman," said Felix Ofosu cheerfully as he poked his fingers into the coiffed thicket on Lucile's head.

The blood pounded in Professor Schiff's temples. "Excuse

me, but how can you even leave in the middle of your shift, on the busiest night of the week?"

"Don't worry, Mr. . . . ?"

"Professor," Lucile corrected him, "Professor Schiff."

"Don't worry, Professor," said Felix Ofosu, exposing his teeth with a wide grin, "they'll manage. That place runs like an ant colony. One for all and all for one." He scanned them one by one with a taunting look, and they stood there in stunned silence, cowed by the onslaught of self-confidence. Only Lucile, after removing his hand from her hair, opened the car door and folded herself into the back seat as if the whole affair had nothing to do with her.

But then, as predicted—or as Professor Schiff predicted—Alissa whimpered, "It's okay, Mr. Felix, Assi and I will take a cab."

"No, no," Tami protested, "absolutely not. I'll join you. Assi can go with them. I'm sure it'll be interesting for them to talk."

"I really don't mind getting a cab," said Assi with a desperate smile.

"No, no, you go with them, Assi. Alissa and I will get a cab." Tami was adamant. She thought this would be a chance to teach Assi a lesson on the politics of migration. She couldn't let it slip away.

And so it was decided.

A few minutes later, Felix Ofosu was sprawled in the front seat with his legs spread wide, Assi and Lucile were each huddled on one edge of the back seat, and Professor Schiff was gripping the wheel. The Honda made its way through the traffic, heading north.

"I liked your vegan hamburger, chef," said Assi, his voice thick with artificial friendliness.

"Happy to hear it, sir," said Felix Ofosu without turning his head back. "Personally, I prefer the real thing. Extra rare, no grilling at all."

Lucile, who had wanted to believe that the infinity of the cosmos was sufficient to remove her from her third husband's sight, began to recognize how wrong she'd been. What had happened between them? Why had she run away from him? These intriguing questions awaited clarification. But meanwhile, Tami Kushner felt sorry for her. Because people like Tami Kushner always feel sorry for those who hide. For those who seek refuge. For the fleers. That had been true since the days of Cain.

Professor Schiff felt no pity. Professor Schiff felt the frustration of a man whose circumstances had flipped on him. Disappointment, yes, and a burning desire to get rid of Felix Ofosu. Or at least throw him out of his home. But instead, he conducted a polite conversation with the guest. Tami Kushner, who had no hidden agenda and could not deny her ideological commitment, sat Felix Ofosu down at the dining table and put a bowl of pistachios in front of him. Professor Schiff poured whiskey. Ofosu asked for ice. There was no ice. Nor any cold water.

"Whisky with no ice? How is this possible?" wondered Felix Ofosu.

Sometimes decency requires an intolerable effort, thought Professor Schiff as he clinked glasses with the third husband. They toasted refugees, asylum seekers, and migrant workers.

The topic of conversation was married life. Mr. Felix Ofosu, the third husband, was merely demanding his right: that his wife, Mrs. Lucile Tetteh-Ofosu, come back to him. Immediately. Without delay.

Indeed, Felix's claim regarding the eternal bond between a man and wife was still largely accepted, explained Tami Kushner in a remarkably friendly tone, but a woman is entitled to decide whether she wants to uphold this bond or end it. "And the law," Tami added sweetly, "supports our opinion, rather than the concept of eternity."

When Tami Kushner said the word *law*, Professor Schiff felt Lucile's eyes piercing him. Was she hinting at something? Was she telling him that Ofosu did not have a lawful status in this country? She was sitting some distance away, and every so often Professor Schiff glanced out of the corner of his eye at the red splotch of her glorious evening gown (a dress that looked like it had been borrowed from a nineteen-sixties Bond girl), only to remember that she was, after all, a princess.

"You know, Mr. Felix, since we're on the subject of the law..." began Professor Schiff.

"Yes? Yes? If we're on the subject of the law..." He gave Professor Schiff an amused look, transferred it to Lucile, then returned it to Professor Schiff. He gulped down his whiskey and refilled his glass.

"Yes, if we're on the subject of the law, let me ask you something," said Professor Schiff. He screwed the cap back on the bottle and removed it from the table.

Tami was alarmed. "No, really, there's no need," she hurriedly interrupted her husband, "it's not necessary. Mr. Felix understands that we're all friends here, and no one has any ill intentions. Isn't that right, Mr. Felix?"

"Right, Felix?" Lucile repeated the question in a screech. "She asked you something! Answer!" She stood up and gripped the edge of the table with both hands. Now the shiny red blob filled Professor Schiff's field of vision. He had no choice but to stand up as well. He could see his reflection protecting Lucile's in the hallway mirror, and the picture flooded him with chivalrous warmth.

"Lucile, please, there's no need to get angry," said Tami. "I'm sure Mr. Felix understands and agrees with the gist of things."

Felix was the last one to stand. He did so with ease, straightening his pants and smoothing out his purple shirt. He rolled his eyes at the clock and then at his elegant wristwatch. "Well, it's late. I won't disturb you any further." He chuckled somewhat shyly, and added, "I can see that my wife is with decent people who like her and care for her, and that I don't need to worry." He shook Professor Schiff's hand and turned to Tami. "Ma'am," he said, bowing his head respectfully, "you are a very noble woman." His expression turned grave and his large eyes glazed over for a moment. "I very much appreciate your wisdom."

"I'm only doing what I understand." A slight flush came over Tami's forehead and neck.

Felix Ofosu was on his way to the door when he turned suddenly. "In Africa, we have great respect for our elders. They are the peacemakers. What would we do without the elders of the family... the tribe..." He walked out and his supple footsteps (the footsteps of a hunter, Professor Schiff thought to himself) echoed down the stairwell.

Shortly before dawn, when the Schiff-Kushners' insomnia roused them, Tami Kushner murmured to Professor Schiff, "But why did he call me an elder? Do you think I look old? How old does he think I am?"

"Maybe you should get a facelift," Professor Schiff said, his voice muffled by the pillow. "How much could it cost? Get some plastic surgery instead of that car Morduch wants to buy you for your birthday."

She did not want a car. Plastic surgery went against her ideology. Her sleep was growing briefer and more interrupted. Maybe she really had aged a little, thought Professor Schiff.

37

Aboagye removed the microphone from Professor Schiff's shirt and put the recording machine back in its case. Their meeting seemed to have been redundant. Nothing much was said. The last hour had been full of silences.

Professor Schiff walked the special investigator to the foyer. "It seems to me, Mr. Aboagye, that the prosecution is pretty stuck with *The Republic versus Schiff*. It's a waste of time. And think of how much money you're throwing away on me."

"That money would have been wasted anyway," said Aboagye, taking off the jacket he'd made a point of keeping on throughout the meeting. The chilly air-conditioning had allowed him to preserve his formal appearance. But outside, the heat was intolerable, even now that the sun was setting. "Are you ready to admit your guilt, Professor?"

"But I confessed long ago," said Professor Schiff.

"Did you really?"

"Yes, I did. My great-great-great-great-grandfather was a slave trader."

"But that is not the accusation," Aboagye pointed out.

"I also confessed that I wanted to claim the ruins of the sunken ship and the relics found in it."

"That is also not the accusation."

"Then what is it? What? Why am I here if not because of your stupid law?"

"Perhaps that is why you are here, yes, due to the Law for Adjudicating Slave Traders and so forth. But as far as I'm concerned, that is not what you stand guilty of, Professor Schiff. Rather, it is the denial of Africa."

"The denial of Africa?" Professor Schiff screeched, "what are you talking about, Special Investigator Aboagye?"

"I'll tell you what I'm talking about, Professor," Aboagye replied calmly. "Africa does not exist in your world. It is merely a myth. A legend. An amusing anecdote. Me, us, the villa staff, the tribunal . . . The city, the country, the continent . . . We are all here to serve as background sets for Professor Schiff. That is the charge."

"No, no, no, I deny *that*, sir! I adamantly deny it!"

"From the moment you began talking to me, to us, you have not stopped prattling on about the book you want to write. The book you're going to write, or might already be writing, while we feed you, protect you, and put on a show for you with our so-very-nice African-ness."

"Do you want to know what I think about your Africa? Maybe it really is time for me to stop fawning and tell the truth, Mr. Aboagye—"

"Ah, interesting, Professor. Very interesting. So what you've been doing up to now was just fawning? Interesting. But why? What did you think you would get out of it? Did you want the black man to like you, as you like him?"

"Yes! I want to be liked! And do you know why, Mr. Aboagye? Because you Africans have an insatiable appetite for pity. More and more and more pity . . ."

"Go on, Professor, please go on, this conversation is finally getting interesting." Aboagye sat down on the stone bench. In his normally impenetrable gaze there was now a spark of provocation.

Professor Schiff sat down opposite him, on the ledge around the dried-up ornamental pond. "It is an appetite that can never be sated. This country longs for pity more than it longs for actual food."

"But perhaps the other side is also hungry? Do you understand what I'm saying, Professor? Perhaps this whole relationship of humanity with Africa, and of Africa with humanity, is based on a mutual appetite that cannot be sated?"

"Like, for example, Africa's appetite for murderous weapons?" suggested Professor Schiff.

"Or the West's appetite for black people . . ." Aboagye countered.

"The appetite of rulers for money."

"The world's appetite for metals, diamonds, oil . . . For quarries, cobalt, uranium . . ."

"Human beings' appetite for middle-class comforts," said Professor Schiff, "for consumer goods."

"And of course," said Aboagye, "the appetite of multinational corporations for contracts, bids, monopolies."

"The appetite of religions for souls, living or dead," said

Professor Schiff, "preferably dead, because that way ownership is eternal."

"The West's appetite for pure, naive, native cultures," said Aboagye, "for photogenic poverty."

"The appetite for atonement," said Professor Schiff, "the appetite for self-castigation."

"The appetite for freedom . . ." Aboagye added.

Kweku walked down the drive toward them, leading a muscular dog with pointy ears and a curly tail. The dog, whose brow was furrowed in contemplation, was apparently a new tenant at the villa. Professor Schiff called him over, but the animal walking alongside Kweku like a model on a catwalk paid no heed to his beckoning sounds and hand signals. Ardent dog lovers like Professor Schiff tend to be offended when dogs won't allow themselves to be petted.

"Is he scared of me?" asked Professor Schiff.

"No, he's just not interested in you, Professor," said Aboagye with a laugh.

"What kind of dog is he, Kweku?"

"Basenji," said Kweku proudly, "one hundred percent purebred."

"Purebred, hey?"

"Certified."

"What are you going to name him?" Professor Schiff asked.

"I was actually thinking of asking your opinion on that, Professor, since you're a writer and all."

"I'll think about it. Maybe I'll come up with some ideas," said Professor Schiff.

Kweku gave him a salute and headed to the villa's front steps. The dog trotted loyally behind him.

"You know, Professor," said Special Investigator George Aboagye, "a few years ago, at the National Archeology Museum in Lisbon, I saw a copper collar. It was made for a human neck—a slave's neck—and it had the owner's name engraved on it. What amazed me was the small circumference of the collar. Was it worn by a boy? A woman? An extremely thin person?" Aboagye stood up, shook out his legs, and put on the elegant jacket that had been lying on the stone bench. "What do you think, Professor Schiff? Maybe it's time to revise the idiom and say that man's best friend is a slave?"

38

Felix Ofosu was back at the Schiff-Kushners the next day, to look for a brass button he claimed had fallen off his jacket the evening before. A few days later he arrived again, because he was "in the neighborhood and wanted to see how his good friends were doing." The following week—another visit. This time he brought Professor Schiff and Tami Kushner a gift: a fresh green coconut, like they eat in the homeland.

Within a remarkably short time, Felix Ofosu had made himself a regular visitor. At first he would drop by unannounced, under various false pretenses, and once he felt he'd promoted himself from distant acquaintance to household member, he made a point of tying his visits to actual events: once to demonstrate ritual drumming on a plastic bucket for Professor Schiff's son ("The reverberation is obviously a little different than when you have a goat skin stretched on a wooden cylinder, but what's important is the rhythm"); another time to help trap a tarantula that had moved in under the cabinet (instead of capturing it, Ofosu murdered it with a wooden plank, then sat down to tell them at length about Anansi, a spider god beloved and admired in his country, and the one responsible over there, in West Africa, for storytelling); and once he taught them how to make green banana fritters.

As expected, Felix Ofosu's visits, which Professor Schiff initially found mildly irritating, eventually became an unbearable nuisance. Not only because he was Lucile's husband, at least on paper, but because he was opinionated, loud, and devoid of all sensitivity to territorial boundaries. In the private sphere, of course.

And yet, he was her husband. Definitively. Unequivocally. Her third husband. And he would not allow them to forget it. Nor *her*. It was only a matter of time, of course—things happened quickly—before Felix Ofosu turned up for an unplanned visit, as he did practically every day, sat down comfortably, grinning and engulfed in a cloud of aftershave, took a handful of roasted almonds from a bowl, and said, "I hear my dear wife is getting married."

"Yes, that's true," said Tami. She refilled the ceramic bowl and added softly, "I'm sure you'll receive a formal notice soon, Mr. Felix."

"Is there going to be a party?" Ofosu tossed the almonds into his mouth one by one, as fast as a machine.

"If there are any festivities, you'll be the first to know. I can promise your name will be on the guest list."

"As a first-degree relative," Professor Schiff clarified.

"Of course," said Felix Ofosu, "and as the man who first has to be divorced."

"I thought you were no longer . . . " said Professor Schiff gruffly. "I mean . . . I thought it was all over between you two."

"Not at all. Nothing is over. But I heard the groom is a millionaire, and that is very important for Lucile, so I completely understand her. As they say where I come from, love without food starves to death. And the opposite is also true, especially when the groom has more than one foot in the grave—"

"What is it that you want, Mr. Felix?" Tami interrupted.

"Some sort of compensation."

And so. Things were about to go off course.

"How much?" asked Tami.

"You tell me," said Felix Ofosu. He gave a pointed look at the empty bowl, and Tami, compassionate as always—toward someone who, though thuggish, still belonged to a "disadvantaged community"—poured out the last of the almonds, which she'd been keeping for the next day. "Yes, I trust you, as a wise and creative woman, and mostly as the head of the tribe."

"Tribe? What tribe?" Tami looked mortified.

"You're the tribe. All of you. The professor, the kids, your friends, the grandfather. And now my wife, too." His eyes suddenly welled up and tears streamed down his cheeks. The tears were real. He was genuinely overcome by an outburst of self-pity that undoubtedly increased his motivation for extortion.

"What's wrong, Mr. Felix?" asked Tami, and she placed her hand on Felix Ofosu's long, ringed fingers.

"Maybe I belong, too, sometimes . . ." he said tragically, and then repeated, "maybe I do too . . ."

"Yes, you as well," said Tami, and she stroked the sobbing Felix Ofosu's hand.

Professor Schiff knew that if it were up to her, if she truly were the leader of the tribe, she would have admitted him as a member.

Felix Ofosu recovered quickly. "I was thinking thirty thousand dollars," he said, wiping the tears away. "Cash. You know, because given my situation I don't currently have a bank account."

Professor Schiff was rendered speechless by Ofosu's audacity. But Tami, quick-witted as always, answered without skipping a beat: "Five thousand."

"Twenty?" countered Ofosu with a chastened smile.

"Ten!" Tami declared.

"Fifteen," Ofosu said and held out his many-ringed hand.

But Tami pushed it away. "My dear Mr. Felix, we will consult and give you our answer as soon as possible."

"Of course," said Felix Ofosu ceremoniously, "of course, take your time."

Before leaving, he did what he always did on his visits: he compared the time on the wall clock to his wristwatch.

"This is bad," said Lucile Tetteh-Ofosu.

"How bad?" asked Professor Schiff.

"Very bad."

Professor Schiff wanted to know if Lucile thought the problem could be solved through spiritual methods. Something along the lines of the mysterious ritual she'd used to get rid of Toga. She said no. Dances would not be of any use here. Nor would roosters. Nor spells, potions, smoke, or noisemakers. Not even mezuzahs or crosses. There was no combination of activities tailored to this particular predicament. Special prayers, recitations, drumming, whistling, the unique voices her grandmother had taught her—none of these would help. Because the spirits and the supreme powers were defenseless in the face of an unwanted husband. It therefore fell to Professor Schiff and Tami Kushner to be the proxies of fate. The implementers of its decree. Plain and simple.

"But how?" asked Professor Schiff. He guessed at the answer, and it indeed arrived.

"Felix has no papers," said Lucile.

But turning in an undocumented immigrant was no small matter. Certainly not for Professor Schiff, who in his own view—and yes, also in society's view, why engage in false modesty—was a human rights activist. At least in theory. But it turns out that righteousness, in this respectable upper-middle-class society of ours, is not always a straightforward task. Professor Schiff therefore spent several tormented days deliberating.

Even once the die was cast and he'd decided to initiate the process of informing on Felix, he had no idea what exactly he was supposed to do. Call the police? Send an anonymous message to the municipality? To the Ministry of the Interior? And if the latter—which department? Which branch? Which special unit?

Then he remembered Attorney Melchior. Melchior! Of course! He must be proficient in the procedures of reporting and deporting. And he would probably agree to manage the nefarious plot. For a fee, of course. And so Professor Schiff found himself talking with the odious man whom only months ago he had sworn to eradicate from his memory.

Attorney Melchior was only too happy to talk with the professor again. He said he'd missed the days when they'd been partners, and he wished once again to express his deep sorrow for the important project's demise, but he hoped Professor Schiff was getting the most out of the agreement they'd signed, and that Mrs. . . . he couldn't remember her name . . . was still compensating him for the emotional distress, and so forth.

Professor Schiff was filled with loathing. The obsequious voice on the other end of the line reminded him how evil and cruel the procedure he was about to initiate really was.

"Yes, my dear man," said Melchior when his slippery preamble was finished, "how may I help you?"

Professor Schiff was about to hang up. But his curiosity—simple, basic curiosity, perhaps the instinct of a writer—made him press on. He related to Melchior the salient points of the situation, and asked if he could handle the affair while preserving his own anonymity. Absolute discretion was an essential condition, he stressed: Professor Schiff's identity must remain secret. Forever.

"Like the person who turned in Anne Frank?" Melchior quipped.

Sweat covered Professor Schiff's burning forehead. He swallowed and said wanly, "There's no comparison."

"Really?" Melchior teased.

"A, we're talking about a blackmailer who might cross a boundary—"

"He already has," Melchior pointed out sardonically.

"Excuse me?"

"Boundary . . . You know, borders . . ." Melchior tried to explain the joke.

"Oh, yes. Funny." He was being forced to seek help from this despicable man, who lacked any principles or ethics, and who now had the audacity to preach to him. "Besides, it's not like we're sending him to his death."

"How do you know?"

"Well, I don't really."

"Exactly, Schiff. You don't know what awaits him there, in the place you're sending him back to." But when Melchior heard the tormented remorse in Professor Schiff's silence, he added, "However, there's also a good chance that you're doing this guy a big favor. A huge favor. And really, who knows? A change of scene, as they say . . ."

"He's actually pretty well set here, I think," said Professor Schiff.

"Home is always best, Schiff. Now let's talk about money."

"I'm listening."

"Well, you know, my billable hours . . . I'm going to estimate three hours here, plus something like five or six phone calls, and a letter we'll have to print out. Well, it's pennies. Negligible."

"And you guarantee his deportation?"

"Don't worry, he'll be deported in two seconds. Trust me."

"And the anonymity? Absolute confidentiality?"

"Don't worry, no one will know."

"How long until he's gone?"

"If I take care of it—a matter of days. Maybe hours."

"All right. So how much is this going to cost me?" Professor Schiff asked.

"I estimate we'll need a few hours at most. But wait, Schiff, I have a better idea. Instead of paying, why not just give me back the idea I gave you?"

"The idea?"

"Yes, the idea, the idea for the film. I gave it to you to use freely, don't you remember? As a token of my apology and friendship. So instead of paying, just give me back my idea and sign a statement saying you won't use it. I'll write something up, and then I'll take care of this Ofosu of yours. Don't worry, just leave all his information with my secretary."

And that was the end of the call.

Three weeks later, a postcard landed in the Schiff-Kushners' mailbox. It was a colorful postcard, sent from Africa, from a country whose existence Professor Schiff had only recently learned of. A row of colorful stamps was stuck on the back. It was evident that the sender had chosen them carefully, wishing to surprise the recipients with a particularly loud gesture. One that would magnify the excitement of getting something in the post other than a bill or a credit card statement.

And indeed, Professor Schiff could not remember the last time he'd retrieved from his mailbox a postcard with creased edges, covered with stamps.

There were only a few words on the postcard, in large, unruly handwriting: "Dear Tami and Professor Schiff, give my love to the whole tribe. Respectfully yours, Felix O."

The picture on the front showed a herd of elephants.

39

"Africa," said Captain de Groot, passing the telescope to Klonimus Schiff, who held it up to his eye.

Tall, slow waves crashed against a sparse copse of palm trees. A few ships and smaller vessels were anchored in the middle of the bay. A schooner with all its sails raised drifted south, its frothy wake clearly visible even from a great distance. At the edge of the bay, on a dry peninsula (or was it an island with a dike leading to the shore?) was a large, beautiful, white fort, its walls glistening in the morning sun. The sea foam seemed to be gathering at its feet. Further east was the estuary of a large river whose waters burst into the sea, coloring the turquoise with gray.

Ladies and gentlemen, members of the Special Tribunal, Madam Attorney General, Head of the Investigation Team:

Strange as it may seem, that was the first time Klonimus Zelig Schiff had ever seen Africa. True, he was a tireless and successful slave trader who had worked in Suriname for more than three decades, and had even taken the name Schiff—which means "ship"—to indicate that the sea was his domain. He had also designed a family emblem depicting a ship suspended atop a massive wave. And yet, as has always been the custom in the business world, the actual labor of buying and transporting goods was performed on his behalf by captains, agents, and brokers. It was they who moored on the coasts of Benin and Biafra, who conducted negotiations, who collected the human merchandise. And it was they who sailed the ships for two exhausting months, carrying these tortured souls across the Atlantic on the route known as the Middle Passage.

It was they—not he. Never he.

Klonimus Schiff was surprised. This was not how he'd imagined the shores of the continent. He had maps. He even had a globe displaying the majority of the world, which the Europeans had cut up into squares, sliced with borders, and given names to. On the globe, as on the maps, the fold in the content known as the Gulf of Guinea was colored orange. Perhaps to symbolically underscore the areas controlled by the Dutch, whose royal dynasty's color was orange? Klonimus had almost childishly expected that the land would somehow connote that orange curve—perhaps orange trees?

The water, part of the same capricious ocean that lapped at Caribbean ports, was slow, heavy, and thick here. This, too, was surprising, and somewhat ominous. Klonimus's head spun. He felt nauseous. It was simple seasickness, no rare occurrence on a naval voyage, and certainly nothing unfamiliar to my great-great-great-great-grandfather, who was extremely sensitive to the rocking motion of the waves. But this time, the sickliness was accompanied by a great sense of distress.

Despite his nausea and dejection, Klonimus gathered all the *Esperanza*'s passengers on deck, and performed the ceremony he'd been planning throughout the two-month voyage. He opened three bottles of extremely scarce kosher wine, which he'd kept especially for the occasion, poured a little for everyone, thanked the Almighty for bringing them to Africa almost unharmed and in more or less good health, recited *borei pri hagafen*—the blessing over wine—and when everyone, including the children, had taken a sip, he outlined the plan he had concocted.

Once they reached the bay and explored it, Schiff explained to his little congregation, they would find themselves a suitable, comfortable corner, and then with God's grace (and possibly some cash), the Dutch governor of this region would allocate a small area where they would be allowed to reside temporarily until they could build a permanent settlement. Missives had been sent to all relevant parties several months ago, and a reply from Dutch Governor Commander Friedrich Franz Ulrich Last had been received even before the *Esperanza* had set sail.

At this point, Klonimus Schiff, who could barely stand up and whose complexion was now a pale shade of green, retrieved an envelope from his jacket pocket. He took out the letter, unfolded it in the light breeze, and read it aloud to the small crowd swaying on deck with him:

"His Majesty's government views with favor the establishment in Dutch-administered African territory of a Jewish settlement and will use their best endeavors to facilitate the achievement of this object . . . " and so on and so forth.

Schiff's knees buckled. He grasped at a rope, put the envelope back in his pocket, turned, and emptied his guts into the waves. He then wiped his face with a perfumed handkerchief and continued.

After carrying their cargo to shore, he said, they would erect a synagogue on the land allocated to them by the magnanimous governor. Around the synagogue they would build their homes. Meanwhile, a research expedition would travel upriver to locate a suitable place for the permanent settlement. The expedition would be led by Mr. Ruben Zwart, who was knowledgeable about agriculture, and by Mr. Lot Met-Zonder, the older son of Mr. Cornelis Met-Zonder, who was an expert in tree logging. They might be accompanied by the trusty Mr. Ajax Witte Voetjes, who would chronicle their findings with his paintings.

When the expedition returned with its recommendations—their exploration would certainly last no longer than two or three months—they would lease the plot of land from the tribe or nation to which it belonged (respecting any local authority, of course, and remaining neutral in any conflicts among the nations and tribes) and then, with the blessing of the Dutch throne and/or the British parliament, would establish the first Jewish town in Africa. Or rather, the first Jewish town in the world outside desolate Judea! And perhaps, with God's help, this new town would also herald the revival of a new nation, which would lead the entire world into a new era of faith and justice.

Amen!

It is difficult to know the extent to which Schiff's words were understood, and how much of his speech seeped into his listeners' minds. Their vocabulary was meager, at least in the language in which their master-leader spoke to them, and even if they did take in the main tenets of his grandiose plan, they were not asked for their opinion of it. They were trained to obey, and that was all. They did not know how to consider. To examine. To ask questions. To cast doubts. Casting doubts is a skill one must learn and practice for years, starting at a young age.

In any case, the end of the speech was signaled by the word *amen*, which they shouted repeatedly with childish glee. Then they kept standing there, ceremoniously upright, even as their rabbi-leader collapsed onto the deck right before their eyes, crawled on all fours, writhed, and vomited bile.

They stood there for another moment or two, not daring to move until ordered to, until two sailors hurried over to the semiconscious Klonimus, lifted him by the arms and legs, and carried him to the middle deck like a sack of sugar.

Someone shouted, "Hallelujah!" This was the sign for the crowd to break into a boisterous song and dance. Ladies and gentlemen, can you imagine the scene? All of a sudden there were thirty people, children and adults, singing ardently while shimmying their hips, stomping their feet, clapping their hands, and drumming on the floorboards: *Praise Him with the loud sounding cymbals; praise Him with the clanging cymbals. Let everything that hath breath praise the Lord. Hallelujah*. . .

In the speech delivered by my great-great-great-great-grandfather, the landowner, slave trader, and would-be leader of a national movement, one can detect more than an iota of megalomania. Klonimus himself, of course, gave no consideration to the remarkably smooth transition from owning human beings' bodies to controlling their souls. But these are rather similar conditions, aren't they? Both purport to give meaning to the lives of those subject to the authority. In the first case—economic. In the second—redemptive. But since the term *self-awareness* has only recently been invented, it would be unfair of us to demand that Klonimus Zelig Schiff be ahead of his time. Expecting him to be fair and merciful and to espouse a morality that meets this tribunal's standards is already a tall order. But a little cynicism and even self-mockery? That seems too much to ask.

Nevertheless, all this time, as I've investigated the man's life—and, in the past few weeks, engaged in a moral reckoning on his behalf—I've often asked myself what my forefather found funny. What made him laugh? I mean really laugh. The way you laughed, for example, when I told you about the people who sang and danced while their leader endured a bout of seasickness. Did Klonimus chuckle upon hearing a dirty joke from a sailor at the port of Paramaribo? Did he smile while watching a commedia dell'arte jester? Did he add his own little giggle to the laughs of children ogling at monkeys playing tricks in a street show?

I'm afraid I find myself absolutely unable to picture him laughing. Do you know what I think? I think that in Klonimus's world, although it was brimming with absurdities, there was no room for comic relief. And I'm sure you can guess why. Because humor cannot exist without compassion. Masters have no need for it. It only gets in the way. And if that is the case, ladies and gentlemen, it should now be clear to us what prevented Klonimus Zelig Schiff from completing his metamorphosis: an inability to laugh. Yes, laughter: that was all that was required of him.

I hope you've noticed, ladies and gentlemen, that in the picture of the ceremonial gathering on deck, a picture I have sketched for you as best I can, young Zipporah is absent. This is because, while the congregation members sang "Hallelujah," stomped their feet, and clapped their hands, Zipporah lay on a couch in her grand cabin in the stern of the *Esperanza*. The African coast surfaced in its full glory through the long, diagonal windows, but Zipporah was not interested. She was indifferent to the continent, to the end of the journey, to the dream now coming to fruition. Because if there was any news of the future, it was here, now, right upon her, attached to her breast, dozing, with Zipporah's nipple in her mouth and a sheer drop of milk on her tiny lips: her daughter.

The baby had been happily born some ten days earlier, in the middle of a hot, sticky, salty night, and the name given to her by her father was Yehudit. All I can say about the birth, which had occurred in this opulent cabin (the shared residence of Klonimus and Zipporah), is that the mother was surrounded by the caressing hands of five women while the sixth, Nelly Suiker, helped the baby emerge with great difficulty from her mother's womb into the world of 1831. It was not easy. Zipporah's screams of agony shook the ship's sails. But what do I, a man, know of childbirth or of contractions lasting for two days? And what do I, a man of the twenty-first century, understand of the terrible dangers awaiting mothers and their babies in those distant days?

The young mother held her beautiful baby close to her body and could not take her eyes off her. She sang her a lullaby in the language of spells and idolatry, the use of which was strictly prohibited. And just as she began, the door opened and the two sailors carried Klonimus in and laid him on the bed. But Zipporah did not stop singing. On the contrary: she sang louder, and to the ancient words of her forefathers she added some Hebrew that she had recently learned. The jumbled mixture of sounds and notes created a perfect lullaby, and Zipporah, as we know, had a wonderfully sweet, intoxicating voice, which experts would describe as a natural mezzo-soprano.

Some time later, very slowly and with great effort, Zipporah got up with the baby in her arms, limped over to the bed, and lay down next to her husband. The infant, now nestled between them, put her tiny thumb in her mouth.

Klonimus woke and asked, "What is that song, my girl?"

He was addressing his wife, of course, not the baby. But the confusion caused Zipporah to burst out laughing. The countless hardships she'd experienced in the fifteen years of her life had taught her to seize on every comic moment she encountered and exploit it to the fullest.

And then a miracle occurred. Zipporah's laughter, the lucid mezzo-soprano bells coming from her throat, struck

Klonimus and activated a dormant mechanism inside him. At first he smiled, then made a little sound, which grew louder and louder until it was an actual bellow. He laughed! Yes, Klonimus Zelig Schiff laughed, for perhaps the first time since he was a little boy.

And yet as he laughed so freely and joyfully, with his beloved daughter beside him, he knew, having finally completed his transformation process, that his life story was coming to an end.

Predictably, the sound of the mother and father laughing disturbed the baby's sleep. She woke up with a start and burst into tears.

40

After a long series of appointments, cancellations, and postponements, Professor Schiff's defense team finally convened in the conference room at the Holiday Inn. The organizer of the meeting was apparently unaware that Professor Schiff was a regular guest at the hotel pool, where he diligently swam a mile every morning. (As we know, Professor Schiff had reached a certain arrangement with the officer overseeing Villa Clark. It was not a cheap arrangement, but after all, he who holds that "a healthy body makes for a healthy mind" must not tolerate physical decline merely because he finds himself in a peculiar legal entanglement.)

As far as Professor Schiff was concerned, it was a most welcome coincidence. On that eventful morning, as was his custom, he completed his daily swim and emerged from the pool with his mind clear and fresh. The important meeting would be held a mere hundred steps from the pool, a short distance by any measure, a distance far too short to allow for any ill thoughts to ruin his post-swim clarity. But when he got to the locker room, he found that the clothes he'd left on a bench were gone. Fortunately, the thief, or whoever had accidentally seized Professor Schiff's shirt, underwear, and pants, had been kind enough—or confused and rushed enough—to leave his glasses and cellphone wrapped in a towel.

After half an hour of searching and angry inquiries, Professor Schiff realized he was late for the meeting. He was therefore forced to abandon the mystery and appear before his defense team wearing nothing but a white bathrobe that barely covered his aging and, one has to admit, slightly sagging body. It was certainly an odd appearance, but once he'd recounted the story to the befuddled team, they opted to proceed despite the mishap.

Three of the people were the ones Professor Schiff remembered: Ms. Sasson (who had undone the red braid coiled on her head like a cinnamon Danish and let her hair fall to her shoulders); the tall young man with multiple pens in his pocket, whose name was Benny Rose and who turned out to be the embassy's legal advisor; and the heavyset man with glasses who, once again, opted to remain nameless and title-less. They were joined by two experts who'd been flown out especially: the historian Joel Shapiro and the legal scholar Louis Mandelbloom, two intellectual giants of great repute, or so Professor Schiff was led to believe. And finally, there was the man introduced as "the proposed head of the defense team," whose dark-skinned face glowed at Professor Schiff as he enthusiastically shook the hand extended to him from a bathrobe.

Ms. Sasson introduced the radiant man: "Doctor Saidu Malik, a brilliant lawyer, top of his field, formerly an advisor to the minister of justice, chair of the Chamber of

Attorneys . . ." When she noticed the flash of surprise in Professor Schiff's eyes, she came closer and whispered in his ear, in a language only their compatriots understood, "Not just black but also . . . you know . . . It can't do any harm. Someone from the local scene."

An aproned waitress served tiny sandwiches, another walked around with a dish of colorful macarons, and a third poured coffee.

"Shall we start?" asked Ms. Sasson.

Hanging on the walls around them were color photographs of young men engaged in a rite of passage ceremony. Some of them had black skin glistening in the sunlight, others were smeared with ash and paint, but they were all extremely tall, muscular, and proud of their naked bodies. The photos had been taken by the acclaimed filmmaker Leni Riefenstahl when she'd visited the Nuba tribe in Sudan. The exhibition was in honor of South Sudan's seventh anniversary of independence. This information was provided by the explanatory text on the wall above Ms. Sasson's red head.

Shapiro was the first to speak: "There have been a few attempts to determine the number of slave traders who operated along the transatlantic route in the eighteenth century, including, by the way, African ones, and the estimates are a few tens of thousands. I find it strange that out of these tens of thousands and their many descendants, the only one singled out happens to be Jewish."

Mandelbloom continued: "From our perspective, it's like putting you or me or any other Jew on trial for what Judas Iscariot supposedly did. And so we're planning to turn the historical, collective charge—the one that has always been based on myths and prejudices—into a central motif in your defense." He grinned and licked his lips, looking very pleased with himself, as if turning the tables and positioning the accused as the accuser was a brilliant legal stunt.

How malicious, thought Professor Schiff. How cynical, how futile! Nevertheless, the facts, absurd as they may be, were correct: the man who had exploited and enslaved black people, backed by a racist ideology and a discriminatory set of laws, was himself the member of a persecuted, discriminated, humiliated minority.

"And your ancestor was not the only Jew, of course. After all, that was the norm two centuries ago," said Shapiro, "but obviously the antisemites are already having a field day with this. Take a quick tour of the Internet and get some perspective. Have you heard, for example, about Judah P. Benjamin, the Jewish plantation owner from Louisiana who served as the Confederate secretary of state under Jefferson Davis? Now there's a historical personage for you! Compared to him, your relative was just one more smalltime trader."

This argument was what set Professor Schiff off. Klonimus Zelig Schiff was absolutely not just another Jewish slave trader. He was an original, daring man who founded his own tribe and created a mission for himself. He was a dreamer. An ideologue. A social philosopher. A leader. A man of great stature. And at the very least important enough for his great-great-great-great-grandson to be asked to narrate his life story at length. No, he was not just one more slave trader.

"For your information," Professor Schiff protested, "I've researched the man's life and found out some important and surprising facts. Facts that will shed light on the circumstances under which he acted . . ."

Shapiro shook his head impatiently and grumbled, "We await the results of your research anxiously and curiously, of course, Schiff, and personally I have no doubt that it's extremely interesting. But is it relevant? In principle, I mean."

"I must say that I completely agree with my colleague," said Mandelbloom, "and in general I find it puzzling that the experts on the other side have not noticed the fishy smell coming from this whole affair. The unpleasant connotations . . . Obviously, the negative feedback is not going to work in their favor." He glanced around the table to gauge the impression he was making. "I already know what I'm going to say in my opening statement. I will say: Your honors, the plaintiff standing on trial today is an entire nation. It is, quite possibly, all of human civilization . . ."

"Oh, it's going to be quite a show," said Dr. Saidu Malik, muffling a chuckle in his double chin. "I can already see what a marvelous spectacle it's going to be." Then he stood up, and his hand, as it reached for the macarons, patted Professor Schiff's shoulder affectionately.

At this point, someone came to inform Professor Schiff that his clothes had been located in the laundry room, and with his mouth still gluey from the cookies and coffee, he asked for a break to change into his clothes and collect himself. The entire team seemed to welcome the suggestion.

"Just a moment," said the nameless, heavyset man, who had not uttered a word or moved a limb thus far, and only the blue dots of his eyes scanned the assembled through his thick glasses. "There is another possibility."

All heads turned to him.

"That this whole story is a fiction . . . "

The heads quickly swiveled to Professor Schiff and back to the heavyset man. He continued, "That most of the details in this case, especially those concerning genealogy, are not just inaccurate but actual lies. That this whole story about the slave trader is an invention. That Klonimus Zelig Schiff never was. That there is no evidence of the man's existence. That Schiff took 'poetic license' and conjured up a fictitious ancestor for the purpose of his literary work." A wan smile appeared on his broad face. "The total baselessness of the facts releases him, of course, from all liability. No case to answer."

Ms. Sasson twirled a lock of hair. Benny Rose nibbled the tip of his pen. Mandelbloom drained his coffee cup. Shapiro drummed irritably on the table.

Dr. Saidu Malik cleared his throat uncomfortably. "And what about the facts?"

"Which facts?"

"And the documents?"

"Fake."

"And the research?"

"Total fabrication. Fantasy."

"Meaning, what you are suggesting, Mr. . . . ? "

The heavyset man ignored the near-explicit request to introduce himself. He took off his glasses and wiped them. For a moment the light-blue dots turned into the eyes of an astounded child. "What I'm suggesting is simple: we argue that the whole thing is a scam and be done with it."

"We can't do that," said Malik.

"Why not?"

Professor Schiff became irate. If they were to dispute the existence of his forefather, would that call his own being into question?

He leaped up from his seat at the head of the table. "I'll tell you why not, Mr. No-Name," he barked with barely veiled anger, "I'll tell you!" The truth is, his injured pride had been simmering since he'd lost his clothes in the locker room.

What happened next was so apt for the situation that it might have been written for a sitcom: his bathrobe sash snagged on the chair leg and the robe fell open like the curtains parting on a theater set. He tried to clutch the robe back and tighten it over his body, but he was too flustered to do that. The others, to their credit, looked down and stared at the carpet. Only Ms. Sasson turned her head sideways, and found herself looking straight at a handsome Nuba warrior with a very long penis. She sheltered her eyes with a feeble hand.

Professor Schiff continued, "I'll tell you why not. Because it makes no difference to history whether or not Klonimus Schiff existed. Because history, sir, has already taken him in and given him a role—an important role, a role that I, as his great-great-great-great-grandson, have confirmed by virtue of being his heir. And this role cannot be changed, and it cannot be replaced, or postponed, or transferred to someone else. I hope you are capable of understanding this."

Now that he'd calmed down a little and his voice had returned to its normal frequencies, Professor Schiff was able to bend over, unhook the sash, and cover himself with the robe. "You can look up," he mumbled.

The first to raise his eyes was the heavyset man. He stared at Professor Schiff with the pair of blue spots behind his glasses lenses and smiled his little smile.

"Bravo, Professor," said Dr. Malik, and he gave a token clap. "Bravo. Wonderful speech. Honestly."

41

The next day, at their biweekly Internet call, Professor Schiff updated his wife, Tami, on the legalistic brainstorming session at the Holiday Inn. Among other things, he told her about his strip show with the naked Nuba warriors in the background.

Tami observed dryly, "Leni Riefenstahl? Really? You found a way to work *her* into your story, too?"

Right after this irritating comment, the Internet went down and Tami's face froze, then vanished, with only her metallic, distant voice still coming through in meaninglessly truncated syllables.

The disconnected call left Professor Schiff brimming with information that demanded immediate release—information that was perhaps intended for his wife but was now available to any listener who happened by. As fate would have it, Special Investigator George Aboagye appeared at the villa a few moments later, without any warning, as usual. But was it really necessary to schedule a meeting with someone who was officially considered a prisoner?

Professor Schiff began speaking even before Aboagye could sit down in the wicker armchair and inquire politely and/or formally into his wellbeing. They sat on the upstairs veranda this time, the one outside Professor Schiff's study, facing the massive wawa tree. A thick twilight was descending on the estate, and the din of birds preparing for the night was at its loudest.

"I met with my defense team today," said Professor Schiff.

"I know, Professor. I was the one who helped set up the meeting."

"I thought you might like to hear what was said."

"Of course, but I believe it would be inappropriate, irresponsible even, of you to tell me. I must advise you to maintain confidentiality."

Nevertheless, Schiff told Aboagye everything, in great detail, trying not to skip a thing. He did this even though he was fully aware that he was disclosing secrets to the opposing party. But perhaps he did so because he hadn't yet decided which side he was on. For the time being, strangely, he felt that he was completely objective, not really supporting either team.

At the end of his confession—to which Aboagye listened attentively, taking notes—Professor Schiff recounted the mishap that had rendered him naked, and reported bitterly on his wife's vexing comment.

"I admit that it's a little strange, the way Leni Riefenstahl wormed her way into my story, a story already so charged and full of details."

"But who is this Leni?" asked Aboagye.

Professor Schiff reluctantly provided a brief encyclopedia entry: "She was an acclaimed German film director."

"I don't remember ever seeing anything of hers."

"You might not have. She found a lot of beauty and poetry in Nazi events. You know, flag parades, torch processions, marching soldiers with their jackbooted legs thrown high . . . She documented all these marvelous spectacles for Hitler, and for the entire enlightened world."

"How exactly does she fit in with our affair, Professor?"

"In the seventies, this former Nazi traveled to the Sudan, photographed young Nuba warriors, and published two coffee-table books that became bestsellers. The Germans snapped them up."

Aboagye closed his notebook and put it in his pocket.

Professor Schiff continued, "And I'm willing to bet that those Nuba warriors are now walking the streets of Dusseldorf or Frankfurt with brooms, sweeping the sidewalks. Or pruning bushes in manicured public parks. And if not them, then their children and grandchildren."

"Not that that changes anything," observed Special Investigator Aboagye.

"You're right," said Professor Schiff, "that remark was unnecessary."

42

Ladies and gentlemen:

I've grown accustomed to the tranquil routine here at the villa. To the slow pace. The subjectivity of time. The torpor of the good people who serve me. I've acclimated to the heaviness of the air. The seething life in the quiet beyond the rattling generator. The insects. Sleeping under a mosquito net. The chatter of birds that wakes me every morning. The peculiar taste of the coffee. The fried plantains served at breakfast. The tasteless yam or cassava pastries, and Esther Efua's touching attempts to satisfy my strict vegetarianism. I'm used to calls disconnecting suddenly. The Holiday Inn swimming pool. Meetings with Special Investigator Aboagye. The microphone he attaches to my collar. His notebook. The quibbling. The cynicism. I'm used to being driven to this air-conditioned building you call The Hall of Justice. To standing here on this platform before you.

I've become accustomed to you, ladies and gentlemen, and to your facial expressions, which frequently evince your dislike of me.

Your concern for my emotional state is very touching. Truly.

You asked if I miss my home. Yes, I do. But only in the

technical sense. In other words, I think about my children and my wife, and about Lucile, and one or two friends. I imagine, I daydream, I wonder what they're doing while I'm thinking of them—but not with the aching feeling that comes with homesickness. Nor do I feel any burning need to share my daily events with them.

On my first days here I was constantly taking pictures and sending them home with long, detailed explanations. I was engaged in feverish documentation. Obsessive, even. But all that photographic enthusiasm waned long ago. I still send pictures. Mostly of myself. Mostly alone. At my desk with my laptop open. At the mirror. Lounging in a deck-chair on the balcony, with Fanon's *Wretched of the Earth* open on my lap. But also with the people who are employed to serve me. To protect me. To investigate me. Here I am with Kweku and his Basenji. And here: a group photo in which I am surrounded by the Villa Clark staff next to the concrete statue in the garden. And here: standing awkwardly between two large women, Fatimatu and Esther, with the wonderful wawa tree in the background, at the far edge of the grounds. And here: with Nana, the gardener, my hand reaching for a curious cane rat that approaches me fearlessly. Here I am again: looking askance at a colorful butterfly that landed on Special Investigator George Aboagye's shoulder while he interviewed me in the villa's front vestibule.

Distinguished members of the Special Tribunal, Madam Attorney General, Head of the Investigation Team:

Up until now I have done the best I could to recount the tribulations of Klonimus Zelig Schiff, my great-great-great-great-grandfather, the progenitor of the male dynasty that bore me. But will you allow me to also say something about the other side? About what I inherited from my late mother, the daughter of a Jewish doctor from Berlin? I wish to tell you about my mother not just for the sake of balance, but also so that you will know something about the legacy of immigration on which I was reared from my first day on Earth. This might seem like a digression from the questions at the heart of *The Republic v. Schiff*, but nevertheless, please allow me an effort to arouse a little empathy.

My mother was an immigrant. What sort of immigrant? A perpetual immigrant. An immigrant who never reached her destination, not even years after she supposedly acclimated to her new country. For some people, immigration is a constant state. A process that never ends. Even after fifty, sixty, or seventy years, something remains open. The suitcase. The door. The ticket. Something is never really shut. Not the new language. Not the culture. Not the landscapes that were supposed to replace the backdrops of previous chapters.

This was the case with my mother, the chronic immigrant, who conducted a daily battle with these breached areas of her mind, with the unhealed wounds. There is no other way to explain the transitoriness that dominated her life. For example, her utter disdain for a tidy house. Her profound but unaware contempt for bourgeois trappings, the ones that are always designed to create an illusion of permanence and stability. She had no need for a shiny, well-equipped kitchen. On the contrary: a collection of dented, crooked, burnt pots was quite enough for her. Worthless knickknacks lived side by side with valuable artifacts whose provenance she could not even remember. The furniture was a random assortment in which finely designed tables and bureaus coexisted with tattered chairs and armchairs that she'd acquired accidentally. Clothes and shoes never found their place in the closet. In short, had my mother ever been forced to leave her home in the middle of the night, she would not have missed a single object. Not one.

She did not even have a room of her own. In every apartment we lived in, she always made do with some corner where she would shove a folding bed or foldout couch, and that was where she slept, supported by a tower of cushions, half-lying half-sitting, as if ready to pounce the second there was a knock at the door.

Yes, I can hear your question. And the answer? No, they did not sleep together, my parents. Was that customary in my country in that era? No. It was not. Married couples at the time did consummate their unions in a shared bed. As a child, all the homes I visited had a door that was always closed, a mysterious sanctum in which the father and mother barricaded themselves. But not in my home. Not at the Schiffs'. Professor Schiff's parents did not share a room. Certainly not a bed. And how could they? A bed is supposed to be a safe haven. A shelter. How could Professor Schiff's father curl up every night with a perpetual immigrant, for whom the only constant was her longing for a distant land?

Yes, I heard that comment, too. Of course they did share a bed at least once. And, if you must know, twice. I have a sister.

But it's true, it's absolutely true. You're right. My father himself was also the son of immigrants. And you've collected enough data about the Schiff lineage and the axes of its travels around the world for the past two and a half centuries. Nevertheless, my father liked to boast of his roots in the new country. These roots were, admittedly, very shallow, but it turns out that his birth in a geographical region adopted by his forefathers did give him a clear superiority. In every respect. And do you know what I think? I think he always chose women who were perpetual immigrants (my mother was not the first) so that his status as a native resident would never be in doubt.

Did the ruse work? Interesting question. All I can say, ladies and gentlemen, is that for almost forty years the man barely left home. Make of that what you will.

But wait, I wasn't planning to talk about the slave trader's great-great-grandson. It's my mother I wanted to tell you about. The chronic immigrant who was afraid of policemen and uniform wearers in general. The woman who kept gold bars in a secret hiding place. Who always kept a window open. Who adopted the voice and cadence of a little girl.

"Don't stay here," she told me over and over again. "Don't stay, Aguri. Leave. There are other places." But in fact, she wanted so badly for me to stay. At least at a distance from which I could easily come home for Saturday lunch.

Well, I've told you everything I wanted to. Now, as I once again see the confusion on your faces, ladies and gentlemen, I slightly regret trying to soften you up with this schmaltz. Feel free to strike the last section from the transcript.

43

The time had come, once again, for the periodic treatment of Grandpa Morduch's ailing eye. The task of accompanying him to the hospital had long ago been redelegated from Professor Schiff to the caregiver and future bride, Lucile, but this time Morduch specifically asked Professor Schiff to take him. He didn't bother explaining why, and Professor Schiff didn't ask. In these strange times at the Kushner-Schiff household, it was easier to simply give in to whims rather than investigate their reason. And since, in his mind, he'd already marked Morduch as the enemy, it's possible that what made him agree so easily to the odious job was his guilty conscience.

On the surface, there was no reason for the task to be so tedious and torturous. The treatment itself usually lasted less than half an hour, including the time spent waiting at the doctor's office. But Morduch viewed these hospital visits as merely an excuse to spend a morning wallowing in a human commotion while stuffing himself with sugar and watching, enchanted, as people went about their frantic consumerism. (Apart from being a place of healing, births, and deaths, the hospital in central Tel Aviv also serves as an entertainment venue, with cafes, ice cream stands, a chocolate boutique, stands hawking computer games and toys, a cellphone vendor, a pharmacy, and of course, a lottery kiosk. Yes, in places like these people tend to test more than one aspect of their luck.)

Professor Schiff was expecting the visit to follow the usual procedure: after the treatment, they would sit down at the cafeteria in the maternity ward, and he would have to watch Morduch devour a double slice of cremeschnitten torte, wolf down some baklava, sip a glass of lemonade, and finish off with an enormous serving of ice cream topped with whipped cream. But Morduch had other ideas. "Today," he announced, "we're going somewhere special. A place that has special meaning to me."

It had never occurred to Professor Schiff that Morduch would drag him to south Tel Aviv, and not just that but to an eatery that provided sugar only in tiny baggies, minute portions that could never satisfy an addict like Morduch. But of course, there was a reason for their visit to this remote and somewhat sad location, where the dirty blades of an electric fan chased the hot winds around.

"Here," Morduch ceremoniously informed Professor Schiff, "roughly where that refrigerator case with the sandwiches stands now, on May 19, 1969, I proposed to the late Dora, your Tami's grandmother."

And so Professor Schiff found himself in the heart of this historic site, where Mordechai Shtil, also known as Morduch, had captured his position in the Kushner family. Professor Schiff remembered that long ago, in the sixties, this had been considered an upscale patisserie, but when he looked around he had trouble reconciling the place's shabbiness with its former glory.

"I have some important things to say to you, Aguri," said Morduch, "man to man. But I trust you to convey the relevant details to Tami."

Professor Schiff scooted his chair closer until their faces were almost touching.

"I'm sure you and Tami are asking yourselves what the meaning of all this is. How your Grandpa Morduch, after all these years, can suddenly meet a woman, and not just any woman but someone sixty years younger than him, and a *schvartze*—"

"We don't say *schvartze* anymore, Morduch."

Morduch tilted his enormous ear toward Professor Schiff and tapped his hearing aid.

"We don't say *schvartze*!" Professor Schiff repeated at a volume that made the other patrons—yes, there were others—turn around curiously.

"Why not? I just said it."

"Yes, but it's derogative. It's an offensive word."

"Offensive? Seriously! She's about to become my wife. And if she's offended by me calling her a *schvartze*, she can call me an old codger. It doesn't bother me. Labels don't bother me. On the contrary, they help us be precise."

Yes, thought Professor Schiff, there was some sense in what he was saying.

"Now please listen to me, Aguri," Morduch grumbled, "and don't interrupt me with commentary."

Professor Schiff raised his hands in surrender.

Morduch nodded gravely and went on. “So, as I said, there are some things I need to explain, or at least that’s how I feel, because you’ve never asked, and we haven’t talked, and it all happened rather quickly.” He put his hand on Professor Schiff’s knee. “Matters of love cannot and should not be explained. But you see, that mechanism doesn’t go away when you age. It’s an ember that never goes out. And if you’re asking yourself what about the . . . you know . . . the energy down there . . . the libido, or whatever it’s called . . . Okay, I understand the curiosity, but that’s not the point at all. What’s really relevant, what really matters, is that once the grand finale arrives, no one wants to be alone.”

The grand finale . . . Strange, thought Professor Schiff. How foreign this term was to Grandpa Morduch’s discourse. Any talk of death, even vague hints, had always been taboo for him. Existential pornography. A vulgarity not to be uttered out loud. For example, when Professor Schiff had to have stents placed in his coronary arteries, not a single word of commiseration or comfort came from Morduch. When Professor Schiff’s mother died, Morduch ignored it. In fact, he kept sending his regards to her for a decade before acknowledging her nonexistence. In short, Grandpa Morduch had completely censored death. And perhaps it was *that*, not the sugar, that was the secret to his longevity.

“But, Aguri, that’s not what I want to talk to you about. Not the grand finale. This is no time for philosophizing. I want to talk to you about something completely different.”

He stirred his weak coffee round and round, and before each rotation he tore open a packet and poured it into the frothy liquid. "You've known me for decades, I can't even remember how many. Add fifteen years to that and you'll get the time I've known Tami, my beloved granddaughter. And after all these years, what do you know about me? Yes, of course you know that I lived in Africa for a while and did business there. I collected objects—they're all boxed up now, thanks to Lucile—and I collected stories. But not the stories you know. Those ones, I made up to entertain you. I've never told the truth. And do you know why? Because there was nothing funny in Africa. Not in the Africa I knew. In the Africa where I did business. That, of course, began when I was a diplomat. That's when I started mediating and peddling. I made a lot of money. But that was just a prelude to the really good years. Good in the financial sense, of course. But you know what, Aguri? I don't need to elaborate. I'll only tell you that the goods I sold were landmines. That was my specialty. Antipersonnel mines. Foot-activated mines. I bought them from various suppliers around the world and sold them to any buyer in Africa. And there were a lot of buyers in those days. My landmines were a continuous hit, and I was raking it in, as they say. But then I got malaria and came home."

So, his and Tami's guess was right, thought Professor Schiff. How dreadful. How he wished they'd been wrong. True, they'd never questioned Morduch about his past, because that was convenient for them. But could they now turn the not-knowing into an indifferent shrug? And after all these years, how much was that self-justification worth? How could they make peace with knowing that the capital that had sustained the Schiff-Kushners and was supposed to ensure their wealth for perpetuity had come from killing machines?

"So now you understand everything, Aguri," Morduch continued, "but I still want to give you the bottom line. Thousands of people lost limbs because of me. The vast majority were innocent bystanders. Civilians. At least a quarter of them were children. In fact, to this day Africans continue to be hit by Mordechai Shtil's landmines. So that's what I'm confessing to now. That's what you didn't know about me, about your Grandpa Morduch."

At least now there was a reason for Professor Schiff's recent resentment of his benefactor. A solid, valid reason. A moral reason. At least Professor Schiff could take some comfort in that.

"So now I'm getting to the point. Now I will tell you what happened to all the money, where Grandpa's fortune went . . . "

The point? Professor Schiff wondered. Where else could this confession be going? He had no desire to know what the hundreds of thousands, the millions, had been spent on, or when and how the bank accounts had evaporated. No desire at all.

Morduch's large hand, which had rested on Professor Schiff's knee as a token of friendliness, was now irritably and awkwardly mussing his thick, white hair. "Here is the answer.

Everything I had, all of it—and I really did have a very great deal, you know that—I donated to an international organization that provides artificial limbs for landmine casualties. That was the decent thing to do, the logical thing to do, and I did it wholeheartedly. Because I knew that's what you would want, too." His blue eyes, sunken inside folds of skin, scanned the cafe. "And that's what Dora, may her memory be for a blessing, would have wanted me to do."

He took out a bill, folded it, and tucked it under the coffee cup. "She didn't know how I got rich, either. She didn't know anything. Because I was ashamed to tell her. At least I can say that in my defense. At least that." He leaned on Professor Schiff's arm and stood up. "All right, let's get out of this place. I feel like something sweet."

44

Ladies and gentlemen, members of the Special Tribunal, Madam Attorney General, Head of the Investigation Team:

At this point I was planning to provide you with the salient points of Grandpa Schiff's curriculum vitae. Something along the lines of: In 1790, at age twenty-five, Klonimus Zelig arrives in Paramaribo, Suriname, as the representative of the family bank founded by his uncle in Frankfurt. In 1794, he starts a sugar export agency. In 1797, he buys his first ship, adopts the name Schiff, and marries Esperanza, née Levi . . .

Well, you get the idea. And although there were a few interesting details in the summary I prepared (for example, initiating the first kosher rum distillery in the world; contending with a rise in insurance costs due to increased piracy in the Caribbean; attempts to evade the ban on bringing slaves from Africa), on the whole this outline turned out to be very dull material. Which is no wonder, because when you condense a person's life into a few paragraphs covering commerce and the accumulation of wealth, it exposes the futility of such a life. Of course, when one lives it, it is full of interest and intrigue. It's only the summary—the damn summary, which always seems to become necessary at some point—that damages the appearance of it all.

Anyway, ladies and gentlemen, I have decided to spare you the bother and skip ahead to 1829, the year in which, after thirty-five years of activity, Klonimus Schiff retires from his business and transfers his fortune to his three daughters and young son. And it's important to note—again, for the sake of factual accuracy—that by the time the idea of leaving has taken seed in Klonimus's mind, he has essentially exhausted all the capitalist opportunities offered by his adopted country of Suriname, and is ready to begin a new chapter. In other words, circumstances provided him with the perfect timing to launch what today we would call a "second career." And, as we know, he made a bold and original decision in choosing to become a national leader.

I say this, however, with no mockery or judgement. Because I myself, having just reached the exact age of Klonimus when he led his small congregation to Africa, am looking for my own "new chapter." In our world, aging writers can possibly take out a loan and open a cafe. I considered doing that. A cafe where there would be no loud music. Nothing but Bach. A quiet place. A place where writers who have yet to open their "new chapter" can write the previous ones.

We left Klonimus Zelig Schiff laughing joyously in his cabin on the *Esperanza* as it swayed in an unidentified bay opposite an unidentified fortress, somewhere on the golden coast of West Africa.

In this happy scene, Schiff is almost sixty-four, the leader of a small but loyal congregation of men, women, and children, all of whom he freed from slavery but enslaved to his national vision. He is the husband of a young woman with whom he is in love beyond all description, explanation, or formulation. And he is the father of a newborn girl. These three states of existence perfectly encompass the new chapter in his life. As a community leader, he is atoning for three decades of trading in human beings and working them to death. As a loving husband, he is rediscovering the emotionality that had seeped out of him and left him hollow. As a new father, he is renewing his own youth.

Oh, how wonderful! This aging man has halted his decline down the slippery slope of old age, a slope that becomes increasingly steep with every passing day. And indeed, in a portrait done at the time, one can clearly see the ecstasy on Klonimus Zelig Schiff's face. Among the watercolors rendered by Witte Voetjes that survived alongside the diary pages, the man can be seen with a shimmering glint in his eyes.

I apologize, ladies and gentlemen. I am aware of how trite that sounds. A glint? What glint? What are you babbling about, Professor? Fortunately for me, however, that portrait is among the artifacts submitted for your review. Here, see for yourselves. Does not this man with the wild beard and the peculiar blend of top hat and sailors cap perched atop his white curls look ecstatic? Is there not an impassioned blaze flickering in his eyes as they gaze out at you?

Incidentally, have you noticed the words scribbled on the margins of the portrait? Read them, please. Do you know what those strange, impenetrable words mean? They are potential names for the new colony that was about to be founded on the African shore: Schiffhafen, Schiffburg, Schiffbay... Klonimusstadt, Klonimusville...You see, it's not by chance that these names are scrawled around the portrait of the man who invented them. I can imagine my great-great-great-great-grandfather holding the artwork, staring at his own likeness, amusing himself with the notion of being commemorated—the founding father, visionary of the slave state—by naming the new colony after himself. I would have been happy if there were one tiny spot on the globe that bore the name Schiff. Yes, it could have been amusing. I wouldn't have cared where it was. Africa would certainly do.

If you look in the corner of the portrait, you'll see the name he eventually chose. There it is, circled: Port Esperanza.

Klonimus Schiff stood on deck waiting for the sun to rise. Fires flickered on shore. The water was colored in shades of pink. The lamp in the lighthouse at the edge of the bay grew slowly dimmer. Orange clouds dragged behind the rising sun.

Captain de Groot leaned on the railing next to Schiff. He took the lit pipe out of his mouth and offered it wordlessly. Schiff's polite refusal was also silent. The rising sun, usually a celebratory occurrence, made him impatient. De Groot put the pipe back in his mouth, and instead offered Schiff the telescope.

Schiff ran the lens across the small port coming to life. Among the dinghies, small sailboats, fishing boats, and two schooners anchored some distance from the pier, he tried to locate *their* boat, the one that had been dispatched from the *Esperanza* two days earlier with the official anchoring request and requisite certificates. Where had First Mate Munk and the two sailors disappeared to? Had their boat gone down in the storm?

Eventually, Klonimus Schiff—the man who let nothing stand in his way besides the turbulent sea—decided he had no choice but to sail to shore himself. He asked de Groot to prepare the second boat. Then he woke Witte Voetjes and Lot Met-Zonder, his faithful assistants, recited the morning prayers with them, and returned to deck.

"Everything is ready, sir," said the captain.

Schiff pulled out his pocket watch and examined his reflection in the gold cover. "I am ready as well," he said. His huge beard was neatly combed. The edges of his moustache had been shaped and waxed. On his sparse white hair, perched at an angle, was a felt tricorn that might have struck the residents of these parts as slightly old-fashioned. It was hard to know. Fads could trickle to even the farthest reaches of the conservative world. Did Africans, for example, still wear powdered wigs, or had that puzzling accessory been abandoned here, too? Schiff considered requesting sartorial advice from Captain de Groot, who was surely better informed then he was, but the etiquette prevented him from asking such intimate questions of someone below him in rank. He therefore had to assume that a handkerchief tied around one's neck was still an acceptable adornment in this part of the world, and that the green (and, in his opinion, extremely festive) jacket, from which a frilly shirt collar emerged, would not give away his provincialism. To be on the safe side, he pinned to his chest a few shiny badges of honor that he'd received from colleagues in Suriname.

In the bag carried for him by Witte Voetjes were a few important papers (including the ceremonial declaration, "*His Majesty's government views with favor . . .*" and so forth, from the Office of the Overseer of Dutch Assets in Africa), a case containing twenty gold guineas (should bribery became necessary), and an old flintlock pistol (in case he needed to threaten anyone).

By the time they departed, it had started raining, and the boat's passengers—Klonimus Schiff in his outmoded gentleman's outfit, Witte Voetjes in his own finest garb (including a wig, which he insisted on, for his own reasons), Lot Met-Zonder, and the two sailors who rowed the boat—were drenched. I assume their appearance did little for the pomp and circumstance deemed so essential by Klonimus Schiff for his first steps on the shores of Africa. He and his entourage looked pitiful. But the people standing silently on the pier were not at their best, either: half-naked laborers whose ribcages threatened to burst through their skin, servant children carrying umbrellas, soldiers in blue uniforms with brass buttons and blunderbuss rifles dripping with water slung over their shoulders like farmers' tools, all standing on the rickety wooden jetty as if for a grotesque welcome ceremony.

But as soon as the boat touched the pier, the soldiers started yelling and waving their arms. All Klonimus could make out amid the uproar of shouts was "No!" and "Forbidden!" One of them put his rifle up to his shoulder and aimed it at the boat.

Klonimus Schiff addressed the person he presumed had the most senior rank, perhaps because he was strikingly tall and was the only one wearing a cape. "I am Klonimus Zelig Schiff, commander of the *Esperanza*. I hold a request for anchor, and a letter signed by The Honorable Colonel List—"

"No entry!" the caped man interrupted. "Sick people here. The port is under quarantine."

"I fear I must insist," said Schiff.

"The port is under quarantine, sir," repeated the cape owner.

"I must meet with the commander."

"The commander is very sick."

"In that case, with his second-in-command, or whoever stands in his place." He felt it was time to use the coins. And indeed, when the man spotted the metal glimmering in Schiff's hand, he motioned for his workers to tie the boat to the pier and ordered the soldiers to clear the ramp to shore.

And then, finally, Klonimus Schiff set foot on the soil of Africa.

It was muddy, sticky soil, in which the rain had carved deep channels. Had his trousers not been drenched, Klonimus Schiff would have certainly bent down to kiss the ground and risked dipping his beard in the mud. Instead of this gesture, which of course was almost a requirement for someone who had brought himself to a sort of promised land, he made do with a prayer. "*Baruch ata adonai, eloheinu melech ha'olam,*" Schiff recited, with his eyes closed and with great intent. "Blessed art Thou, our Lord, who has granted us life and sustained us, and brought us to this time." From behind his wet shoulders, he was answered by two hoarse voices: "Amen."

The five men were led to a hut that housed the port office and apparently also served as an occasional inn where visitors could undress, dry their clothes at the fire, and sip some gin.

No one rushed the visitors. Matters proceeded here sedately, as though the formalities were simply part of the homey atmosphere. Like the smell of tobacco smoke. Like the bubbling samovar. Like the hunched servant in her apron, who draped the guests' wet coats over the backs of three chairs she moved in front of the fireplace.

The man who introduced himself as deputy commander of the port sat down at an ornate desk. Two crossed flags hung behind him. He spread out the papers Schiff handed him and studied them at length. Then he dipped a feather in ink and began writing his own document. He wrote slowly. Meticulously. With the effort of a diligent student.

It was all so quiet. Sleepy. Even the monotonous noise of the rain was pleasingly serene. Not a word was uttered. And then, through the doorway, Witte Voetjes eyed a cart drawn by two donkeys. The cart was piled with corpses.

Witte Voetjes tugged at Schiff's sleeve. "Rabbi, sir . . . " he said and pointed outside.

Schiff turned to look. He had seen dead people before, occasionally as a result of his own commands, but he had never seen them led away in a heap like refuse from a slaughterhouse.

The deputy commander added his looped signature to the paper, folded the corner, dripped wax on it, and pressed an iron seal into the wax. "Well then," he said, and when he looked up he noticed the startled expressions of the elderly gentleman and the dark-skinned young man.

The cart of cadavers was gone, but the deputy commander understood.

"Plague," he said, and crossed himself.

45

"Professor Schiff," said Special Investigator George Aboagye, "if you claim to love us so much, then go ahead and join us. Yes, come and join humanity's eternally degraded."

"I'm up for it," said Professor Schiff. "How do I join? What's the procedure?"

"Let me think . . . In order to become African you do not have to undergo any conversion ceremony, nor fill out any forms or pass a test. The problem is that you . . . How do I put this delicately . . . you don't look quite right. However, while you may not have the correct color and features—which is a problem that will be hard to get around—you do have that chronic chip on your shoulder, and you are in a sort of permanent conflict with the world. And those traits certainly make you one of us."

"But if that's the case, maybe I should settle for being part of the Jewish people?" Professor Schiff mused out loud.

As always, Special Investigator George Aboagye had arrived unannounced. Except that this time, he invited Professor Schiff to join him on a drive, and Professor Schiff obediently followed him to the official car—an extremely ostentatious hunk of metal that was an affront to good taste.

Professor Schiff assumed Aboagye was taking him on an educational tour. He knew how important it was to the special investigator to challenge his ignorance regarding this country and its culture. But Aboagye, as befitting a man who was both historian and lawyer, divulged the true purpose of the excursion only gradually and in reverse order.

"I have bad news and good news, Professor. Which would you like first?"

"The bad news," Professor Schiff answered without hesitation.

They were sitting next to each other on the back seat, inching through the usual afternoon traffic. Professor Schiff was trying to guess where they were going and why, or whether they would ever get anywhere at all.

"So here's the bad news. Ready?"

Professor Schiff nodded.

"The parliament of a certain neighboring country has recently passed an identical law to our own."

"It's starting to look like a fad all over this part of the continent," Professor Schiff observed.

"Fad or not, the point is that yesterday the attorney general's office received an extradition request from this neighboring country."

"Extradition? Of whom?" From the corner of his eye Professor Schiff could see Aboagye scrutinizing his reaction.

"Of you. They want you."

"Why can't they find their own slave trader descendent?" Professor Schiff snapped. He'd never had much patience for unoriginality. Two-bit plagiarizers of this kind disgusted him.

"I'll explain, Professor Schiff. It's all a matter of foreign relations. There is no extradition agreement between us and this country. Now, one of our biggest criminals—the former CEO of the national oil company, who stole public funds for years and also took bribes—was arrested there, at our request, and his passport was confiscated. But they're only willing to extradite him if they get something equivalent in return. You know, one must keep the scales balanced." Aboagye shifted so that it would be easier for him to lecture Professor Schiff. "Anyway, our side, meaning the Ministry of Justice, came up with a fair exchange. Your name was mentioned as a possibility. Our neighbors considered it and concluded that it's worth discussing."

Professor Schiff was astonished. "*Me* in return for a thief?" he spluttered. "You're giving me up for a common thief?"

"If I were you, I would not take things so personally, Professor."

"But what about the historical importance? The national value? The educational principle? And all that long testimony? And the media? And the glass booth?"

"Yes, the whole business is extremely embarrassing," Aboagye conceded, "and, as you can imagine, I personally was vehemently opposed. But I'm sure you will not be surprised to learn that there are some people on the upper floors who are growing a little tired of this whole affair."

"But why didn't anyone ask me? Don't I have a say?"

"You're right, Professor, I'm with you one hundred percent."

"Didn't I make an emotional investment? Didn't I sit in that lousy villa for five weeks waiting—yes, waiting with bated breath—for a decision?" asked Professor Schiff bitterly.

"I thought you liked the villa." Aboagye dug through his jacket pocket, took out a packet of peanuts, tore it open, and offered some to Professor Schiff. "By the way, I forgot to mention," he continued coolly, "that one difference between our law and the neighboring state's is that theirs stipulates capital punishment."

Professor Schiff moved his gaze to the window. He chomped violently on the tiny peanuts and bit his lip. After a few more minutes of moving slowly through the traffic jam, he dared to ask, "What's the good news?"

"Ah, well, the good news is this," said Special Investigator George Aboagye in a dryly official tone, "upon the recommendation of His Excellency President Vincent Matu Ayeh, the parliamentary committee for ceremonies and honors has decided to award you the Friend of Africa medal, as well as honorary citizenship in the Republic. The decision was passed unanimously. Congratulations."

Professor Schiff stared at him in disbelief. He was expecting to see at least a shadow of the familiar sardonic smile, but Aboagye maintained his vacant expression, with the only movement being his jaw moving slowly up and down as he munched the peanuts. Eventually, Professor Schiff managed to convince himself that Aboagye was not poking fun at him.

"A medal?" he mumbled. "'Friend of Africa?'"

"I was also asked to inform you that the decision will have no effect on your legal status and the tribunal sessions will continue as usual," said Aboagye with a mouth full of peanuts.

The crawling convoy came to a standstill. Then it suddenly started moving, sped up, and stopped again. Professor Schiff felt nauseous. "So where are we actually going?" he asked.

"To parliament. To receive the medal."

Forty minutes later, the car circled Republic Square, and through the front window, over the driver's head, they could see the domed roof of the parliament building and the four-colored flag languishing atop a flagpole. They drove along a boulevard of palm trees, slowed down ceremoniously, and stopped at a barricade. An armored vehicle was parked next to a checkpoint manned by soldiers in berets.

George Aboagye held up his invitation to the event and showed it to the soldier who leaned in at the window. On the other side of the vehicle, another soldier scrutinized Professor Schiff's bearded face and compared it to his passport picture. He waved them through, and they coasted along the boulevard to the marble path leading to a columned vestibule outside the building, where two women in blue uniforms popped out of nowhere and walked up to the car. One opened the door for Professor Schiff and the other for Special Investigator Aboagye.

Professor Schiff's head was spinning. He was exhausted by the long drive and confused by the conversation. He stretched his legs and filled his lungs with the warm evening air. Then, troubled and weary, he walked next to Aboagye up the wide staircase leading to the parliament building. They walked through a security checkpoint, showed their papers again, walked through a glass door, then another, took things out of their pockets, picked them up on the other side, and then, once they were in a large hall adorned with colorful wall hangings and bronze sculptures depicting idyllic scenes of tribal life, a rotund man walked up to Professor Schiff and blocked his way. "Excuse me, sir, I will have to ask that you leave," he said. He put a walkie-talkie to his cheek, mumbled a short command into it, and within seconds an armed security guard in military uniform appeared and grabbed Professor Schiff by the arm. He might have been a celebrity, but no one recognized him here. The man continued, "You are dressed inappropriately, sir, to say the least. Your attire is an insult to the dignity of the parliament; it demeans the legislature's status and disrupts public order. I must therefore ask you to leave the site immediately."

It should be noted that Professor Schiff had arrived at the important event wearing his usual professorial attire: jeans, black T-shirt, and not very new sneakers. But the truth is that even had he been aware of the occasion ahead of time, he couldn't have dressed according to the required standard because he did not now and had never owned any finer clothes, certainly not a formal wardrobe of suits and ties.

Aboagye, who had walked ahead, came back. "We're together," he said, "for the event in the auditorium. I'm from the Ministry of Justice." He dug through his pocket, took out the crumpled paper he'd showed the soldiers earlier, and waved it in the rotund man's face. The paper was embellished with the green and red of the Republic's emblem. "Here, we have an invitation."

The man snatched the paper and ripped it. "Now you don't," he said, and turned his back.

The security guard walked them to a side entrance. Aboagye phoned the driver, and a few moments later the car arrived and collected them into its luxurious embrace.

"So, do you still believe Africans walk around naked, Professor?" asked Aboagye.

Professor Schiff said nothing. Not only was he forced to confess the sin of haughtiness (his shabby clothes were not a sign of modesty in this case, but quite the opposite), but he'd also proved that he was unworthy of becoming an honorary citizen of the Republic. Much less a friend of Africa. For it was unacceptable to wear an emblem of friendship on a faded T-shirt. Simply unacceptable. Not here.

The disappointment, the insult, and the shame had stolen his capacity for speech. He wanted to turn into an insect, fly out the window, and vanish into the viscous air of the tropical evening.

Later that night, sitting alone on the veranda watching the almost-full moon extricate itself from the clouds, Professor Schiff thought its flattened face was sending him a message of fraternity: two whites in Africa.

46

Oh, Lucile!

Just as suddenly and grandiosely as she had burst into Professor Schiff's life, so she left it. Although this time, there was also heartbreak. This is how things unfolded:

Informing on Felix Ofosu—a simple, fast, discreet procedure, one fell swoop like a kosher slaughter, intended to sink into the annals of history without a trace (apart from that crumpled postcard with the elephants)—turned into one dramatic segment in a tragic chain of events. Because, having apprehended the husband, the immigration authorities tracked down the wife: Mrs. Lucile Tetteh-Ofosu.

One Saturday morning, policemen knocked on Mordechai Shtil's door, and Mrs. Tetteh-Ofosu was asked to pack up her belongings and accompany them to the detention center. Morduch was frantic. He was convinced there'd been a case of mistaken identity, but of course his attempts to persuade the officers that the lady was his fiancée, meaning his future bride, and in fact, his very-near-future bride, were unsuccessful. The police had no doubt that the old man was making a fool of them. Or of himself. As on previous occasions, the assumption that a wrinkled face indicates an infirm mind precluded any fair evaluation of the facts. Moreover,

Morduch's unruly behavior, or rather his violent outburst, proved to the officers that he was indeed suffering from dementia. He pulled out a gun—yes, a gun! No one knew he'd been keeping an old Parabellum pistol at the bottom of his bathroom cabinet. Grasping the cocked weapon in his shaking hand, he threatened he would shoot to kill if they didn't let his fiancée go and leave the premises immediately.

The policemen laughed. They literally laughed, as if they were watching a staged prank. Morduch lost his wits and fired the pistol. Pieces of plaster fell from the ceiling and crumbled on the policemen's shoulders. He fired again. One of the two officers leaped on him and pinned back his arms. Another bullet was fired when Morduch dropped the gun. The officer was startled. He pushed Morduch, knocked him to the floor, and put his knee to the old man's neck. In the silence that followed, the only sound was the feeble beeping of an alarm clock in the other room.

"He's dead," said Lucile.

"Dead? But I barely touched him!" said the policeman.

"Dead," Lucile repeated, and tears filled her heavy-lidded eyes and rolled down her round face that seemed to have been sketched with a compass.

The second policeman lifted Morduch's limp hand, checked his pulse, and confirmed that the man was dead.

"But he was pretty old anyway," said the first policeman. "How old was he?"

"A hundred and four," Lucile spluttered through her tears.

"Oh well." The officer stood up and brushed off his pants.

Morduch's death did not prevent Lucile's arrest; it merely delayed it by an hour and a half. When the ambulance drove away with Morduch's body strapped to an orange stretcher, so did the police van with Lucile Tetteh-Ofosu in the back seat.

It took time, too much time, before Professor Schiff found out about the incident.

On the morning when Morduch was buried in the reserved plot next to Grandma Dora, Professor Schiff was dashing around Tel Aviv's detention centers with Attorney Melchior. He was equipped with an injunction issued by a judge, a checkbook, and a bundle of cash, but he could not find Lucile Tetteh-Ofosu. Not that morning, nor the next. Nor on the day after, or any other day. And not a single official, policeman, or administrator knew where she'd been taken or where she was being held.

Professor Schiff mourned. Yes, he sank into an angry and frustrated bereavement. But even in his grief he did not lose hope that one day Lucile Tetteh-Ofosu would reappear, without any warning, miraculously, magically, regally—just as she had done the first time.

And then Professor Schiff went to Africa.

47

The sky after midnight was clear, but over the beach the darkness was tarnished with smoke from dying fires. Professor Schiff marched obediently behind Luther, the presidential secretary. Luther carried a large backpack, the kind usually used by young hikers, and Professor Schiff did his best to keep up with the silhouette of the backpack and place his feet precisely where Luther stepped, to avoid the potholes and obstacles on the way. Interesting, he thought: Luther's assertive steps bore no resemblance to the gait of the man he had last seen wearing a stiff suit and tie in the national colors, dancing around the president in an unnamed village's square. When was that? When had that wondrous helicopter flight "to get to know the African soul" occurred? So much time seemed to have passed.

They took a flight of steps from the neglected concrete promenade down to the beach. The sea at the foot of the white fort—the slave castle—chased little waves to the wooden piers closing in on the bay. Long dinghies with their noses lodged in the sand absorbed the water's motion with moans and creaks. A floodlight swiveled from somewhere in the distance, exposing the colorful pictures on the sides of boats setting out for nocturnal fishing trips, and quickly made them disappear again.

Young men and women were sitting in a circle drumming with their hands on plastic buckets and cans. Among the tin shacks, under lengths of fabric or shelters made of palm branches, people slept: children close to their tired mothers, hardworking men with limbs askew, babies in cradles improvised from cardboard boxes. Dogs scratched themselves. Goats munched. Roosters crowed at each other from either end of the bay in regular half-hour intervals. Flags, rags, laundry, and fish hung on lines stretched out between poles and masts.

Professor Schiff and Luther crossed the crowded fishing village without arousing much attention, probably because it was so late at night, but also thanks to their clothes. Luther had insisted that Professor Schiff wear a black beanie and pull his shirt up to his nose to hide his white beard. The heat was intolerable, and as soon as they were past the piers and the row of warehouses, Professor Schiff freed his face from the disguise.

Beyond the eastern tongue of the bay, the port lights twinkled. On the closer hilltops, the wealthy neighborhoods' homes were lit up with white beams meant to keep away the less fortunate. Farther away, in the center of town, the presidential palace glistened with thousands of lights, and to the men walking on the beach it looked like wonderful, strange diamond-studded jewelry. Behind them was the white fort, also bisected by floodlights, and Professor Schiff thought he could feel the warmth of those beams on the back of his neck.

They padded among dead fish, piles of rolled-up nets, and trash, until they reached a wooden structure with its back on the slope and its front supported by stilts. Luther signaled for Professor Schiff to stop. Professor Schiff obeyed. They waited. And then, out of the darkness, from between the decaying wood posts, emerged a heavyset figure who resembled President Ayeh in every way except his black clothes and black cap. But indeed, it was Vincent Matu Ayeh. He and none other.

"Your Excellency!" exclaimed Professor Schiff.

"I wanted to bid farewell to you, Prof," said Ayeh, who had not been the president for almost forty-eight hours. "I'm leaving tonight, probably forever."

"I'm moved," said Professor Schiff, very genuinely.

"I am, too. And sad."

"That's understandable, Your Excellency," Professor Schiff said.

"Please, you can call me Vincent now. I have to get used to it. In fact, Prof, I wanted to take this chance to tell you that your visit here was very important to us. We learned a lot from you. And personally, I not only enjoyed our conversations, but I've also been inspired by you."

He looked thinner, although he couldn't have lost much weight since being deposed in a military coup two days earlier. His face was bruised. A streak of congealed blood on his forehead was clearly visible even in the dark.

Ayeh noticed Professor Schiff's worried look. "Oh, it's nothing, Prof. Really, don't worry." He flashed a toothy grin. "Just a silly fall down the stairs." The former president touched his wound gingerly. "I must admit that there was no real violence. Not against me and not against anyone else. Everything was conducted with perfect order and relatively peacefully. No shots were fired and nothing was destroyed. To General Kossi's credit, I must say that he organized this coup in the cleanest possible way."

Ayeh started marching toward the port lights and signaled for Professor Schiff to walk by his side. Luther followed at some distance, with the backpack.

"You have a mission, Prof," said Ayeh, "you're doing an important public service for this country. There's a reason I recommended you for the Friend of Africa medal and honorary citizenship. There's a reason. Thanks to you, we can have an orgy with our ghosts and thereby forget the present, which is—now I can admit this—rather disappointing most of the time." As he walked heavily, lurching from side to side, Ayeh put his hand on Professor Schiff's shoulder in a show of friendliness. "You know, Prof, I was president for seven years—a relatively short term by African standards, by the way—and until you landed here, with your grandfather's grandfather's grandfather, I did not understand how important the past is and what a useful resource it can be. A charge sheet, an excuse for failures, an existential reason . . ." He stopped, looked into Professor Schiff's sweaty face, and said, "If by any chance you put me in your book, please try to be fair."

They walked on silently for a few minutes, until a light suddenly began to flicker out at sea.

"Right on time," said Luther. He responded to the flashing light with his cellphone. And then they heard a rattle, which grew louder and louder, until a small motorboat emerged from the blue darkness. A blurry figure waved.

Like in an old spy movie, thought Professor Schiff. Even the intrigues in this country have a romantic quality and the sweetness of nostalgic drama.

"What are your plans now, Your Excellency?" asked Professor Schiff.

"Clementine is waiting across the border. We're booked on a flight to Europe. I myself don't know exactly what the destination is. But don't worry about us, Prof, we'll be fine. We have enough. More than enough. I don't need to look for a job coaching girls' soccer in some godforsaken place like Tel Aviv." He patted Professor Schiff's arm and laughed. "I read your mind, Prof, didn't I?"

Luther removed the large backpack and, once again, as he had that day on their waterfall excursion, he knelt down, untied the former president's shoelaces, and removed the shoes from his feet.

"Yes, I made sure we had retirement funds," Ayeh went on, "enough to live an immigrants' life, far from the homeland, far from Africa. I prepared myself for the worst-case scenario. But I know full well that money, even a lot of money, can never make up for homesickness."

Vincent Ayeh bent over with some difficulty, reached out beyond his belly, and slowly rolled up his pants. Then he swung the backpack over his broad shoulders. "The new president, Rupert Kossi, allowed me to leave on condition that I do not come back for the next twenty years."

He shook Professor Schiff's hand and then Luther's, who held out his shoes.

"Don't forget to send us your book, Prof. With a dedication," Ayeh said as he waded into the water and made his way to the rocking boat.

"Of course, Vincent, of course," shouted Professor Schiff to the figure padding heavily through the frothy waves. "Good luck, and my best to Mrs. Ayeh!"

Luther and Professor Schiff headed back along the waterline. The light from the fort showed them the way. They walked in contemplative silence, each with a heavy heart for his own reasons. When Professor Schiff looked back, hoping to see the motorboat carrying away the former president, he saw only their own footprints in the raked, glistening sand, which was nothing but pulverized seashells.

When they passed the structure on stilts where they'd met Ayeh, Professor Schiff remembered the backpack. He'd been curious from the start. "Excuse me, Mr. Luther, would you mind if I asked you a question?"

"Go ahead."

"What was in the backpack you gave the former president?"

"That's a personal matter. I think it would be unprofessional of me to tell you."

"Money? Diamonds? Gold? Jewelry?"

"No, certainly not."

"Luther, the president's gone, he's fled and he won't be back soon. Your association with him has come to an end."

"I am still obliged to maintain my professional discretion."

"Don't worry, Luther, your secret will be safe with me forever, I promise," said Professor Schiff. But he knew he would have trouble keeping his promise. In fact, he had no doubt that whatever Luther told him would have to go in the book. The book he wanted to write. The book he might have already been writing. The book that would never be sent to former President Vincent Matu Ayeh, with or without a dedication.

Luther finally acquiesced. "All right then. The backpack contains the trophies Vincent Ayeh won as a young soccer player, and medals he received when he was a penniless boy in the slums of Shuffle Park, when he'd just started making a name for himself."

They walked on silently for another moment or two.

"Yes, that's what was in the backpack," Luther murmured.

On the outskirts of the fishing village, Professor Schiff looked back again and searched for his footprints. They had mingled with dozens of other prints on the ground covered with urban refuse. Professor Schiff remembered a poem by Longfellow, which as a boy he'd had to learn by heart in English class:

> Lives of great men all remind us
> We can make our lives sublime,

And, departing, leave behind us
Footprints on the sands of time.

But there are already so many footprints in the sands of time, thought Professor Schiff. Perhaps it's for the best that life blows on them, washes them away, and erases them, to make room for new ones.

48

Distinguished members of the Special Tribunal, Madam Attorney General, Head of the Investigation Team:

Perhaps it was not the plague, but a different deadly pandemic? All diseases are alike anyway, and their treatment is always the same: cold compresses, ground nutmeg, bloodletting, and above all, prayer. Ultimately, it all depends on God's will.

Nevertheless, Klonimus Schiff, who like most men of his era preferred faith to a confrontation with the mysteries of biology, did not dismiss the dangers lurking on shore. He decided to return to the *Esperanza* immediately. But first he made Ajax Witte Voetjes, Lot Met-Zonder, and the two sailors promise to keep the plague a secret, so as not to alarm the passengers. He was primarily concerned for the women, he said, who of course were inclined to excessive emotionality. What's more, the heated anticipation of the moment when they would disembark on the shores of the old-new land "makes hearts beat faster."

They filled two barrels with water from the well near the port office, bought a sack of yams, some almost-fresh cornmeal, a crate of coconuts, three baskets of fruit (bananas and other fruits they were unfamiliar with), six dirty chickens cramped into wicker cages, and a goat with its feet bound. They had not learned the fate of the first expedition, but since they were in a hurry to get back to the *Esperanza* and avoid the plague, they did not make too much of an effort.

All night long, Klonimus and his crew rowed through high waves, and at dawn they reached the ship, which welcomed them with sorrowful creaks of her masts. The supplies were hauled on deck, and Klonimus shut himself in his room, consumed with fears and dilemmas: Should they anchor in place and wait for the disease to die down and disappear (as diseases do)? Or would it be better to sail on and look for a different site where they could fulfill their dream of settlement?

All morning, he wrote in his diary. He wrote and wrote and did not stop until his hand hurt and the tip of his quill was worn down and dripped black spots onto the paper. What did my great-great-great-great-grandfather write? It's hard for me to guess. Perhaps he sensed that the voyage had reached its end. Perhaps he understood that his mission was over. Was it, then, a will? A summation? A farewell to his wife and daughter? Or perhaps he filled the pages with quotes from the writings of the Hebrew prophets, his ancient predecessors, whose legacy he purported to continue?

The chickens were slaughtered, and in the evening the congregation welcomed the Sabbath with a feast and hymns. Zipporah was honored with the lighting of the candles. After dinner, they heard from their rabbi-leader about the beauty of the land they were about to settle. He described again the synagogue they would very soon construct at Port

Esperanza—a magnificent house of worship that would be just as glorious as Herod's Temple. The most beautiful city in the universe would spring up around it, and they—the members of his little congregation—were fortunate enough to be the pioneers. He talked and talked until their eyes glistened with tears.

On Saturday morning, dead rats were found on the deck. No one on board viewed this as particularly interesting or unusual. Certainly not a portent of disaster. They were used to rats, their regular companions since their days of enslavement in Paramaribo, brethren to their poverty and degradation. And of course, they could never have imagined that these dead ones, which had surely come aboard the *Esperanza* in the sacks and baskets of food, were carrying the plague.

It was only a matter of time now.

One of the children—was it Isaak Met-Zonder?—picked up the rodents and tossed them into the sea. And he was the first to complain, the next day, of a headache and swollen glands. On Monday, twenty dead rats were collected and there were four sick people bedridden in the middle deck. At noon on Tuesday, the child Isaak died, and most of the ship's passengers were lying in their hammocks burning with fever, their glands swollen and their fingers black. On Wednesday, two died. On Thursday—seven. On Friday—twelve.

The next evening, when the Sabbath ended, the dead were joined by the young Zipporah and her baby, Yehudit.

Ladies and gentlemen, is there any way to describe the pain felt by Klonimus at the loss of his beloved wife and daughter?

I can probably use the hackneyed expression *heartbreak* to convey the ripped, tight feeling in his chest, and I can recruit the word *shock* to portray the vacuum into which his thoughts were sucked. Yet these words would be merely perfunctory.

He walked among his dead, who lay scattered throughout the ship, victims of the Black Death. He leaned over each of them—men, women, and children—stroked their faces, murmured the Kaddish prayer for the dead, and wept. These people who had been his slaves, and who had sworn allegiance to him when he'd given them their freedom—they were now beyond his sphere of influence. He could not even bury them.

Captain de Groot, an experienced and unsentimental naval officer, demanded that the bodies be thrown into the sea. Klonimus refused. They were Jews, all of them, in their lives and especially in their deaths, and he knew that only those who return to the earth gain eternal rest and the chance to one day awaken on the day of resurrection.

De Groot threatened mutiny.

Klonimus Schiff begged to at least be allowed to take his wife and daughter ashore and bury them in the soil of Africa, under a gravestone.

But by the time the Sabbath ended, all the passengers apart from Klonimus and Captain de Groot were dead. There was no one to bury them and no one to mutiny. The captain and the rabbi with no congregation were the last ones standing.

"Your honor," said Captain de Groot, "I believe my duties are done. I ask that you release me from our contract."

"You are released, Captain," whispered Klonimus.

Captain de Groot saluted. "I'm taking the boat, Mr. Schiff, sir. Will you join me?"

But Klonimus Zelig Schiff merely waved a weary hand, as if his arm had filled with lead, and turned away from the captain, trembling with tears.

He had only one option left: to sink the *Esperanza* and go down with it.

But how do you sink a massive merchant ship?

Stunned with grief, Klonimus Schiff lit an oil lamp and, still sobbing, faltered down the three flights of steps to the belly of the ship. He was hoping to find a crack he could expand, or a loose floorboard he could pry up. He felt certain he would be able to sink the ship that way.

He had never before been down to the hold of the *Esperanza*, never descended into the depths below the water-line, never shown any desire to see what was there, in the belly of his own ship, two stories beneath his feet. He had never visited the slaves' cells, those low-ceilinged caverns where the goods were stored—the human goods. He had never seen with his own eyes the suffocating quarters where they housed the captives, who were doomed to live as slaves or die an agonizing death on their journey westward.

In the lamp's dim light, Klonimus could see iron chains and handcuffs still fastened to the posts. Ropes dangled from the low, sooty ceiling. Rat carcasses were strewn across the muck-covered floorboards.

In one corner, Klonimus saw a dent carved in the wall. He held the lamp closer and found a deep, wide gash. It was clearly the work of a desperate prisoner who had somehow found the strength to hack at the wood with his own iron shackles, attempting exactly what Klonimus now wished to do: puncture the hull and sink the horrific prison in which he was trapped.

The ocean waves pounded above Klonimus Zelig Schiff's head. He channeled his pain over the loss of his beloved and their daughter and his grief over his lost congregation into the figure of this anonymous prisoner, a stubborn and courageous man condemned to slavery, who, like Klonimus, had heard the waves and longed for the water to breach the ship and wash it away. He had yearned to reach the ocean's depths, where he would be freed from his torments.

Next to the indentation in the wall, Klonimus noticed engravings. Marks left by the slaves. For whom? For the next batch of captives?

Holding up the lamp, Klonimus walked slowly along the row of notches, touching and scrutinizing each one, as if he were reading a story written especially for him in hieroglyphics. Here was a sun, a moon, a tree. Here an eye. A face, perhaps the artist's. And a human figure. No, two. Was it a woman? Yes, of course, a woman. And beside her a boy. Or perhaps a girl? And then there was another face. The etching in the wooden boards was very distinct. The face looked familiar. Yes, he'd seen this figure before.

Suddenly his breath stopped. It was he himself! He clearly recognized his own likeness engraved on the wall. The lamp fell from his trembling hand and the flame went out. Klonimus felt his way to the steps and climbed back up.

Violent waves struck the *Esperanza* as he reached the deck. He clung to the ropes and watched the clouds rolling in over the land. The storm rattled the ship, which was lifted to enormous heights and knocked down into great depths. Fierce winds drove frothy water over the deck. The goat broke free and was washed away in a fast-moving current. Barrels, dead rats, tables, chairs, chicken cages—they all churned about in the watery upheaval.

The anchor was dislodged, and within minutes the ship was shocked by a massive blow and uttered a painful groan of furniture breaking as its underbelly was ripped apart by a reef. The *Esperanza* tipped over on its side and began sinking quickly.

"It's about time," said Klonimus Zelig Schiff to the waves that buried him.

49

For once, Special Investigator George Aboagye arranged his visit to the villa ahead of time. When he arrived, he informed Professor Schiff that the attorney general was closing the case in *The Republic v. Schiff.* Professor Schiff was a little disappointed by the sudden decision. Even though he'd been awaiting it, or rather, had become used to awaiting it, he now felt as if his plans had been scuttled. He'd been sure that over the summer, when the attorney general's offices were closed for vacation, he'd be able to relax in the serenity of Villa Clark and finish his book. The book he'd begun writing. The book he was, in fact, deep into writing.

At their previous meeting, Professor Schiff had asked Aboagye to read a thirty-five-page précis, which he'd translated into English with great effort, and give his opinion. Aboagye had agreed, though not very enthusiastically. He would read the text as part of his professional duties, he explained—absolutely not as a favor for a friend.

"Did you read it?" Professor Schiff now asked with a glint in his eyes.

"Yes, I did."

"And . . . ?"

"I can't say that I was surprised," said Aboagye, "this text is in perfect alignment with your personality profile, as indicated by the investigation."

"Meaning?"

Aboagye kept silent for a long time and looked straight into Professor Schiff's eyes. Finally, he spoke softly, accentuating every syllable: "Professor Schiff, you are a racist."

Professor Schiff's mouth felt parched. "A racist . . . ?"

"Yes," said Aboagye, "and I suggest that you not publish this book. It is insulting. Disgusting. Ridiculous."

Professor Schiff was overcome with painful disappointment and injured pride, which pounded in his temples and made his legs shake.

"There are three elderly white men in your book," Aboagye continued, "each belonging to a different era, each of whom falls in love with a black woman. These elderly whites are authoritative, wealthy men of stature, and of course they represent—each in his own way and as befitting his own era—Western society, while the black women they fall for are inferior, primitive, and narrow-minded. One of these women is a beautiful shaman—well, of course, how could you not resort to the folklore of sorcery and superstition—and the other is a helpless, disabled young girl. Precisely the stereotypes that drive racists like you, who pose as unbiased observers."

"But there are other things . . . " Professor Schiff protested.

"And the other characters? Stupid, one-dimensional African caricatures."

"But . . . but . . . " Professor Schiff said feebly. "But . . . " He struggled to defend the work he had labored over. The work that had occupied him for so many hours. Upon which he had pinned so many hopes. "But . . ."

"Professor Schiff," Aboagye proclaimed, "your book simply disgusts me."

"But I love the people here, and I love your country, and your culture . . ." murmured Professor Schiff, his eyes brimming with tears. "I love you all so much . . ."

"Yes, you do, I believe you, Professor. You love us just as a master loves his slaves. I think we've already discussed this issue, haven't we?"

Aboagye was right. Yes, the special investigator, who was neither a literary critic nor a friend—was right.

"If it's any consolation, Professor, I don't think you ever stood a chance. Because when a white European author writes about Africa, he is unwittingly reenacting an exploitative act. Literary colonialism, I would call it. I have no better description." He held out his hand.

"Thank you for your honesty," said Professor Schiff, and his cold, flaccid hand was crushed by the special investigator's sturdy fingers.

And that same evening, Professor Schiff began packing his bags.

50

Ladies and gentlemen, members of the Special Tribunal, Madam Attorney General, Head of the Investigation Team:

I thank you profoundly for devoting all these many hours to patiently hearing me speak. If I have rambled here and there, if I have allowed myself to digress, it was only because I wanted to give you the story of Klonimus Zelig Schiff's journey and atonement as fairly and accurately as I could. I hope I have convinced you to extend him a little credit, even if he does not deserve forgiveness.

I admit that I had to fill in a few of the facts myself. Perhaps even a great many of them. Please forgive me for that, ladies and gentlemen. Remnants from sunken ships, pages from an ancient diary, family trees sketched on parchment—all these are not enough to expose the deep shadows in our souls. Besides, I see no point in telling a boring story. That goes against my principles.

I, for one, am glad the affair is over. And yet I am also sad. Firstly, because I've become accustomed to standing here before you. And although I did not have the opportunity for a genuine conversation with any of you, still I allow myself to include you among my acquaintances. In fact, you are more than acquaintances. You are practically friends. After all, we've been meeting regularly for almost two months. I know your facial expressions. Your body language. I am more attached to you than I am to my neighbors back in Tel Aviv, whom I've been nodding hello to for twenty years.

I am also saddened by the revocation of the Law for Adjudicating Slave Traders and Their Accomplices, Heirs, and Beneficiaries, only six months after it was passed. But what choice did you have? The notion that legislation can represent some sort of universal, timeless morality is, how can I put this . . . a little presumptuous. Not to mention the desire to rectify in a district court a historic wrong that tormented millions of human beings. It's as tenuous as it is touching.

Incidentally, I do not believe that the citizens of the Republic, for whom this trial might have provided a little entertainment, are all that interested in historic justice. They want justice now. Or perhaps not justice, but a few basic things without which it's very difficult to live. You know which things I'm referring to: employment, education, healthcare, housing, transportation. But I'm not here to preach or to instruct. I'm certainly in no position to do that, being the great-great-great-great-grandson of a slave trader.

I will miss you, ladies and gentlemen. I will miss this courtroom. The whir of the air conditioner. The checkerboard of lights, burnt-out bulbs alongside lit ones. I will miss the father of the nation, the Republic's first president, smiling in the portrait that hangs next to the flag. And the louvered blind forever stuck diagonally over the main window. The ticking of the large clock. The bottle of water placed on the stand. The fly that always starts buzzing around me just as I begin speaking.

When I came to your wonderful country, to your little republic, I was almost a complete ignoramus. If not for the family matter that brought me here, I would have been just another camera-toting tourist. But in these two months, I have come to understand something. I now know that there is a great deal of malice in that ignorance. Because not only does it erase the acts of theft and plundering committed by my forefathers against the inhabitants of this continent, but it also enables the theft and plundering committed at this very moment, in my name and on my behalf.

There is one more thing I know: human turpitude touches us all, and none of us can elude it. Ever.

51

On the flight back to Tel Aviv, Professor Schiff dreamed that he was in a tiny village on the ocean shore. He saw no palaces, only what was left of a round structure, perhaps a lighthouse. Farther down the shore there were remnants of a crumbling pier and decaying fishing boats with colorful paintings peeling on their sides. When he asked where he might find Mrs. Tetteh-Ofosu, a crowd of excited children gathered, grabbed him with their little hands, and pulled him to a hut with a corrugated tin roof at the edge of the sparse village. It looked exactly like all the other huts, except for a bright stretch of fabric hanging over the doorless entrance.

Professor Schiff lifted the fabric, leaned on the doorway, and glanced inside. He had trouble making anything out in the dark. The first thing he noticed was a cluster of white spots on the floor. It was a handful of seashells, and invisible fingers were scattering them onto a straw mat. The hand slowly became visible, and then, from within the darkness and his memory, his eyes gradually pieced together the complete figure of a woman sitting in the back of the room with her legs crossed: Lucile!

He remembered how her image had come together in stages the first time he'd met her, too, like a picture slowly appearing on photographic paper in a darkroom.

She quickly gathered up the seashells from the mat. "Professor? Is that you? Why are you so late?" Her big grin spoke to him as if her mouth were an independent entity emerging from the shadows.

"Am I late?" Professor Schiff asked. "If so, I apologize."

She stood up and hugged him. Oh, Lucile! Lucile, the exiled princess! They stood embracing in the entrance, deeply inhaling the smells of each other's necks.

In the two months he'd spent at the villa, two months of quarantine, two months in which he'd been forced to abandon his routine and the characters that normally populated it, his yearnings had swelled and grown like a tumor. Yet he hadn't even been aware of them until this moment. Now he released something into Lucile's embrace—just a miniscule portion of the longings he'd amassed.

"Okay, Professor," she said after a long while, "that's enough." She pulled back from his arms, pushed him away, and scanned him with a probing look. "You've changed," she said.

She, though, had not changed at all, except for a few silver coils in her curled hair, which might have been there before and he simply hadn't noticed. Even her clothes, the gym shorts and faded T-shirt . . . Her bare feet . . . It was all diametrically opposed to the regal grandeur she usually cultivated, but it was the uniform she'd worn when he'd first met her. Her beach attire. Her seashell attire.

"You've changed, Professor," Lucile repeated, "there's something different in your angry face. Some new expression, but I'm having trouble saying what it is . . ."

Guilt? wondered Professor Schiff. But that guilt—the guilt that he could now proudly display and even boast of, thanks to his slave-trading ancestor—was a difficult emotion to express visibly. It weighed on his heart, it was in his thoughts, but his face still evinced the same arrogance of a Western man secure in his happiness, his assets, the portion of the world he holds on to, his proprietorship of humanity.

Lucile said, "Oh, I know: it's the expression a baby gets when he understands he's been born."

"What are you talking about, Lucile? Babies don't have expressions."

"Please do not argue with me, Professor. That's not what we took this whole long journey for."

"I'm sorry," said Professor Schiff, "you're right, as usual."

They looked at each other for some time.

"So, are you willing to start a new chapter?" Lucile finally asked.

"Absolutely."

"Yes," Lucile said, "that's what the seashells told me."

Lucile was once again involved in a transaction. But this time it was a simple barter: the Tetteh family estate, consisting of two huts, the ruins of a lighthouse, a crumbling fishing pier, and a tiny strip of shore on the Atlantic Ocean, in return for an apartment in Tel Aviv. The papers she'd brought to sign were on the straw mat, weighted by a stone so they would not blow away in the breeze.

"You know, Professor, I never really lived in this hut.

But now you will live here for me, if you understand what I mean. And I'm very, very happy about that."

For the first time in his life, Professor Schiff knew with complete certainty that he was in the right place. He was perfectly suited to this hut, to this sleepy village, to this strip of shore on the Atlantic. The chronic alienation he'd endured ever since coming into his own had vanished. Never in his sixty-three years had he felt such peace of mind.

He removed a round, shiny object that looked like candy from his pocket. It was the mezuzah he'd bought from the gatherer at Shuffle Park three months ago. He held it out to Lucile and said, "I know you like these things."

She took the mezuzah and put it to her lips.

"I knew you'd be happy," said Professor Schiff.

"No, it's not for me, Professor, it's for you." She held the cheap plastic mezuzah up to the lintel, and deftly fastened it with a thin piece of rope. "When you get the chance, pop into town and buy some nails and a hammer. There are some things you should always have around the house."

Professor Schiff had already informed his superiors at the university that he was taking early retirement, and they very quickly—too quickly, perhaps—found a replacement. But he did not mind. He was *here* now, and a new chapter had begun. Tami would arrive soon. Just for a visit, of course. At least for now. And the kids, who were busy as usual, would also come. Of course they would. Anyone who wished to stay here with Professor Schiff was welcome. Assi and Alissa would pay a visit. Alissa would build sandcastles while Assi sampled the local cuisine. Kweku and Esther would come, and they'd bring the dog. George Aboagye would stop by with his audio device, and they would record the screeching seagulls and not disturb the ocean sounds with their talk of Professor Schiff's guilt.

Duke would come, of course, more than once. He would probably stop by every time he happened to be in the area. Dr. Malik would visit, and so would Dr. Samuel Baidoo, as well as Luther, who was rumored to have left government service and opened a tourism agency.

Former President Vincent Matu Ayeh would come—theirs was a friendship that had to live on—but only if he was promised immunity from prosecution for bribery and breach of trust. It was ridiculous, honestly: everyone knew the measure of honesty demanded from public officials was excessive. The last time they'd talked, Ayeh had promised to give Professor Schiff a few soccer lessons. "It's never too late to start playing ball," he'd said. His wife, Clementine, would join them, in between her fashion shows and human rights conventions.

Oh, and Ilana Sasson from the embassy would also visit. She'd already expressed her interest in the remote coastal community—a community of one. Shapiro, the historian, would come, as would Mandelbloom, the legal scholar. Ali would come, of course, with Fatimatu and the kids. And Nana the gardener, and the young guy with the pens, and the heavyset man—they would all come to visit. Attorney Yoel Melchior had already written to Professor Schiff to say he would like to stop by. The members of the Special Tribunal were invited, of course, with or without Madam Attorney General and the distinguished Head of the Investigation Team.

"Do you know what you're going to do in Tel Aviv?" Professor Schiff asked Lucile.

"Of course. I'm opening a voodoo school. I already have a group of beginners and a very long waiting list." She poked her fingers into the tower of hair perched on her head like a frozen fountain and dismantled it in three quick moves. "And you?" she asked. "What will you do here on the African coast, Professor? How will you live out your next chapter?"

"Oh," said Professor Schiff, "I'm not going to do anything. I'll just keep remembering. I'll remember and remember and remember . . . Until the memories run out and history begins."

ACKNOWLEDGMENTS

My heartfelt gratitude to all my hosts in Africa: Juliana Yorke, Kwesi Amoak, Nana Asase, Professor Esi Sutherland-Addy, Kofi Akpabli, Nana Awere Damoah, Fritz Baffour, Chief Nana Ansah Kwao, His Excellency Jerry John Rawlings, Bright Kissy, Dr. Nathan Levine, Lynda L. Donald, Martin Egblewogbe, and especially to Ambassador Shani Cooper, who graciously introduced me to all of these contacts. I hope very much that you like this book. And if I have made mistakes or erred with hyperbole, I can assure you my intentions were good and pure. Either way, I apologize for any embarrassment caused by my words. I also thank Ms. Abiba Kone, for sharing her stories with me.

Special thanks to my friend Professor Adam Rovner, from whose research on Jewish autonomies in Africa and Suriname I drew much inspiration. I also thank him for his helpful comments.

Thanks to the readers of earlier versions of the manuscript: Ruti Kantor, Halelah Schiff, Liri Schiff, and Deborah Negbi, who devoted their time and offered their feedback.

Special thanks to Saray Gutman, my Hebrew publisher and editor, who believed in this book even before it was written; to Michael Z. Wise of New Vessel Press, for bringing this book to a new readership and for putting up with my whims; and to Jessica Cohen, an excellent translator and a dear friend.

AGUR SCHIFF, born in 1955 in Tel Aviv, is a graduate of Saint Martin's School of Art in London and the Rijks Art Academy in Amsterdam. He has worked as a filmmaker, started writing fiction in the early 1990s, and has published two short story collections and six novels. Schiff, professor emeritus at the Bezalel Academy of Art and Design in Jerusalem, has been awarded the Israeli Prime Minister's Prize.

JESSICA COHEN shared the 2017 Man Booker International Prize with author David Grossman for her translation of *A Horse Walks into a Bar*. She has translated works by Amos Oz, Etgar Keret, Dorit Rabinyan, Ronit Matalon, Nir Baram, and others. Her translations have been supported by National Endowment for the Arts and Guggenheim fellowships.

Distant Fathers
by Marina Jarre
This singular autobiography unfurls from the author's native Latvia during the 1920s and '30s and expands southward to the Italian countryside. In distinctive writing as poetic as it is precise, Marina Jarre depicts an exceptionally multinational and complicated family. This memoir probes questions of time, language, womanhood, belonging and estrangement, while asking what homeland can be for those who have none, or many more than one.

Neapolitan Chronicles
by Anna Maria Ortese
A classic of European literature, this superb collection of fiction and reportage is set in Italy's most vibrant and turbulent metropolis—Naples—in the immediate aftermath of World War Two. These writings helped inspire Elena Ferrante's best-selling novels and she has expressed deep admiration for Ortese.

Untraceable
by Sergei Lebedev
An extraordinary Russian novel about poisons of all kinds: physical, moral and political. Professor Kalitin is a ruthless, narcissistic chemist who has developed an untraceable lethal poison called Neophyte while working in a secret city on an island in the Russian far east. When the Soviet Union collapses, he defects to the West in a riveting tale through which Lebedev probes the ethical responsibilities of scientists providing modern tyrants with ever newer instruments of retribution and control.

And the Bride Closed the Door
by Ronit Matalon

A young bride shuts herself up in a bedroom on her wedding day, refusing to get married. In this moving and humorous look at contemporary Israel and the chaotic ups and downs of love everywhere, her family gathers outside the locked door, not knowing what to do. The only communication they receive from behind the door are scribbled notes, one of them a cryptic poem about a prodigal daughter returning home. The harder they try to reach the defiant woman, the more the despairing groom is convinced that her refusal should be respected. But what, exactly, ought to be respected? Is this merely a case of cold feet?

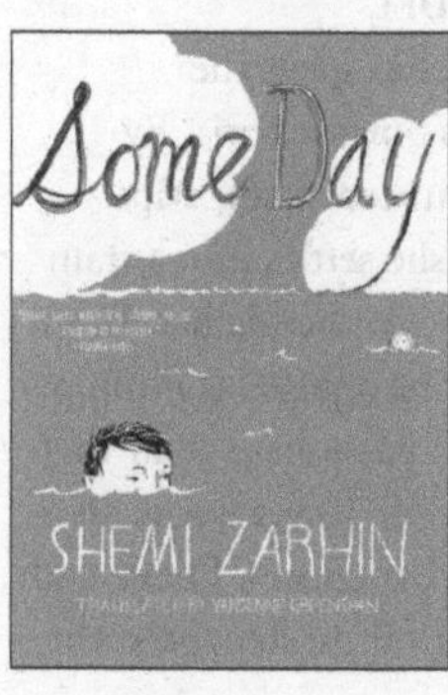

Some Day
by Shemi Zarhin

On the shores of Israel's Sea of Galilee lies the city of Tiberias, a place bursting with sexuality and longing for love. The air is saturated with smells of cooking and passion. *Some Day* is a gripping family saga, a sensual and emotional feast that plays out over decades. This is an enchanting tale about tragic fates that disrupt families and break our hearts. Zarhin's hypnotic writing renders a painfully delicious vision of individual lives behind Israel's larger national story.

Alexandrian Summer
by Yitzhak Gormezano Goren

This is the story of two Jewish families living their frenzied last days in the doomed cosmopolitan social whirl of Alexandria just before fleeing Egypt for Israel in 1951. The conventions of the Egyptian upper-middle class are laid bare in this dazzling novel, which exposes sexual hypocrisies and portrays a vanished polyglot world of horse racing, seaside promenades and nightclubs.

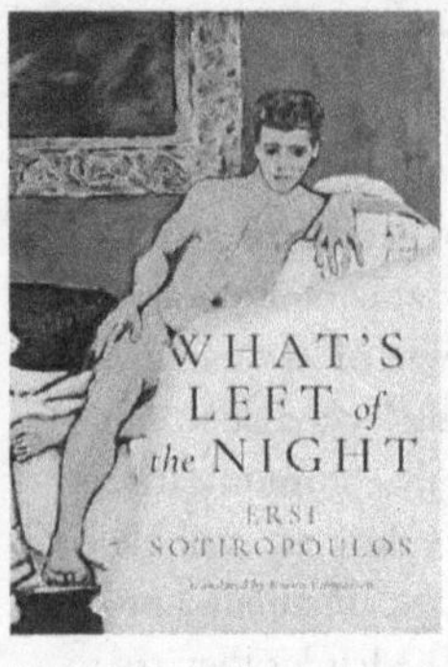

What's Left of the Night

by Ersi Sotiropoulos

Constantine Cavafy arrives in Paris in 1897 on a trip that will deeply shape his future and push him toward his poetic inclination. With this lyrical novel, tinged with an hallucinatory eroticism that unfolds over three unforgettable days, celebrated Greek author Ersi Sotiropoulos depicts Cavafy in the midst of a journey of self-discovery across a continent on the brink of massive change. A stunning portrait of a budding author—before he became C.P. Cavafy, one of the 20th century's greatest poets—that illuminates the complex relationship of art, life, and the erotic desires that trigger creativity.

The 6:41 to Paris

by Jean-Philippe Blondel

Cécile, a stylish 47-year-old, has spent the weekend visiting her parents outside Paris. By Monday morning, she's exhausted. These trips back home are stressful and she settles into a train compartment with an empty seat beside her. But it's soon occupied by a man she recognizes as Philippe Leduc, with whom she had a passionate affair that ended in her brutal humiliation 30 years ago. In the fraught hour and a half that ensues, Cécile and Philippe hurtle towards the French capital in a psychological thriller about the pain and promise of past romance.

The Bishop's Bedroom

by Piero Chiara

World War Two has just come to an end and there's a yearning for renewal. A man in his thirties is sailing on Lake Maggiore in northern Italy, hoping to put off the inevitable return to work. Dropping anchor in a small, fashionable port, he meets the enigmatic owner of a nearby villa. The two form an uneasy bond, recognizing in each other a shared taste for idling and erotic adventure. A sultry, stylish psychological thriller executed with supreme literary finesse.

The Eye

by Philippe Costamagna

It's a rare and secret profession, comprising a few dozen people around the world equipped with a mysterious mixture of knowledge and innate sensibility. Summoned to Swiss bank vaults, Fifth Avenue apartments, and Tokyo storerooms, they are entrusted by collectors, dealers, and museums to decide if a coveted picture is real or fake and to determine if it was painted by Leonardo da Vinci or Raphael. *The Eye* lifts the veil on the rarified world of connoisseurs devoted to the authentication and discovery of Old Master artworks.

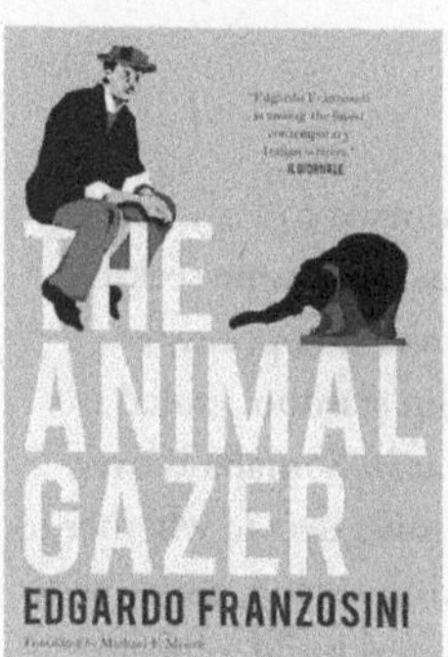

The Animal Gazer

by Edgardo Franzosini

A hypnotic novel inspired by the strange and fascinating life of sculptor Rembrandt Bugatti, brother of the fabled automaker. Bugatti obsessively observes and sculpts the baboons, giraffes, and panthers in European zoos, finding empathy with their plight and identifying with their life in captivity. Rembrandt Bugatti's work, now being rediscovered, is displayed in major art museums around the world and routinely fetches large sums at auction. Edgardo Franzosini recreates the young artist's life with intense lyricism, passion, and sensitivity.

Allmen and the Dragonflies

by Martin Suter

Johann Friedrich von Allmen has exhausted his family fortune by living in Old World grandeur despite present-day financial constraints. Forced to downscale, Allmen inhabits the garden house of his former Zurich estate, attended by his Guatemalan butler, Carlos. This is the first of a series of humorous, fast-paced detective novels devoted to a memorable gentleman thief. A thrilling art heist escapade infused with European high culture and luxury that doesn't shy away from the darker side of human nature.

The Madeleine Project
by Clara Beaudoux

A young woman moves into a Paris apartment and discovers a storage room filled with the belongings of the previous owner, a certain Madeleine who died in her late nineties, and whose treasured possessions nobody seems to want. In an audacious act of journalism driven by personal curiosity and humane tenderness, Clara Beaudoux embarks on *The Madeleine Project*, documenting what she finds on Twitter with text and photographs, introducing the world to an unsung 20th century figure.

Adua
by Igiaba Scego

Adua, an immigrant from Somalia to Italy, has lived in Rome for nearly forty years. She came seeking freedom from a strict father and an oppressive regime, but her dreams of film stardom ended in shame. Now that the civil war in Somalia is over, her homeland calls her. She must decide whether to return and reclaim her inheritance, but also how to take charge of her own story and build a future.

If Venice Dies
by Salvatore Settis

Internationally renowned art historian Salvatore Settis ignites a new debate about the Pearl of the Adriatic and cultural patrimony at large. In this fiery blend of history and cultural analysis, Settis argues that "hit-and-run" visitors are turning Venice and other landmark urban settings into shopping malls and theme parks. This is a passionate plea to secure the soul of Venice, written with consummate authority, wide-ranging erudition and élan.

The Madonna of Notre Dame

by Alexis Ragougneau

Fifty thousand people jam into Notre Dame Cathedral to celebrate the Feast of the Assumption. The next morning, a beautiful young woman clothed in white kneels at prayer in a cathedral side chapel. But when someone accidentally bumps against her, her body collapses. She has been murdered. This thrilling novel illuminates shadowy corners of the world's most famous cathedral, shedding light on good and evil with suspense, compassion and wry humor.

The Last Weynfeldt

by Martin Suter

Adrian Weynfeldt is an art expert in an international auction house, a bachelor in his mid-fifties living in a grand Zurich apartment filled with costly paintings and antiques. Always correct and well-mannered, he's given up on love until one night—entirely out of character for him—Weynfeldt decides to take home a ravishing but unaccountable young woman and gets embroiled in an art forgery scheme that threatens his buttoned up existence. This refined page-turner moves behind elegant bourgeois facades into darker recesses of the heart.

Moving the Palace

by Charif Majdalani

A young Lebanese adventurer explores the wilds of Africa, encountering an eccentric English colonel in Sudan and enlisting in his service. In this lush chronicle of far-flung adventure, the military recruit crosses paths with a compatriot who has dismantled a sumptuous palace and is transporting it across the continent on a camel caravan. This is a captivating modern-day Odyssey in the tradition of Bruce Chatwin and Paul Theroux.

New Vessel Press